GAMMON

Library of Congress Cataloging in Publication Data

Bosak, Steven.

GAMMON

STEVEN BOSAK

St. Martin's/Marek
New York

Design by Paolo Pepe

Library of Congress Cataloging in Publication Data
Bosak, Steven.
  Gammon : a mystery

  I. Title.
PS3552.07568G3 1985   813'.54   85-2554
ISBN 0-312-31629-1

First Edition

10 9 8 7 6 5 4 3 2 1

For Emil, who didn't bet Burmbagoo,
but especially for Jennifer,
who, in her own way, did.

———— ONE ————————————————

I was dreaming out my den window that morning into the cold March fog that huddled along the Chicago lakefront. The park and beach, only a block away, were nearly obscured in mist and sporadic white leaps of Lake Michigan as it crashed into the cement breakwater. My backgammon advice column, "Backgammon Clinic with Vernon Bradlusky," was hours behind newspaper syndication deadline and lay half-finished in the typewriter carriage. I sipped coffee. It was raw and wet outside, and I couldn't get comfortable with the idea of finishing my work and delivering it to my editor downtown. Spray after spray of angry wave lurched up and over the breakwater. My phone rang, just next to the typewriter and my elbow: it was my partner, Toby Kale.

"Say that again?" I asked, still watching the weather, only half listening to Toby's monotone.

"We stand to make ten or twenty thousand. Easy," he said flatly, chewing something as he spoke. From the hollow quiet in the background I figured he was holed up at Murphy's Pub, pay phone wedged between his shoulder and ear. I heard him slurp at his beer as someone in the background coughed and hacked away. Toby went on to explain that he'd been out on the Coast and that all I needed to do for a cut in the profits was to pick up a package for him at the Post Office, take the package home, and wait for him to call.

"You want me to pick up some huge parcel of cocaine or some other shit and drag it to my apartment? The Post Office box is being watched and you want me to get whatever it is you have stashed there?" I said, damned irritated, figuring what the slob was up to. Toby was always after one scheme or another to

1

make a quick buck, and I often took the chances, but this sounded too good, too easy, and way too much over my head. Ten or twenty thousand for picking up a package at the Post Office? "Deal me out this round, Toby. This sounds like trouble," I went on.

"Bradlusky," he sighed, "you can be a genuine candy-ass at times. I'm telling you, I already took all the risk. No cops are watching the P.O. box, and I guarantee it has nothing to do with dope."

"My column," I used as a last defense and hit the space bar until the carriage bell rang.

"You and that Mickey Mouse column. This is *real* money I'm talking about, not sucker pay. More than you could ever hustle in months. Why am I even making you the offer?" he bitched. I just laughed. It was easy to laugh at Toby.

"I'm glad you can laugh off thousands of dollars. There's a key here at the bar, in the Slim Jims box. If I could leave it for anyone else I would, but," he stammered.

"Toby?" I said, but he'd hung up. Just as well, I thought. A bogus drug deal, no matter how he tried to convince me otherwise. What else could that kind of a setup be? The last drug investment he had gotten me involved with had turned out to be a few ounces of talcum powder and Italian baby laxative. At any rate, this latest escapade was sure to be illegal, and although I'm not exactly a member of the Crime Commission, jail time was all I needed at that point. And like I said, Toby's schemes were always running short. When the two of us stick to hustling backgammon games we do just fine. Fine enough for me, at least. A great team, actually, him playing the loud, thick idiot that wins and wins and wins from me, waiting for a mark to get thirsty, interested, so that when Toby steps away . . . But this other scam I didn't need to hear about. I finished my coffee and that week's backgammon treatise with: "But all good strategies come full circle. The game that's won with one attack can be lost with the next." Perfectly awful. But perfectly me. I dressed, put in my loose bridgework and fed my fish—a big white angelfish and half-a-dozen cheap but hardy goldfish.

Downstairs, the mailman was smoking a joint in the foyer. He let out a long drag.

"Smoke?" he offered politely, the joint cupped in his hands.

"No, thanks. Mail?"

He reached with his free hand into his mail pouch. "Cold damned day. Just a little break in here where it's nice and warm, you know?" he explained as he handed me my mail, his eyes watery.

It was typical March mail: overdue account notices, a menu for another new pizza joint around the corner, and a blue envelope, scented with gardenia, that I knew would be Caroline Brodin. Or as the return address maintained: Mrs. Caroline Massad, Villa Massad, Lux Praia, Albufeira, Portugal. Gardenia-scented mail, indeed. She's married to one of the wealthiest men in Portugal and she splashed rummy schoolgirl perfume on a long-distance love letter to me. I dumped all the trash mail but Caroline's into a can at the corner of the parking lot. From that open, windy spot I could look across the lot and see that two guys in coveralls were busy on my Buick Regal, hood up, door open. I counted off the months I was behind on the payments as I strolled down the aisle of cars.

"A yellow, a fuckin' yellow?" the guy under the hood screamed, throwing his hat at the engine block in frustration, a tangle of wire in his other hand. I walked right past them, looking back at the car only when I heard it turn over. What the hell, the brakes squeaked and the transmission rumbled. And my car getting repossessed that afternoon was just the very beginning: all it took was an El ride downtown for another dose of grief. It wasn't enough for my editor to chew me out over my missed deadline. No, when I got to Sid's office in the Prudential building he gave me a few minutes with a whiskey and water before looking over the tops of the pages just finished for that week and, with a cold-as-meat glare, informed me that my column was in trouble. He couldn't place it in any newspapers. Not nearly as fast as it was being dropped all over the country, anyway. In fact he told me with a tight-jawed grin just chock-full of maliciousness that he'd been forced to run a reprint that day. A reprint of an older column. "As few people as are really reading this turkey," he said, tossing the finished column on a stack of dailies on the floor, "I don't think any one of them will notice a reprint. As memorable as this crap is," he chuckled before reaching in a vest pocket for a roll of antacids. I tried to convince him: not one more missed deadline; I'd be on time; but Sid wasn't buying that. Seems he felt backgammon was losing readers no matter what. Wasn't the fad it had been when he signed me up after the tournament win in Mexico City in '74. Backgammon was so much the rage then that the AP wire story in which Elton John announced his bisexuality ran with a picture of him pensively bent before what was clearly a backgammon board. Sid signed me, and my column saw a lot of action those first years. In fact I spent so much time on the column I lost my edge in a few important tournaments. I completely choked in the Canadian Open the next fall. And now Mexico City had already become nearly four long years ago. I hadn't been in a good tournament in a long while. And here I was in Sid's office about to lose my column as well. I asked for a little more time. I'd zip up the column—somehow.

"A month. Maybe less," he told me, too chicken-shit to give me the final deadline by looking me in the eye. He swiveled to gaze out his window at the drizzly city. "If I can't recoup some more papers for the column by then, it isn't worth my time. And maybe not yours." He shrugged, smirking. "The doctor column. When the readers start to drop off, a few columns on glands . . . a series on ovarian cysts." He popped another antacid from the roll, still looking into the gray city, the dripping steel and brick. "Too bad you can't get a few ovarian cysts in your columns, huh?" he said, crunching down loudly on the tablet. He swiveled back and said serious as straight whiskey, "Think about it."

On the train back north I drifted asleep only to be jolted awake at each stop. I slumped in my seat and lay my head against the window, my breath steaming up the glass rhythmically, blurring out the broad brick backs of the warehouses and offices along the early stretch of the elevated.

The train squealed as it rounded a sharp curve. I drew my

feet up onto the baseboard of the car, hoping the vents there would kick up more heat. I cleared a porthole in the condensation in the glass. The wooden stairways of uptown three-flats, littered with broken bicycles, old brooms, rugs frozen to banisters where they'd been flung to dry and forgotten, flickered past as we pulled to another stop. Damn. I wanted the tournaments back, I realized. What did I have when the column folded? Just hustling games in the Rush Street bars. And even those games were getting few and far, far between. I needed to get back in the games. Get the tux out. I wanted to get on a plane, check into one of the tour hotels, spend time in the bars with the other players. And the games themselves, winding down in the early morning hours, leaving you with a light-headed glow. I needed to feel the sharp clack of dice in the dice cup, the subtle aroma of fine leather game boards; the elegant, diffuse light of casino chandeliers; the heavy, nearly narcotized hush of voices breathing in the air around your smoke-wispy head, as your hand—foreign-looking, enlarged in your eyes, its fingers vulnerable and ivory-looking, poking from the stiff sleeve of the tux, out over the points of the game board and the dice—picks up and puts down and moves with such preciseness that it seems to do all the thinking. The tournaments.

The El jerked me awake and forward, snapping my face into the metal back of the seat in front of me. I brought my hand up and felt a warm rivulet of blood. It was no wonder: anything, including spicy Mexican food, could give me a nosebleed—perforated membrane, the doctor had said. I searched my pockets, but all I could find to stop the bleeding was a napkin left on the train's floor, unfolded and flattened to the floor with a heel mark of dirt. I plugged the nostril with it, though, even as a few fellow passengers gave me sidelong looks and a few disgusted winces. I snorted back blood, swallowing. Toby's proposition was beginning to sound good, long shot and trouble as it probably was. But what did I have to lose that morning, nose hemorrhaging, car repossessed, my job as a columinst as secure as my bad bridgework? If nothing else, the kind of money Toby was talking about could set us up in Vegas where the hustling was better and more forthright. Maybe even enough money to practice, hone, get back in the tournaments. But I had no money and no prospects. What a combination. What a dice roll to work with. Where'd Toby say he left that P.O. box key?

I walked the three blocks from the El to Murphy's Pub in rain so cold it might as well have been snow. I stomped in the door. Sandra was writing a check out for the beer driver, who tucked it away in a down vest I wished I'd had enough sense or money to buy. I pulled up a stool, the only customer.

"Did you check dates on the beer?" I asked her when the driver had left. I had worked the bar when she opened it a few years back, tending bar nights, writing the column in the front window in the afternoons. That relationship had led to another that included living with her in the upstairs apartment for a few short, sweet months.

"My beer is *my* business," she said, and the mock hard-ass curl to her lips, the way she flicked back a bouncy swath of her strawberry red hair; the clear gray of her eyes that she shot me as she reached for a glass and filled it with Bushmills shook me like a chill: I wished I were still living upstairs, looking across late-morning coffee and the kitchen table at her.

I put my hand out to hers as she poured my drink. She ignored my gesture, put the bottle away.

"You slob," she said, eyeing the blood-sopped paper in my nose. "When are you going to get that operation, get this nose taken care of, huh?" She shook her head, pulled the matted napkin from my nostril, and pressed a cold bar rag to it.

"Hold it," she told me firmly, and motioned for me to put my head back. I only tilted it back enough to placate her. The bar clock leered down at me: it was nearly three feet across, backlit, and bore the photo of the late Mayor Richard J. Daley, his expression warm, his eyes mirthfully twinkling over bulldog jowls; the minute, hour, and second hands splayed across Hizzoner. It was nearly two O'Daley.

She turned to the register and a stack of invoices, her white sweater catching the yellowed light of a beer sign behind the bar. She tapped at her chin with the end of a pencil, concentrating on a column of figures. I sipped my whiskey slowly, lowered my head, and cautiously removed the bar rag. The bleeding had stopped. I felt she was deliberately ignoring me.

"So what's so urgent about the paperwork today?"

She rested her chin in her hand, let the pencil drop to the papers, and "harumped" at me, riffling the hair across her forehead. She was finally looking friendly, relieved to be able to smile.

"Sorry. A lot on my mind lately," she said and walked back over to me, tossing away the bar rag.

"Why don't you take the day off. Call up your part-time bartender. I got a lot on my mind too. We could—"

"Forget it," she said quickly, but reached over and picked a stray scrap of napkin from my cheek.

"I thought a steak dinner, dancing," I went on. It did sound good.

"Neither of us dance," she countered, still smiling, still amused, still not wholly unconvinced. She looked me square in the eye. "You'd like to have me back, wouldn't you?" she teased, finger trailing lightly over the smoothness of her neck.

"There's a lot of things I'd like to have back today," I admitted. She chuckled gruffly, fluttered her eyelids sarcastically, knowing how much in love I was with those opalish gray eyes and that Irish-white skin.

"You should have thought of that before you started screwing Caroline again." She winked and pushed my drink to me with one finger and a smirk, turning to mix herself a Bloody Mary.

I guess she had a point. But her sister and I had been screwing each other so often—ever since college at Northwestern—that we scarcely saw why it upset so many other people. We screwed through junior and senior year, even when I was tail-wagging over some debutante from Winnetka; lived together after graduation when the euphemism was "shacking up" and not the casual in-thing to do; had intermittent meetings at motels when my first marriage and her affair with some stockbroker were hitting low. And then, after she was safely married to her present husband and tucked neatly away in Portugal, she flew into Chicago on a visit—to see how Sandra's new business was doing—and the two of us ended up doing what we do best together atop beer cases in the storeroom, long after closing. Empty quarts clinked chimelike beneath us in their boxes as the overhead light went on; Caroline froze in my arms in midgrind. I gasped as I felt the pitcher of beer splash at the small of my back, through the cheeks of my ass. I bolted upright and out of Caroline, dripping beer, as the door to Sandra's apartment at the top of the stairway slammed shut. I stood shivering and looking up the stairs of the storeroom as if Sandra would come back out. Not that night. Just my clothes and typewriter.

"You know how your sister is." I shrugged at her, I have to admit a bit more than embarrassed, even a year later.

"Yeah, right. Blame it on Caroline," she scoffed, stirring her drink with an obscenely large stalk of celery.

"Hey, I don't even provoke her. Look," I said, pulling Caroline's letter out of my pocket as if it were evidence. "She's still writing me letters. A married woman and all," I went on.

"Positively shocking," Sandra feigned, slitting the envelope and flipping open the letter without even so much as a nod of permission on my part. "Fucking cheap perfume," she mumbled, sniffing the air, wrinkling her nose.

I downed the rest of my drink and walked around the bar to help myself to the bottle. I poured, glancing over her shoulder and catching a glimpse of more paper than the one sheet of blue stationary.

"What is it?"

She raised a finger, her lips playing over the words as she read. "You won't believe it." She laughed and handed it to me, keeping whatever else was in the envelope in her hands. I read:

> Vernon,
> (Love calling you by your first name!!!) I'm
> in trouble. Bet you're saying that broad is
> always in trouble, so what. But this time my

*trouble can do you some good. It's my husband,
Gregory. Seems since his brother was killed he's
been in sad shape. Losing weight. Business
slipping, and I don't trust his partner. Which
brings me to you. Gregory had scheduled a
backgammon tournament for the casino this
month. Southern European Championship, or
title bout, or some crap, I don't know, it's you
boys who know that business. But since he's
been slipping . . . At any rate you should play
the tournament and maybe keep an eye on
things for me. For Gregory. I'm just afraid things
will happen. If it weren't for this backgammon
crap I'd never have met Gregory. We both owe
you a lot. There's a ticket enclosed and I've paid
your entrance fee to the tournament.
Love and hope to see you soon,*

Caroline.

"And I suppose you should go dashing to her rescue,"
Sandra said after I had finished reading, placing the ticket atop
my glass of whiskey. TWA to New York to Lisboa. My mouth
must have been open, for she stuck the celery in.

"That's just what you'd want, huh?" she said.

"Yeah, a tournament," I answered in disbelief, tossing the
celery to the bar. She had turned her back to me, straightening
the potato chips on the wire rack, her shoulders working under
the sweater.

"Yeah, you haven't lost in a big tournament for a while,
have you?" she said without turning. Sharpness in her voice.
Chips on top, pork rinds in second row, barbecue next, the cel-
lophane rustling in her quick fingers and the clips that hold the
bags.

"So maybe it's time to win one. If nothing else it's a ticket
out of this stinking town for a few weeks." I held the ticket up
to the dim bar light as if looking at counterfeit money. Which

reminded me . . . a tournament like that would take cash, even if the air fare and entrance fee were paid.

"Toby," I said. "Where has Toby gotten to?" She walked down to the end of the bar, began to straighten out the liquor bottles, checking for dead soldiers or near empties, and pulling them out of the crowded tiers.

"Who knows." She shrugged, dumping a bottle in the trash with a muffled splat.

"He called from here this morning," I said.

"We weren't open this morning," she said quickly, the same tone I'd heard from her when I walked in.

"He told me to pick up a key here at the bar."

"I don't know anything about a fucking key," she said. Testy. Nervous. Me and women, I'm always walking a line: that damn letter from her sister was only a vivid reminder of that night in the storeroom.

"But—"

"But I had to pick up the slob from the airport," she said, turning her anger now on Toby. "Drags me out to the airport, wouldn't spring for a cab. I let him make a few calls and have a beer or two with that shady friend of his and then—"

"What friend?" I asked. Toby's easy ten or twenty thousand was starting to sound even less worry-free, suddenly crowded with an outsider.

"Short, wiry black guy. Yellowed eyes. Sick-looking, actually," she said, hunching her shoulders in a shiver at the thought of him.

"How sick? Like a junkie, maybe?"

"No," she said curtly going back to her work, remembering to be pissed off at me. "Sick like living too long in this damn climate without the proper clothes. All the guy had on was a silly dashiki and ratty old jeans."

"And he came in on the plane with Toby?" I couldn't figure who in the hell he was involved with, unless it was some characters from New York, his old neighborhood in Queens.

"Different airline. Didn't say much. Caught up with us at the terminal. They had beers and left just as my food vendor came in." She poured me another drink, then walked stiffly to the other end of the bar again, searching for more empties, slamming bottles down, a fresh jolt of her temper rising amid our otherwise innocuous conversation. Caroline's letter, her presence, attached like brown, warted barnacles to every exchange between us. I picked up my drink as she began dusting the bottles again with a scrawny lick of feathers. I walked around the bar and she glanced up, sniffling. I spread out my arms.

"That night," I said, closer, slowly approaching. "I'm sorry." Realizing I'd never really apologized. Not in so many brittle words, ever.

"Hey, just come on . . ." She waved at the air with her arms, as if to scoot me away like a puff of smoke. I grabbed her hands and she tried to wriggle them free.

"I'm sorry about that night. Sorry about taking so damned long to tell you I'm sorry. Shit, I'm just plain sorry," I said.

"You got that part right," she answered through her teeth, wrenching her hands free, her elbow jerking back, knocking over the Slim Jims box on the counter. They spilled over the back counter, down over the slats behind the bar. I stooped to help her pick them up, stuffing them roughly into the box again, and found the key that Toby had mentioned—the P.O. box key— sitting like a pearl on the bottom of the box. I pocketed it.

"I don't guess it should matter now anyway," she said. She sniffled a laugh, looked at me, both of us crouched behind the bar, Slim Jims between us. Her gray eyes glowed pewter, a few tears left. "You're no better or worse than one of her cars. Furs. Hell, you should be just as pissed at her as me. Maybe more. You stupid asshole." She smiled and pushed me back from my haunches to flat on my ass with one shove.

TWO

I did exactly as Toby told me. I went to the P.O. and picked up the package—wrapped in brown paper and the size and shape of a good-sized department-store catalog. I looked uneasily around the Post Office, expecting the sleazy friend of Toby's, the one who met up with them at the airport. Or a plainclothes cop. A guy in a sharkskin suit and a yellow silk tie looked like a candidate but he cruised past me without a flinch, whistling "Lady of Spain." I got the package home where I could shake it, and it did rattle a few times. Reassuring; dope wouldn't rattle. At least not any I was familiar with. But what could it be if not dope? I kept my word to Toby and put the damn thing up on the fridge next to the black bananas and the empty ice cube trays.

I tried to reach Toby: no luck. I fixed myself a drink and dialed my father's number in Phoenix, taking the airline ticket out of my pocket and spreading it on the table in front of me.

He answered on the fifth or sixth ring.

"Who the hell is it?"

"Your son."

"The jackass in K.C. or the hustler in Chicago?"

"The newspaper columnist, you mean," I corrected him.

"No self-respecting columnist would run a repeat. Not any good columnist, anyways," he snorted at me. I heard a woman's high, thin voice attempt to trace an opera melody which played bravely on a phonograph, but her voice was no match as it cracked, faltered, and took up again despite such ear-rending failure. My father told this woman, named Doris, to shut up, and the opera continued unaided.

"So what you want? A couple hundred or something? Don't

ask, I'm flat out till next month, Vern. They've raised the rent on this trailer plot again. Shit, you'd think it were a condo in Fort Lauderdale. Should've bought there, come to think of it. But I ain't got buck one. Livin' on Doris's government check now. That pension of mine gets to lookin' more and more like one warm beer in a Friday night union hall. So I'm sorry, can't help ya, kid. Next month. Maybe. No tellin'."

"No. No loan, Dad. I got good news. I'm going out on a tournament again. Portugal this time. It sounds like high prize money. I leave the day after tomorrow. Thought I'd let you know, just in case you decided to call."

There was a long silence from him which the opera managed to flesh out before he spoke.

"Portugal? That's where that slut—what's her name?—the slut you been chippin' off and on for the years? Didn't she find religion and get respectable and married over there?"

"Yeah, well," I began to explain, "she got me in the tournament. She needs me to take care of a little business for her too. Sort of two birds with one stone."

"I'll just bet," he chuckled softly, wheezing. He hadn't quit the cigars. "Watch where that fuckin' stone lands, too."

"But the tournament. Haven't had a chance like that in years."

"Yeah. That sounds real nice, Vern. Get you off that column for a while, huh? Must be running out of ideas what with selling columns you already had printed."

That was the first time I'd given the column a thought. I rushed my father off the phone and gave Sid a call at home. It took me a while to convince him that I could just as easily write the damned thing in Portugal. And my being at a real tournament had an advantage. I could throw in colorful sidelines about the games themselves and the *international* ambience of the whole freak show. He asked for gossip. Lots of gossip. I didn't argue although I should have. For some reason the greasy backgammon hustler was suddenly feeling respectable. I fell asleep, drink in hand in an easy chair, dreaming of the tournament.

*   *   *

When I woke to the ringing phone, I expected Toby, hungover, apologetic, to be on the other end. I was wrong. It was Ted Singer, a bartender at Zorine's, a Near North Side club that Toby and I hustled on occasion.

"I'm tellin' you, Vern, this guy is ripe. Out of town. And if you ask me, he deserves to be picked. He's been takin' quite a few customers in here. He even asked *me* if I knew any good players." Ted was my eyes in Zorine's; if he saw anyone Toby or I could hustle, he'd give me a ring, but he always found reasonable grounds (the mark was a loud drunk, was bad for business, looked at Ted the wrong way) to single a man out for us. Any piddling reason would do, so long as neither of us brought up the understanding that he would receive a ten-percent share of anything Toby and I managed to win.

"What time is it?" I yawned into the phone.

"After eight. You'd better get down here before he gets bored."

I tried to get hold of Toby again, thinking this was a good setup for a team, but he still wasn't in. I walked down to Sheridan Road, then realized I'd better flag down a cab if I wanted to get to Zorine's in any time to play Ted's man.

I got out down the block from the club, at the light. Rush Street: it was changing, always changing. When I first made a trip there it was the day Kennedy had been assassinated—right there on the TV that hung over the bar, and right in the middle of my lunch of beer nuts, a corned beef, and a dry martini. Weird lunch. Two days after my twenty-first birthday. Girls then went into bars accompanied, *escorted.*

I walked the block and a half to Zorine's, realizing that here on Rush even the air had changed. Back then you could catch the smell, the faint trace, of an expensive cigar or women's perfume. Now the air smelled of musk, marijuana, and charcoal broil. The sidewalks were full at night not only with businessmen and servicemen but with gay hustlers in the same jeans and baubles as the secretaries who prowled the sidewalks for laughs and for a vicepresident or commodities whiz kid to sink their claws into. And of course, now as well as back then, the hookers.

The doorman took his time recognizing me, and even asked for identification. Zorine's is semiprivate—a few rock stars have had fist fights on the dance floor, a president's son granted a magazine interview at the bar where he described his experiences with drugs, and a prime minister's wife (at least wife at that time) was first photographed in the arms of some jet-set hermaphrodite crooner just beyond the very doors I entered— and with that reputation to uphold, the management couldn't let just *any* slob wander in off the street.

The place was respectably crowded for midweek, and I nudged my way to an open spot at Ted's end of the bar. He worked his way toward me, managing to fill a glass with ice and Bushmills on the way.

"Our friend's still here," he shouted to me over the blare of a disco number that pounded heavily in the Lauren- and Halston-scented air. Heads, arms, torsos glazed with just the polite amount of perspiration bobbed to the music. Ted filled a customer's glass with some creamy blenderized slop and nodded toward the rear of the club.

"He's playin' one of our regulars. Commodities broker. Young kid, comes in about once a week."

"Do you think he's hustling, is he a hustler?" I asked him, catching an elbow in my side as a girl in Danskins and a wrap-around silk skirt made her way to the bar. I felt like a challenge that night—something to test my mettle. I knew Portugal would eat me alive if I weren't prepared for professional play.

"Hard to say if he's a hustler or not. He beats most everyone he comes up against."

"What else, where's he from?"

"Says New York, but he doesn't sound it if you ask me," Ted answered, refilling two Scotch-and-sodas.

"New York?" I couldn't figure why a New York hustler—if indeed our friend in the back was a hustler—would be in Chicago, when the Big Apple had all the action you could imagine.

"Yeah. Says he's a developer. Couldn't get much out of him or his broad. And what a set of luggage she is . . ."

"What does he drink?"

"You want me to spike it?" Ted winked.

"Hell no," I chuckled. "Just give him a refill on me once we've been playing awhile." I slapped a twenty on the bar. "And if this guy works out there'll be *fifteen* percent in it for you." He looked away as he slid the bill off the bar. I think I embarrassed him.

I made my way through the overdressed snobs on the dance floor. Hell, I was the only person in the joint wearing a cheap polyester suit; you'd think the least I could get would be a dis-believing stare for looking so out of place among the gold chains, narrow silk ties, and French collars. I stepped into an arena of tables, booths, and a battery of sound-absorbing hanging plants. Most tables were taken with couples, drinks, and conversation. One backgammon game was in play near the left wall, but right away I knew it wasn't the action I was after: both men carefully pondered each of their dice rolls as if they were studying the entrails of some sacrificial animal for a divine portent; they smiled, joked, and talked casually between moves—much too slow, chatty. I faded farther into the alcove and found what I was looking for. In a corner, nested below the lush cloud of a Boston fern, two men and a woman were bunched around a backgammon set. The younger man was unaccompanied, and he nervously bounced his leg, pumped it up and down beneath the table as he rolled, paused, moved his men, and returned to his drink all in one long sweep of his hand. His opponent was older, white-haired, and sporting the bronze tan that you get only in the deep Bahamas or the Virgin Islands—it wasn't that quick-fading Miami Beach orange. A pair of wire-framed glasses with lenses as thick and opaque as chunks of ice nearly hid his eyes, which made fleeting, overmagnified appearances across the thick lenses like fish swimming too close to aquarium glass. A sturdy, sharp nose held the enormously weighty spectacles. On a smaller, less confident-looking man such a pair of glasses would mark him as a wimp, an easy pushover, and to be sure the lu-dicrous glasses almost did the same for this guy but for one striking, compensating factor: one entire side of his face was a maze of scar tissue. Scars that resembled blued and purpled eruptions pitted the drawn cheek all the way to the ear, pocked the flesh from under the thick lens and down to the very line of his jaw, where some of the scattered gouges seemed capable of being as deep as the jawbone if you had the stomach to look down into them long enough. There was scarcely an inch of healthy skin on that side of his face and the tinge, the healed-over tinge of that flesh reflected in the thick edge of the spectacles, underscoring the shadowlike flittering of the eyes.

On the other hand, "that broad" of his whom Ted had likened to a piece of Samsonite was anything but excess baggage. Women like her are difficult to construct in even the most leisurely of dreams. It wasn't a pert nose or creamy skin or any addition or subtraction of features that leveled me so thoroughly. It was the overallness of her: the delicate yet suggestive angle to her wrists, the movement of her slender, wispy hands; the darkness of her that began in her auburn hair, a velvet like some lush, cavernous night that cast itself over her angular, spare features. There was in her, all around her, a brooding, pacing nature; she looked capable of cuddling and then equally up to swallowing you whole. Her lips were glossed gold, as were her eyelids, which seemed to reflect the same sensuous angles and points as her wrist and lanquid fingers, which now stroked the white-haired gent's jacket, traced a circle on his arm. She leaned to him, his good side, to his ear, where she either nibbled or whispered. I pulled up a chair from the next table, keeping a respectable and impartial distance.

It was the woman who noticed me: she shot me a quick, too-easy smile with those gold-glossed lips, while her dark, deep eyes glared as alertly as a predator's. A chill ran through me: I wanted this woman and felt like running away from her at the same eerie moment. Keeping one watchful, stoic eye on me, she leaned once more into the gentleman's ear and this time I was close enough to hear her whisper despite the bombardment of disco from the dance floor. He looked up, an oiled, precise turn of the head away from the board where the young opponent was executing his next move with a heartburn wince. The gentleman offered me what could have been a smile. I did not see all of that smile though, as it was tangled into his scars and the white of his mustache. The woman tucked a sheet of her hair behind one ear. The man returned to the game, turning the good side of him to me again, and I noticed an incredibly large diamond earring in his lobe. I don't know how I had failed to see it before: a two- or three-carat diamond studded into his tanned lobe, the very one his woman tended as she whispered once again to him. He nodded as he rolled the dice, and then I could see the white corners of the mustache smile, bristle. The board revealed his reason for being so pleased: he had the nervous kid backed up on the far side of the board, blocked four of the kid's pieces with a near-prime, a solid wall of his own men in home court. The kid did not have a chance.

"Man, oh man, are you lucky," the kid breathed, advancing only one of the four men free from the trap, but just barely on the other side of it. Luck. If the kid believed that luck was the supreme power in this game, it was no wonder he was losing. Beginners—at least beginners who are in love with losing money—ascribe every move of the good player to that magical, elusive quality named luck. Their moans are predictable: *If only I had some, Mine just isn't with me today,* or *If only you didn't have so much,* when all along what the winning player has is skill and as long as the amateur chalks it up as luck, the winner can come back and skin him again. The ignorant amateur, believing luck to be like the weather or his underwear and subject to change every day, will throw himself in with the winner again and again, never knowing it was skill that battered him. So a pro likes to hear luck mentioned by an opponent. I myself allow the dice their due, but figure a course or courses that let me have most of the say. The kid, in uttering the simple, innocent word *luck,* had made himself transparent, breathless as a jellyfish washed up and marooned on a beach. The white-haired gentleman made short and neat work of him, removing his own pieces from the board and leaving the kid unable to even move out of the winner's home and into his own home board, assuring the white-haired gentleman of not just the game or a *gammon,* but a rare and satisfying *backgammon.*

The kid, to his credit, calmly passed a thin packet of bills under the table where the girl retrieved them wordlessly and tucked them into the front pocket of her tight jeans. The kid squirmed in his chair, drained the watery remains of his drink, and patted his forehead and cheeks with a monogrammed handkerchief. The gentleman stirred his own drink and took a sip. "Another?" he asked, but the kid was already standing, tucking a stray medallion into his open shirt front, and sliding his chair up to the table.

"No, thanks; no, thanks," he said, offering a weak smile that twitched with self-pity.

"It was nice playing you, sir," the gentleman called after the kid as he disappeared out of the alcove and into the crowd on the dance floor. I was glad that the gent had sharpened his claws on such an easy mark, perhaps he would be less wary of me. He stood, offering me the kid's seat with an outstretched hand, tanned right down to the fingernails.

"I'm Moreno," he said. His accent was foreign-sounding for a New Yorker. His girlfriend, whom he introduced as Justine, was resetting the pieces as I settled into the leather chair with my drink and introduced myself. He sent Justine off for more drinks while we discussed stakes. The kid and he had been playing one hundred a game. The stakes couldn't be doubled; of course, a gammon paid double, and a backgammon, such as the one just played, netted three times any wager. When I agreed to the one hundred per game but suggested that we use the doubling cube, his otherwise smooth, cool expression leaped into a sparkling display of expert dental work; he liked my idea: there was no need to wait for a gammon or backgammon again; he could get greedy whenever he liked.

"Yes, yes, the doubling cube it is," he agreed. Justine returned with our drinks, drawing a cold glare from a passing waitress.

We played the first game closely. We each took the safer moves and did our best to stay close to each other without seeming to hold back. Neither left men open in dangerous territory. He was trying to feel my type of game as I was holding back and attempting the same: we did not want to appear too experienced or eager. I felt ridiculous, and twice I had to bury a grin behind a long swallow of whiskey; we were pulling at our chains. All through the game I felt him applying subtle pressures then suddenly drawing back, like some pickpocket. I too was careful, neat, even making subtle yet carefully planned errors designed to show—if he took advantage—at what level he was playing. He may have spotted such a move one time as I split a point close to the safety of my home board yet within striking distance of one of his men. His roll allowed him to strike my open piece, but by doing so I would quickly regain ground and perhaps end up in a better position. To his credit, Moreno did not entirely ignore the invitation; to do so would have signaled his wariness. Instead he complained of what a conservative game he played and how hitting my exposed man would not really help him so much and didn't I really think it better that he use the dice roll to advance his other men? We both chuckled, and for the same reasons, I'm sure, for he advanced his men in such a manner that they would frustrate any attempt on my part to recover if he had made the other move. It was a strange feeling, as if I were playing into a perverse mirror in which my every move became ten or twenty and he could see each clearly. Justine sipped her drink, let her eyes wander over the cheapness of my suit, the sparseness of my hair; the very plainness of me seemed like some horrible defect she was inspecting. I shifted uncomfortably in my seat, the leather slippery under the polyester of my pants. Why should I feel self-conscious when her *amore* there looked as if half his face had been steeped in battery acid for a fortnight.

He won the first game, but narrowly enough for me to ease up on moves at the end. Staying close while losing was a good maneuver on my part; it told him that even when he played a lackluster, purposefully unaggressive game, he could beat me. That was the type of confidence I hoped I could build in him. To help him in that direction even further, I looked up at him, shaking my head with a gee-golly-shucks motion as he removed his last man and won the game. "The dice sure were with you the last few moves," I said, hoping I wasn't obvious. He smiled, as Justine whispered into his ear once again. She reset the pieces as Moreno sipped daintily at his drink, gazing over my shoulder and out onto the dance floor.

"Another?" he said vacantly. "Perhaps one of us will have the opportunity to use the betting cube this time." There had been opportunities in the first game. He was playing very modestly.

"That would make things more thrilling, wouldn't it Mr. Bradlusky?" Justine said to me, her first words to me, fixing me again with her eclectic combination of cold, austere stare and gentle, supple smile. I continued to ignore Justine's whispers and her fingers tapping lightly, seemingly playfully, at his shoulder, the nape of his neck, and told myself that it was Moreno I was playing and that I should concentrate on the game regardless of diversions. He made some fine moves, displaying a greater skill in utilizing his dice than in the first game. He was beginning to risk showing such plays. But he risked a little at a time, calculated risks that provided big gains if an inferior player failed to realize what trends they indicated. I bit down hard and ignored those risks, making myself lamer and lamer in his eyes. Midway into the game his placement of points forced me to leave a man open, a blot. He hit the exposed piece. As a result of the way in which he had blocked the most common and useful spots of the board for my piece to reenter, the six, seven, and eight points, I was unable to move with my next roll.

"Double," he said nonchalantly, reaching to the center of the board and righting the cube to show a two. Two hundred dollars would nearly tap out the cash I had. Justine sipped from Moreno's drink. I had to agree to the challenge; if I refused his double—as rules have it—I would forfeit the game.

I wasn't in such bad shape, however. Most of my pieces were in lower-numbered slots at home board than Moreno's pieces were, and either he was not aware of the overall situation, or he was certain I was such an inferior player that it would make little difference. Justine tapped a swizzle stick against the glass rim, one-two-three-four, sending beads of perspiration sliding down the glass sides. In some respects, this hit might afford me a chance. A chance only if Moreno (or Justine?) continued to underestimate me. I rolled low, as I had hoped, and was unable to get onto the board. This had a giddying effect on Moreno, and he moved some of his more strategic outer points closer in toward the home court. Justine, meanwhile, whispered and tapped so much that her actions lost all semblance of affectionate play. Moreno drew his pieces closer to his home court, abandoning any blocking strategy for a clear run at what he and Justine obviously thought by now was an easy victory. I received a high and low number, moving my trapped piece snug against some of Moreno's advancing men, while I moved the high number on my home end of the board. He took the bait, an insulting and disastrous thing to do to a pro. As he moved quickly for that kill, a smile puckering the taut scar tissue, I sensed in Justine a jerk, a twitch to her otherwise languorous calm as though she were jabbed, hooked through the mouth, but when I turned to her nothing reflected in those watchful, dark eyes, and she even took a long, lazy swallow off Moreno's drink to prove she was ignoring his mistake. From his taking that bait, I knew he wasn't wise to me. Sure he had knocked me off the three point, but from that position it was easiest for me to roll a four (a very common number) and hit his then exposed man. As quickly as his "luck" had alighted upon him, it turned to me: I rolled the four I needed.

"Double," I announced to Justine's blank, cool stare.

Moreno extricated himself from my end of the board three rolls later, and as if the act of raising the wager were all it took to regain face and a semblance of control over the game, he reached for the cube and announced once again, in a cool, nearly melodic lilt, "I believe I have to double up once again." This despite his obviously poor position on the board. Who was I to argue with such ballsy determination? I simply reached over in my turn and with a phantomlike hand righted the cube once again. "And I must double on that," I said after a single move, trying desperately to sound sarcastically apologetic while stilling the simple mental calculations that scorchingly informed me that, with that little twist of the wrist, that outwardly serene and calm gesture of turning over the doubling cube once again, I had transformed a single one-hundred-per-game diversion into a sixteen-hundred-dollar investment. But he took his move despite a visible flinch from Justine. He touched his finger pensively to the doubling cube.

It was then that the drinks I had ordered arrived in the chalky white arms of a waitress. Moreno, who had been regarding the field of battle and the "sixteen" that loomed up from the doubling cube that I had placed at his end of the bar on the gameboard, found the fresh drink in his hand and looked to Justine for confirmation that she had hailed for the round; but as it dawned on him, slowly crept up on him, when Justine denied ordering his drink with a sparkling shake of auburn hair, he chuckled. Slightly and to himself, but as his amusement gathered strength, he turned to me and lifted his glass in a salute.

"Justine," he nearly shouted in a childlike screech. "We've been took! Hustled! Us, do you *be-ah-leeeeve* it!" Justine smiled at me, except this time she seemed to mean it. I had expected some indignation, some petty moralizing—not the outpouring of affection and admiration that drew a few stray glances from the surrounding tables. Moreno regained himself but still insisted on smirking and humming his disbelief. He reached into his coat pocket for a wallet.

"That last double of mine," he said as he counted out crisp one-hundred-dollar bills. "That last double of mine usually scares them off. Most refuse."

"Those stakes are pretty stiff; can you blame anyone?" I asked, watching him slip the creased wad toward me. I pocketed it without counting. Moreno told Justine in a pouting whisper to give me six more please. I watched her dig the bills out of her jeans. She passed them to me without watching me take them.

"I *knew* you had the upper hand, you understand," Moreno went on. "But I can usually scare down the average player with such a high double. You know, they think of the stakes so much that they haven't the brain left for the game." He tapped lightly at his temple. A look passed between Justine and me: humor him.

"And Justine whispering in your ear?" I asked.

"I guess I wasn't distracting enough, was I?" she said dryly, mocking herself with a long, lascivious swipe of her tongue across her lips. She knew I knew and played the lie like a ham, an inside joke between herself and me. Moreno was an outsider.

"I admire your own subtlety," I said to Moreno, looking at Justine. I could have crawled into those dark eyes and died.

"Ah," Moreno sighed, and took a long swallow of his drink, relaxing into his chair from the stiff-backed posture assumed for the game. "This is a nice, subtle calling card. Having the drink sent over like that."

"Some hustlers, remember that obnoxious, perspiring Greek," he said to Justine before returning to me. "Well some hustlers will just let you go. Not tell you a word. Let you think that you've lost fair and square. Not Justine and I. I let Justine tell them though. Softens the blow. Just mention how long I've played the game, or how I've won money all over this continent and that continent. Got to tell the mark though," he sighed. "It's not, well, *polite* if you don't."

"And the kid before me," I offered as a test to his honor.

"The kid," Justine told me, "was informed of Mr. Moreno's amazing skill two days ago." Her voice was burnished.

"And he came back today?"

"Back today, and I'm sure tomorrow." Moreno grinned slyly. The crowd on the dance floor had swelled into the doorway of the alcove. The music had increased its decibel level to the point where I could feel the bass in my shoes; however, our nook was quiet enough to continue our converstion.

"Then you're *not* a real estate developer," I said.

"I am, I am, among other things," Moreno disagreed quickly. "I play—Justine and I play backgammon for its excitement. It's so much fun to *hustle*," he said, drawing out and thoroughly caressing the word as if it were a mint dissolving on his tongue. "We have so many *diversions* between us," he said pointing the pitted side of him to me, petting it with a quick hand.

"Fun," I repeated flatly.

"And your costume," Moreno marveled at my polyester

suit: the only suit I had left in the closet, the only one clean enough to wear at any rate. "If I were more alert tonight I should have guessed just by the disguise. I mean burgundy polyester, gauche enough to be pure *camp*. I don't know why I didn't pick up on it," he continued, his tone drifting from sincerity to a kind of self-parody; I couldn't tell if he were on the level, if he were mocking me, or if I had simply had too much Bushmills. I ruled out the Bushmills. Who was acting and who was on the level? I couldn't decide from word to word. Not even my own.

"Yeah, most of the suits I use for hustling games are a real scream," I said staring him straight in the eye. He cleared his throat and excused himself to the john.

When Moreno reappeared, he was followed by a massive, muscular black dude in a skin-tight T-shirt and designer jeans: not your Zorine's attire at all. Moreno seemed oblivious to this shadow. Justine stood and walked over to Moreno, a few yards from our table. The black man swept past Moreno and smashed into Justine, causing her to fall backward onto another table; the couple seated there was forced to relinquish each other's hands and watch as Justine fell, upsetting drinks—her face, her expression, however, as passive, as stable as if she had just gotten up from a good night's sleep. Moreno spun to face the assailant; the black man looked the shaken one. He ran a quick hand over his oiled short afro. Glinting in the soft spotlight he found himself caught under, his eyes went directly to the moltenish mess of Moreno's face, the black man's lips pursing and causing a velvet black horrified hole in the already wood-dark complexion of him. Justine got to her feet and advanced on the man, took the elastic collar of the T-shirt in her fingers, and twisted. She spoke sharply to him, her voice like some buffeted dandelion seed in the gush of music from the dance floor. I could not hear one word, just the harshness, the consonance, the fierceness of her attack. The black guy nodded, looked to her, to Moreno, and back to her, his eyes quick and nervous and his posture turned as if ready to bolt at the first opportunity. Moreno stood, hands planted firmly on lapels of his jacket, face marvelously coarsened—if that's possible—by the blue bath of light thrown down across the craters and rims of his scars. The black man disappeared from Justine's fingertips as if he were on some rubberband that she had been holding taut. The crowd, the shifting dance floor, parted and took him in.

"Accident?" I questioned as they sat down, no trace of the incident evident on either of their faces.

Moreno shrugged. "Clumsiness." He forced a smile.

"A lapse in intelligence. Stupidity," she disagreed firmly, eyeing the seam in the dance floor through which the man had escaped. Moreno put a hand to her hand as she nervously twisted at her swizzle stick. This did not soothe her. The hand took up a drink glass, that perfectly sculptured hand, and brought the glass down so hard that it shattered in her grasp, backgammon pieces popping up from the board, two or three rolling to the floor. She held a fanglike fragment of the glass, the rest scattered across the backgammon board like odd-shaped, ill-placed game pieces. I stood to leave.

"Thanks for the game." I nodded to Moreno who seemed to be ignoring Justine's outburst, in fact seemed visibly cowed by it, sinking quietly into his seat. Justine batted her eyes and released the fragment, brushing her hands as if pleased.

"Another game soon?" she asked.

"No, sorry." I tried to smile into those dark eyes of hers. "Leaving the country."

"If you know of any other players, Mr. Bradlusky, any *good* players in the area, be sure to let them know Mr. Moreno would like to play them. Please." She dropped the last word like a personal promise rather than a request. "We leave in a few days for New York," I heard her say to me as I made my way toward the music and the crowd. I managed to elbow a spot clear at Ted's side of the bar. He put a drink and a message into my hand. After Moreno and Justine, and the sixteen hundred that bulged in my pocket like a fat little heart, I was numb from the neck up. Ted's hands appeared in my narrowed plane of vision, unfolded the message, and smoothed it out neatly in front of me: "Sandra called. At Murphy's. Return call immediately."

"So you lost," Ted said as I finally looked up at him. "No

reason to act like a zombie, a sore loser." He shrugged and tapped at the message on the bar. "Call the girl, *loser*. A good woman will take the edge off. I didn't promise you the guy would lose."

"But," I tried to explain, my hand over the bulge of money in my pocket.

"Cut the shit and call the girl," he said, sliding the house phone to me from behind the bar.

"Yeah, call the guffin' girl," a cute and very drunk blonde drawled loudly to me over the blaring music; Ted was pouring her a Manhattan two spaces down the bar. I dialed Murphy's. The noise—both at Zorine's and at Murphy's—was enough to make communication nothing but a series of staccato yelps between the two of us, even with a damp cocktail napkin wrapped around my finger and crammed into my other ear.

"I said it was Caroline!" Sandra screamed for the third or fourth time.

"Caroline?" I couldn't tell if Sandra was still on the same peevish topic as that afternoon at Murphy's. After all, screaming into a phone deadens subtlety.

"I don't want to talk about Caroline."

"No. No. She *called*. All the goddamned way from Portugal. She has to talk to you."

"When?"

"She says she'll call back. Your place. In an hour."

"Did she say what it was about?" I yelled into the receiver. The blonde was watching, craning to overhear, her drunken eyelids heavy with blue eye shadow.

"Probably wants to know which little finger you'd like to wrap yourself around when you get there."

"Sandra!"

"All right, I'll lay off. See me, Vern. See me before you go," she finished, and the line clicked dead.

"What'd the gal say?" the blonde asked me as soon as I hung up the phone and passed it to Ted.

"The gal said I'm *not* a loser tonight, and that I should buy you a drink." I peeled off Ted's percentage, which he hurried into his pocket with visible embarrassment. I seemed to be the only person leaving.

The air outside was crisp with the smell of Lake Michigan on it. A cab, whose driver was possibly clairvoyant, stuttered to an uneven stop before I approached the curb. I climbed in and told the cabbie to head up Lake Shore Drive—I'd fill him in when we got close to anything that interested me. He pulled away as I sank back into the ample seat, Moreno's thirteen hundred warm, safe, and fast asleep in my pocket. I was comfortably congratulating myself: a tournament in Portugal was ahead and I'd just fleeced a freak for enough to make my trip reasonably successful. The only thing that could have completed the evening was a long, warm night with that incredible woman of his. I rubbed at my forehead and the tension that had accumulated there during the game: increment by increment it had built and now I tried to caress it away. Calculation branching from calculation branching . . . I rested my head far back onto the seat, eyes closed, seeing again the glass shards scattered on the game board, the pocks and scars of Moreno.

——— THREE ———

I rolled down both back windows. The cold blast of air was like some Jacuzzi. The cab slid into the light traffic on the Drive as a comforting drizzle began to fall. The high-rise apartments, condos, and co-ops flicked past the window, lit with haphazard patches of gold and blue or garishly ablaze with a slice of spotlight. On the other side of the Drive tufts of trees, dimly visible, hugged the lakefront park, giving way to vast open smears of beach illuminated by infrequent mercury-vapor lamps which cast such intense amber light that a woman walking her poodle seemed pinned in a photograph. Christ, Caroline had phoned! I had the plane tickets and the spending money. It was the night before I was due to leave for Portugal, so only one thing could possibly make her call—bad news. The tournament had been called off. Portugal was having more domestic problems, like rioting and looting in the streets. Or, as my fertile, paranoid imagination felt more likely, an august and pinch-browed assemblage of elder players had determined over brandy and Havana cigars that Vernon Bradlusky, whatever *that* was, could not attend the tournament. And there was at least an hour between me and whatever news Caroline actually had. I couldn't bear waiting for it at my apartment, staring into my fish tank or at the late news on TV, so as the cab rounded the bend at Broadway I gave the cabbie directions to Toby's. If I were going to get bad news from Caroline later on, I might as well chew out Toby and kill some time as well.

Toby's den window, facing the courtyard, glared down through the bare branches of an oak; his was the only apartment lit. The foyer door was jammed open with a handful of department-store flyers, and I climbed the three long, creaking flights of stairs up to his apartment. His radio echoed down the stairwell, saxophones groaning through the door, which was ajar. I went in, crossing the dark hallway and dining room until I finally reached the back of the apartment, and stepped into the den. From where I stood, just inside the door, one hand on the back of an arthritic-looking, splitting naugahyde recliner, I could smell the sour, thready weight in the air. Sweet-sour smells. In shirt-sleeves and his shorts, he was slumped over; his head lolled to one side; he sat in the chair, which had been, seemingly, shoved from the desk up against the wall. Stray, stiff tufts of his hair jutted from his scalp. Blood, like a bright bib, spread down his powder blue shirt and all along his boxer shorts where a nest of gray-yellow intestines had spilled from the wound in his abdomen. I stepped closer to the corpse. Everything I saw in the wide, steely wash of the desk lamplight looked somehow removed, as if I were viewing everything through the smudged pane of an exhibit case. I seemed to grow taller, I was looking down on the corpse, the air around sticky with the blue lamplight, thick as if full of blue dust. Toby's head, on its side, stared up at me, eyelids missing, cut deftly, lower and upper, away from the eyes. The lips also had been removed, the teeth smiling almost puckishly from nostrils to nearly chin, gums wrinkling in the air, graying. Those eyes and that smile went through, seemed to physically poke into me, setting me back from the lamplight. I staggered away, gripping my own hands for some reason, rubbing them together for warmth, although the room was hot. When I drew away from him my eyes went to his desk—the originals of some of my backgammon columns lay scattered on it, scissors bright and open across the yellowed newsprint. His picture of Marilyn Monroe, nude against red velvet, glowed faintly down from over the desk, shades darker, beyond the full reach of the lamp. His sports coat—yellow and blue plaid, left on the floor—was suddenly wrapped up in my feet as if it had slithered across the floor to crawl up my leg; I bent down, dizzy, seeing the puddle of blood under the chair, a dark puddle with the lumpish shreds of Toby's lips in it, the puddle spread out under the chair as if Toby had pissed blood right where he sat. I fell onto that floor, and the very fall sickened me, my stomach leaping, my breath short and shallow. I realized I had tried to stop breathing, the air was so thick with the acrid smell of the death of him, molecules of him rising in the very blueness of the air, from the wounds, from the opened flesh. I flicked the sports coat away from me, toward his bookcase, got up on my hands and knees only to retch thinly, nothing to squeeze out of me, my eyes tearing and my breath still short despite my trying to take in air, the floor under me growing round, rounder as if I were atop the swelling back of some huge animal that was drawing in deep breaths. I clutched at the shag throw rug under my hand, found loose cloth in one hand to wipe my mouth and realized it was one of Toby's powder blue socks. I held it a minute, wet with my vomit, looking at it as though this were a cut-out chunk of his flesh, threw it, and found myself racing out the door and down, down around and down the landings. I burst out into the courtyard as if I had broken the water's surface, gulping cold, medicinal-tasting air. I pressed myself againt the courtyard gate, the bars solid behind each ear, down my back; my breathing sounded metallic, bell clear in the canyonlike courtyard; wet snow was falling steadily now, reassuringly, gathering white in the grass yet dissolving in the crisscross of cement. "I must go back up," I might have said aloud, voice like some fading radio station, popping in and out. Muttering. "Go back up. Call the cops. Up and call." I would have gone just then. I know I wouldn't have run off, I would have gone to do the right thing if it hadn't been for the sudden shrill laugh of a woman and the sharp clacking of heels as she and her hulking escort had suddenly exploded in the quiet. The sounds of them sent me in the opposite direction toward the business lights of Sheridan Road. I fell in with the spreading fan of people that the all-night theater had just cut loose onto the sidewalks. I slackened my pace, walking, at least for appearance's sake, calmly in the direction of my apartment. Whatever it was that Toby had told me he was up to (that damned package atop the fridge?) it had gotten him killed. I was mixed up in it, whether I liked it or not. I could see myself explaining what I *didn't* know to a detective, crew-cut and gum-snapping, during a bare-knuckle interview. ("I swear, Officer, that's all my partner told me—pick up the package and wait for a call." "Sure buddy, let's take it from the top, now what was in the package? . . .")

I would be a *suspect*. I shuddered. What a word. What had I touched in the apartment? I thought my way into the apartment in slow motion, the way I had entered, what I had seen, I shuddered again, seeing him under that light. Shot. Had to be shot. What else would push out a hole like that in his gut? The lips, the eyes bloodless. Slit under the throat. I found myself walking faster and faster as I recalled his face, what there was of it. I forced myself to slow, to take it one step at a time, feeling other people behind me, walking the street in my direction. What had I touched?

I looked over my shoulder at the well-lit intersection, its theater marquee, two bars, and all-night grocery. Snow fell heavily in the lights. The movie crowd dispersed into the darker side streets. I stopped in the doorway of a closed beauty shop, a permed and smiling advertisement watched me breathing heavily, perspiring. I calmed myself by counting to ten—backward and forward—by watching the traffic glide past. Yes, Toby was dead. No one had seen me enter or leave his apartment. But Toby was dead. "You stupid fuck," I said, as if he'd blown a move, overbet a game, or spent two hundred dollars on another loud plaid sports coat. I kicked a candy wrapper off my heel where it had stuck.

I walked the remaining few blocks to my apartment as casually as any other pedestrian, but mad as hell—mad at Toby for getting himself killed over something I was certain would turn out to be out of his league, mad at myself for leaving the scene, and, most of all, angry that I had been unable to prevent any of it. It only took three seconds for me to go from anger to shock—the time it took to open my apartment door. Someone had paid me a visit while I'd been out and left the vacuum cleaner from the hall closet directly in the doorway so that I could trip over the hose and land in the rest of the closet contents that had been piled onto the floor. I grabbed the doorjamb and pulled myself from the tangle of hangers and clothes to the light switch. The hallway had been so thoroughly ransacked that the electrical wall plates had been removed, great jagged swaths of wallpaper had been torn loose and the overhead light fixture had been unscrewed so that the shade hung crookedly on the half-exposed bulb. My den looked as if it had been ground up and spit out onto the floor—everywhere were my old columns, the stuffing from my recliner, the scattered pieces of my backgammon sets, two overturned plants, the contents of my desk drawer—pens, pencils, paper clips—atop the pile. In my bedroom the mattress, pillows, and clothes had been slashed open. My suitcases were slit along the seams, padding bulging. In the kitchen, even the cornflakes were poured out onto the floor, a bar of soap sliced open. The phone rang, and I waded through the debris in the dining room to the phone in the living room; I found it under a drift of foam rubber that had been the sofa. I sat down as I plucked the receiver out. It was Caroline. Unmistakably Caroline.

"Vernon," she said. Caroline was the only person I would ever allow to call me by my full, lumpish first name; somehow when she used it my bald spot disappeared.

"I've been frantic. I couldn't let you get on the plane tomorrow before calling," she continued, her voice sharp despite the frazzle of transoceanic static on the line. The neck of a bottle peered out from the pile of foam I was nested in. Amazingly, the bottle was intact, half full. Leaving tomorrow. I sighed and took a slug. Everything was happening at once, I had nearly forgotten about the flight the next day. Toby dead, and whatever the deal was with the package that got Toby killed was still up in the air. I had won thirteen hundred in a game at Zorine's. And yeah, I was supposed to be on a plane to Portugal the next afternoon even though everything I owned, everything I loved was sliced up, ripped apart, leaking away. She might have been talking for hours, but when I picked up her conversation again she said,

"But things are worse than I let on. In the letter . . . Gregory. It's Gregory—he's gone over the edge. I mean he's absolutely crazy. He stays up in his room all day and comes out at night, prowling around like some ghost. After his business went down the tubes and his brother, his brother was killed in Africa, brutally killed." Her voice sounded just the way I felt, maybe that's what drew me back to what she was saying and away from Toby's death and the mess I was squatting in. "I need your help. Some papers at the Chicago office. Some blueprints and papers from the Chicago office we need here in Portugal. Before his leech of a partner gets them. You could pick them up on the way to the airport."

"You want me to do *what*?" I asked, recorking the bottle.

"Pick up some damn papers! His office in the Kraft building downtown!" She grew impatient along with the trembling. "Are you drunk?"

"Not yet."

"Please. Pick up the briefcase tomorrow at the Chicago office. Get here safe," she said softly, her plea barely audible in the crackling connection.

"Toby's dead," I said simply, like telling what I had for

lunch or when I was due for a dental exam. I drank, pulling the cork out again, swallowing, replacing it.

"What?" she asked. But she had heard me. You always say *what*, I guess, when you hear someone is dead. A respectful question, a polite denial.

"The guy you thought was a slob. The one who wore the loud sports coats and ate too much and thought you were too snooty for me." I went on explaining who he was when she knew damned well.

"Oh my God," she said plainly.

"He was murdered," I said, *murdered* sounding somehow too clumsy a word for what I had witnessed. "I found him and I just left him there. I left the goddamned scene of a—of a murder and walked right out on the stupid sonofabitch sitting dead like that, and I could be a suspect." I found myself talking loudly. "The fucking clown"—I waved the bottle in the air, a gesture she was unaware of (I was talking to myself)—"mailed me some fucking package, can't find the goddamned thing in the mess here, I bet, my goddamned apartment torn up. Over this fucking package I'm telling you. Someone after that damn package. Cocaine probably, the fucking clown!" I rambled on like that until I caught myself, took a swig off the bottle, and listened to the astonished silence, the hollow echoing of the overseas line.

"Vernon, God, Vernon," she whispered, static rising around her unsteady voice. "Get over here while you can. Get out of the damn apartment. Get over to my sister's. Just get the hell out."

"Why? They got what they wanted, whoever the hell they are. Killed Toby. Killed his ass but good, Caroline. You should have seen it. Killed his ass and ripped up the place here until they found whatever the stupid shit had stuck his neck out for. Why leave? Hell, I'm getting to *love* it here," I went on, bitter, too loud, standing in the debris of my living room. "And besides, I have to bury the sorry sonofabitch. Gotta plant him, no one else to do it. All the rest of his family in New York."

"You have to get over here quickly," she barked. It startled me.

"You don't understand," I complained.

"You have to get over here for two very simple reasons," she said firmly. I was in the mood to listen to reason; I'd run fresh out of my own. "The first is that you can't help Toby, can't find who killed him if you're in jail. The second reason is that I saw Toby here—right here in the Algarve just last week."

——— FOUR ———

I stood dumb and numb and slugging back off the bottle. Somehow the news of Toby's being in Portugal seemed even harder to imagine than Toby dead and mutilated. That enormous paunch covered in loud blue-and-yellow plaid, the doughy face, and gin-washed eyes patrolling a sun-drenched beach? I shuddered, recalling Toby's lidless eyes.

I don't know what made me look for the package—naïveté, the triumph of reason over the queasy panic that was beginning to grip me, or simple stupidity. Nevertheless, I looked on top of the fridge and felt along the empty ice trays for the brown package, finding nothing. I pulled out the folded shopping bags that were crammed into the space between the refrigerator and the cabinet. Nothing but bags. And a roach, scooting for safety behind the coils of the refrigerator. I slapped out my foot at him, thrusting the tip of my shoe at his escape. I missed, but I stubbed my toe on something wedged between the Freon coils. I wriggled my hand back there and managed to pull Toby's package free. I ripped it open as I sat there in a clutter of spilled cornflakes and silverware and shopping bags. My hands drew away from the contents, startled; the box lay in my lap. I was afraid to open it, my hands hovering over the brown wrapping paper. Whatever was inside had gotten Toby killed, no doubt. Get rid of it, why open it? I could just get rid of it. But while I was saying "Get rid of it" over and over in my head, my fingers had already begun to peel off the tape and paper.

My old traveler's backgammon set. A worthless twelve-by-twenty-inch fold-up leather backgammon set was the cause of all this grief? I opened it, looked in the dice cups, the marker trays. I couldn't believe it. Only thing out of the ordinary was part of a yellowed clipping of an old column and diagram I'd written:

> It is plain by our diagram that white does not have a chance. Black, as you can see, has locked white's remaining pieces into black's home court and black is ready to move his men off the board. It's only a matter of whether black gets a *gammon* or *back-gammon* at this point. Next week: betting strategies.

The column. Yellowed. I recalled the scissors and the newsprint on Toby's desk, oddly crisp in the metallic blueness of the desk lamp. Had he made up this package after he returned from the Algarve? But Sandra had told me she picked him up from the airport when he came back from New York and the package was already in a P.O. box by then. I tried to reread the column but the print swayed and grew fuzzy. I looked up and became aware that I was hyperventilating again, just as I had when I had found Toby's body. I grabbed a shopping bag and breathed into it, leaning against the cabinet, my legs stretched out. I picked up the column once more. What the hell could Toby mean by it? I went through the wrappings and discovered the package had a New York postmark. He must have cut the column out before his trip to New York and Portugal. Was it anything to lose a life over? I turned the scrap of paper over in my hand. Only thing I could think was that Toby had meant for the column and the diagram to serve as some code. I went through several alphabet substitutions for the gammon points in the diagram and came up with gibberish and nonsense every time, scribbling possible solutions on the paper bags, swigging off the bottle, first one leg then another falling asleep on me, perhaps whole hours passing away before I thought to search the backgammon set itself.

I took a steak knife from the rubble around me and carefully sliced away each stitched point from the game board's face. I took up the whole leather covering next and poked through the foam padding and the metal strips that made the magnetic markers stick to their positions. Nothing. I stripped the thing down to its plastic frame. I took the game markers up, black first, and pried the soft magnets from the backs. Nothing. I stared at the ripped foam, leather, and markers until my eyes burned. I went back to the idea of a code until I realized, after all, Toby didn't have to send *my* column and diagram to figure a code unless it was something in the contents of the column that made the difference. I finally folded the damned thing up and got up from the floor. I found myself avoiding the open windows of the apartment as I readied to leave, as if I were the intruder. It didn't feel like my apartment and I felt guilty—an unnamed yet palpable guilt that twitched and prodded at my lungs from up and under and threatened to send me into another spell. Most of my suits had been ripped open at the seams, pockets thoroughly snipped out and examined. My razor and shaving mug were on the bathroom floor undamaged, though the toothpaste and denture adhesive were squirted from the tubes all over the sink and toilet top where the goop had been smeared around like finger-paints—if I were a detective I probably could have lifted some prints from the mess. I grabbed the least destroyed suitcase and threw in the razor, my underwear, and any shirt or sock that had been spared. As I showered I cussed myself for packing the razor, running my soapy hand over the loose, beard-toughened flesh on my neck, my chin. I dried off slowly, standing in the debris of aeresol cans, toilet paper, and towels. I cleaned a spot in the steamed mirror and combed my hair over my bald spot in back. The rings under my eyes were dark, bruised-looking. I was the color of cornflakes left overnight in a bowl of milk. The only thing I needed was a week of sleep, but even my mattress was torn to shreds. Besides, the house made me uneasy. I flinched at each groan of a floorboard. What if they returned? I wandered back into the living room. I had until late next morning for the flight to Portugal. I took out the ticket and checked again, just to be sure. To be sure of what I don't know. That I was really leaving my best friend's body behind? That I had the right time? Where the hell could I pass time until the plane? I stood in front of the fish tank, its motor humming patiently. Christ. Even the fish had been cut open. They floated belly up, the milk-white clouds of their guts spread out behind like party streamers. The water was pink with their blood. I scooped them into my hands and flushed them down the john, spitting a stale, sour taste out of my mouth into the whirlpool.

Outside the air was still and the snow that had been falling stuck to tree limbs and grass; the cement, the streets, were clear but wet. I sniffled as I turned out my side street. It was as quiet on that street as in the apartment. I felt again somehow the intruder, interloper, as if I had to walk through the streets so as not to disturb the hush around me. The air was as heavy with moisture as quiet, and each streetlight and courtyard light threw off starry yellow points in the mist-blurred air. Crossing an intersection, I could hear the stoplights click and whir as the timers switched through their sequence. A bus whispered for attention a long way down Sheridan Road. I felt compelled to trot across the street until I was in the relative safety of a darker section, down some even quieter side street just half a block from the apartment. I crossed to the other side but not before a car barged down the street at full throttle and swerved just as I stepped out of its path, my back to a parked car. It halted with a yelp of brakes and backed up to me. The back door swung open. The guy who got out was truly awe-inspiring at that time of the morning and in my condition: he was well beyond large, his chest alone nearly half his bulk, all presided over by a face that seemed perpetually about to sneeze; his lips, nose and eyes wrinkled as if to really snort a good one, and he sported an Afro that was short, oiled, and businesslike. The guy had on a long dashiki and blue jeans, but way before I could notice any of that, I took a long good look at the length of brown rope that he held taut between the globes of his fists. About the right length to wrap around my neck and jerk sharply. The driver rolled down his stubborn electric window and popped his skinny, too-kind face out the window to say something in a very foreign language to the gorilla and to give me a look. Yellow eyes. The dude Sandra saw with Toby.

"Mr. Bradloozkey," he mispronounced my name. "Please get in the car." And his head popped back in behind the crinching of the motorized window. My good, big buddy peeled me off the car I'd been trying to actually lean *through* and dumped me and my bag into the back before getting in next to me. I hugged my suitcase and with one hand tried to feel for the back door handle. There was none.

"There is no back door handle," the driver said politely, lifting his head to peer at me in the rearview, a band of green dash light illuminating his thin, parrotlike face: rounded beak of a nose, walleyes, and a tiny slope of a forehead that barely managed to support another of those tight, oiled afros. No way these black dudes were from the South Side, though. Hell, not even Gary, Indiana, or the West Side, for that matter. No black hood I knew of. Something besides their dress, their manner of doing business. A truly *strange* accent or dialect that they spoke. I could feel more than see my companion take up most of the back as the car slowly rumbled down the darkened side streets. He hadn't said a word. I assumed, with a sinking, twisting feeling, that this was it. The big IT. Toby was dead and it was my turn. They were both silent for a convincing stretch of time. Enough to convince me that I would be spending the evening and many evenings to come at the bottom of a river. I felt my unshaven neck and wondered, for some reason, if the rope would hurt less if the skin were shaved smooth. Less friction on the hemp. Cleaner break. While I was making such calculations, the driver spoke. His accent was thick and nearly musical. Odd tones.

"My name is Josef and this is Mobotiak. So very fine meeting tonight." He flashed me a smile, the turn signal splashing on his thin neck and face as he made a corner. The streets seemed to be getting darker, if that were possible. Almost as if he were able to drive deeper and deeper into the city, finding the darkest corners, then still darker, winding down as if spiraling into a pit. The cones of the headlights caught the stark flashes of the phosphorescent licenses of parked cars, sharp flares of reflection from bumpers. It was if we were spiraling down to the floor of the ocean in one of those exploratory submarines, new sights leaping before the lights, only blackness around, and the tight, heavy air inside. My stomach tightened down on itself just as I tightened my grip on the suitcase. Shit. Josef and Mobotiak. Up until then Toby's murder had been without a face. Literally. Here were two.

"Sorry if we have put a fright on you. We need a few things to know from you. Such small things Mr. Bradloozkey," he said. The "small" thing next to me snorted.

"Small things," I repeated, and it was good to hear my own voice. The nervousness in me let up a bit.

"I see you are taking a trip," Josef nodded.

"Yeah. Portugal," I found myself telling him. I felt, just then, safer than I had in my own apartment. Perhaps it was the realization that this was the end of me, the very final end of me. I no longer had to tiptoe, as it were. Despite my initial shock at Josef and Mobotiak's appearance, I was beginning to feel friendly toward them.

"Ah, *Port-u-gal*," Mobotiak said, his first words, with enough bass to rattle the partial plate out of my mouth. "It is so cold, wet in this Chicago."

"Yes," Josef went on, attempting to get down to business. "Before you go, you would be so kind as to leave it up with us."

"Huh?" I asked, barely deciphering the slop of the sentence in the thickness of his accent.

"You would be leaving up the items that Mr. Kale so nicely managed to get for us."

"You can cut all the bullshit and just kill me," I said, honestly thinking they were pulling one on me before Mobotiak played twist-tie with my neck.

"These items mean life to you? Why not turn them over?"

he implored and pulled the car over to a very dark, very deserted and, I imagined, uninhabited length of the city. He turned in his seat.

"Mr. Bradloozkey, we can't kill you."

"No. Cannot manage that tonight. Not even as a big favor to Mr. Bradloozkey," Mobotiak said with a percolating chuckle.

"Listen, I know you got in my apartment and roughed it up and killed Toby, so why not just cut the preliminaries and make it a full and fruitful evening for yourselves and do me in. Right here. Before I start to get nervous again. It's been a long, lonely, scary evening, and I don't want to have to shit in my pants one more time. You've got me at a good time. I'm ready." I let the suitcase slither down my shins to rest on my shoe tops. Mobotiak put a heavy hand on my shoulder; my body jerked.

"Mr. Bradloozkey to be very silent for a moment as Josef recites the items he must recite."

Josef cleared his throat, rubbed at those nostrils again, and coughed wetly. "We will not—cannot—kill you, Mr. Bradloozkey. But there are others who will. There are some items which your friend Mr. Kale agreed to turn over to us once he made it into these United States. It seems he changed his mind. When he changed his mind he got dead. But not from us."

"No, not from us," Mobotiak repeated, giving my shoulder a fresh swack.

"Not you, then who?" I asked. Another car suddenly lit the street, muffler snarling, its lights bobbing from the surface, and casting a light on Mobotiak that caused his eyes to squint farther. When the car rattled off, Josef continued, his voice patronizing.

"I cannot tell you that, Mr. Bradloozkey. It would merely complicate your thinking. You must concentrate on one thing only: returning the items. Then you will be safe, yes?"

"Maybe I'd be dead. If I know where the items are, then."

"Oh yes, I believe I have seen similar ideas. But let me assure you," he went on, an annoying *tsk*ing sound to his voice, "the items will be found one way or another. And all for naught you will be dead. Give us the items. We are the good guys, I assure you. Even Mr. Kale believed us to be the good guys. But then a lapse in his finer judgment."

"Lapse," Mobotiak repeated. There was a decided increase in pressure, his fingers pressing into the shoulder joint.

"But why did you rip up my apartment? What makes you so sure I have what Toby promised you."

"We did not rip up your apartment. They did."

"Who?"

"The people who murdered Mr. Kale," Mobotiak said impatiently.

"And what items am I supposed to have?" I asked, shrugging off his hand and getting ticked off at all the tap dancing. There was a long, hungry silence.

"You mean to be saying that you have no idea what items Mr. Kale meant for us to have, nor do you have possession of such items?" Josef said in a thinner voice, rearranging himself on the seat and sighing a pepper-and-garlic-reeking sigh.

"Yeah. Not a thing in the apartment." I continued to bluff him. "So what?"

"Then you will be dead," Mobotiak said. "You sure you did not get a package from Mr. Kale?"

"Yeah. But whoever tore up the place must have gotten it," I lied. I even shrugged my shoulders, and I only do that when I am deep in lie.

"No package," Josef moaned, and turned back to the wheel, restarting the car.

"But Toby's place. Go check Toby's place. What makes you so sure he was sending anything to me?" I asked.

"If they have the package, then you needn't worry about another thing, Mr. Bradloozkey. The contents in their hands, you *will* be as dead as Mr. Kale." He set to driving again, taking street after street.

Dead, huh? I honestly wanted to help them and get my neck out, but what could I do? Toby had obviously crossed me too. An old backgammon set and a faded column I'd written a year ago. The "items" were nowhere. I wished I knew what I was doing and even said it aloud to them. Silence. Mobotiak coughed as he lit a cigar, a cloud of smoke billowing toward me.

"What country you guys from?" I asked. Silence. The car drifted into an alley.

"Toby was in Portugal. So you guys must be Portuguese, right? Never met Portuguese people. Better circumstances, huh? Need better circumstances than this ball of shit we all seem to be involved in tonight, huh?"

The car burst from the alley onto the next street. Toby's street. Four squad cars, beacons flashing, straddled the middle of the block. I sank in my seat, all the activity, the sudden glare and sound of it cowing me. Policemen in black rain slickers and boots marched on the sidewalk before Toby's apartment; the static of the police radio scratched roughly at the air. A dog, bewildered by the police lights, jerked his head about and started to howl a long, clean note somewhere between B flat and sheer misery.

A policeman, his face wrinkled sourly, eyes dull and sleep-swollen, stepped from between parked cars, rapped on the windshield with his flashlight, and barked at Josef, "Get the hell out of here. Street's blocked off. Go back around!" Josef paused, his foot on the brake as the transmission clunked into reverse.

"If he did have the items in his apartment it is too late now," Mobotiak said.

"I think it's been too late for a long time now," Josef sighed.

"If you gentlemen are not going to fill me in on anything, and you seem to be done bullshitting around with me, drop me off at the next light," I said. Josef pulled over and turned his head.

"We will stay in touch, Mr. Bradloozkey. As long as you remain healthy. I only wish we could have finished the business that Mr. Kale had so promised us. You see, he had access to so many more resources than us. You do also. I have confidence that you may indeed yet prove to be useful in finishing off this affair." He shook my hand. Mobotiak let me out his side. He also shook my hand, but I didn't like the feel of it—something too sincere and final. He tapped a long cigar ash onto Devon Avenue before grunting back into his seat and slamming the door. I tapped on his window and he let it down.

"Just give me a clue. Who killed Toby? You got to give me an edge. I'm out here alone, I don't know a thing."

"Best that way, best off. Go on to Portugal, Mr. Bradloozkey. Just keep yourself alive," Josef said from behind his closed window, Mobotiak blowing a cloud of smoke out his. They took off, did a slow U-turn, and headed down Broadway.

Standing on the foggy street, tux over my shoulder, suitcase in hand, I felt as if I had just been dropped off in the middle of someone else's dream. I brushed Mobotiak's cigar ash off my pantleg. I *was* in a dream, or a delirium; since my packing at the apartment, I had given no thought whatsoever as to where I would knock off time until my flight to Portugal. I was just tip-toeing around again, in someone else's dream, on someone else's street, looking for someone else's "items," anxious, cat-nervous. I had left the house without realizing I was headed for Murphy's bar. Really headed to see Sandra. Of all the things that were someone else's, she was the least hostile. Her place was safe. I could decide there, I could wait there. That was all I really had on my own: time and a plane ticket and my winnings from the odd couple back at Zorine's. I walked the three blocks to Murphy's, knocked on the scarred entrance door in the alley, and waited. I heard the bolt unlatch.

"It's Vern," I shouted through the door, surprised at how loud my voice was in the narrow alleyway. Sandra opened the door; she returned to her cluttered desk in the back room without speaking to me, a small reading lamp throwing a spot of light onto the invoices she was totaling.

"Have a seat," she said, not looking up from her work. I sat atop empty cases piled against the back wall. The odor of stale beer hung close in the air.

"Toby's been killed," I told her, not knowing where to start. She scribbled a total hastily and looked up from the paperwork.

"What did you say?" she asked, an annoyed twist to her face. She brushed her red bangs back from her forehead. She looked overworked, tired. But then everyone looks tired when you go without sleep yourself.

"I said Toby's been killed. Murdered."

"Christ, I don't have time for your damn jokes. Why don't you just get the hell out of here. Isn't my sister waiting for you right now in Portugal? You and Toby go play your little pranks on her, huh?" She returned to her calculator. I dropped my suitcase on the cement floor and threw the tux over it.

"I need your help," I said.

She stood up slowly, crossed over to me and gripped me by the elbows. She took a Kleenex from her pocket and dabbed away a tear that had found its way into my eye.

"Who? That guy who was in here, the yellow-eyed creep?" she asked quickly, shaking at my coat sleeve as she held it. Her eyes were big, excited as she spoke. The more questions she asked the harder it was for me to explain anything.

"No, not him. I don't know, it could have been him," I found myself babbling. I just confused things more as I tried to explain how I'd found Toby, the package he'd sent me, and the ride I had taken minutes earlier. But she listened patiently, holding onto my arms, giving me a chance to tell her all.

"Upstairs. Let's go upstairs," she told me, leading me by the arm toward the back. I realized how weak I was when I climbed the stairs.

She fixed coffee, pouring me a large cup but opening a beer for herself. She sat across from me, her expression one of worry and sadness. I sipped at the coffee, feeling her eyes on me.

"What were the two of you up to, Vern? What was in the package? Damn. Why do the two of you get into these things?" she said tensely, like a mother looking for the truth in her children.

"Everyone thinks I know the answer to that question."

"What are you going to do? The police?" she asked, turning the beer bottle in her hands.

"Nothing."

"Nothing? Your best friend is killed and you're not going to do anything about it? You're withholding evidence, Vern. You're in trouble."

"That's why I have to get to Portugal."

She sighed disgustedly, got up from the table, and stared out her window over the kitchen sink into the dark alley. Her face— tired, sad—was reflected in the glass.

I got up from my chair, emptied my cup into the sink, and wrapped my arms around her shoulders. I pulled her to me, but she refused to move, staring out into the night through the reflection of us both in the windowpane.

"Don't you see? Everything points to Portugal. I can't stay here and answer—try to answer questions for the police. I don't know anything, I don't know enough to find Toby's killer. What good would I do him in jail? Who could I help?" She turned into my arms, leaned back against the sink.

"I just don't want you hurt. All of this is so crazy." She placed a hand wearily across my shoulder, tickled at my neck with one lazily circling finger. "And Caroline. I'm afraid—" she stuttered, and I gathered her more closely into my arms, her head pressed against my chest.

"Caroline," I said aloud.

"It's not just that. I have to tell you something," she said, unbuttoning my shirt. She did not even glance up at me as she spoke.

"Mmm." Was all I replied.

"I have something to confess."

"Uh-ohhh," I kidded, or tried to, as she twirled her long nails through the hair on my chest. Reaching up into the knit top she wore, I unhooked her bra, ran my hands across the smoothness of her back.

"Do you remember when your wife found you and Caroline in the motel, that motel in Waukegan?" she asked meekly. I stretched my hand down under the top of her jeans. Hell yes, I remembered my wife finding us. It's not one of those days you easily forget.

"I was the one who told her where the two of you were staying," she said, abruptly halting her caresses. "But it was to get back at Caroline. I didn't want to break up your marriage—it was Caroline I was after."

"That wasn't what broke up my marriage," I assured her, nearly chuckling. Secretly, I had been happy to be rid of my wife. Things had never been the best between us.

"Caroline." Gone was the tinge of apology, the coquettishness to her voice. "Caroline had ruined me a few weeks before the day at the motel." She kissed my chest again; I hugged her. Ruined. "When I was young—out of high school a year or two—I went out with this older man . . . God, all us girls have at least one *older man*. He had dark, curly hair. Mohair sweaters. Drove a Thunderbird. You know the type." She winked, running her hand through the hair at the back of my neck. I nodded, yes I knew the type. I sure hadn't been one of them myself back then.

"Well, he liked photography. And I, uh, posed for him. Lots of pictures. Tight-sweater shots—they were popular. Satin sheets. Half nude. One night, after a big birthday party for him at the Blackhawk Restaurant, I posed with some of his friends. Two of his friends. You know the kind of pictures. I could say I was drunk and he took advantage of me but that would be a lot of bullshit. I wanted to do it. At least, *then* I wanted to do it."

I nodded again, even though she could not see. Her voice trembled.

"So that was years before I met this other guy. Bond broker. Lots of money. Fun to be with. God, he had a sense of humor." Her voice drifted off nostalgically. "Tipped the maître d' at the Prudential three leaves from the potted palm that blocked the skyline view from our table one night. God . . ." she sighed, her breath warm. She raised her head, fixed my gaze in her green eyes. "And Caroline mailed him the pictures," she said coldly, with a sniffle. "Mailed him the pictures when she found out we were engaged."

I tried to say something, but she put her fingers to my lips, watching as she traced the slope of my nose, the stubble under my chin. "I don't know how she got ahold of those pictures," she went on, tears catching on the corner of her mouth as she spoke. Her face was expressionless. I rubbed at the back of her neck, between her shoulder blades, her muscles tight under my circular massaging.

"Why the hell would Caroline do something like that?" I managed to ask. I couldn't believe Caroline could be so needlessly vicious.

She shrugged. "I don't know. She would never say. We had made a game of stealing each other's boyfriends in high school—perfectly normal, catty adolescent behavior, that kind of thing. But that . . . I think she even went out with the photographer. I don't know. But sending those pictures went way beyond any dirty tricks we played as girls." She shook her head slowly before looking at me again, this time with the beginnings of a smile on her face. I nudged away the tears with a knuckle and kissed her.

"But I wanted you to know it was me who told your wife. And I wanted you to know what Caroline's capable of. I don't think she ever let you see that side of her, not in all the years you've known each other."

I had to agree—Caroline had never shown, hinted at that type of unprovoked maliciousness.

"You're not trying to say—" she pressed her lips to mine.

"I'm not suggesting anything. But Toby is dead and you're mixed up in this, and you yourself said everything points to Portugal."

"But Toby was killed here, not in Portugal. Your sister *is* in Portugal."

"I just mean that you should be careful. I don't want you dead," she whispered, staring at me oddly. A lot of people seemed concerned with my mortality that night.

We made love on the kitchen table, clothes scattered among the chairs. Afterward she led me down the hallway to her front parlor and sat me down in a pile of cushions and pillows. The front curtains were open; she leaned across me as I lay there, propped up to the half-sitting position with an armful of the pillows at my back.

"A candle," she said, lighting one on her coffee table, her voice a sudden but soothing sound in the quiet apartment. The orange glow cast by the candlelight made her skin look powdery, somehow smoother than it had felt. She lay her head against me, her breath quavering over my chest as she stared into the candleflame. Street noises—truck brakes, a car stereo, the rumble of an old car—barely drifted up to the tiny living room even though it faced Devon Avenue below. I traced the half-moon of a scar that I always noticed on her shoulder blade. I was fond of it, actually.

"Pushed down," she explained.

"Are you sure?" I asked, thinking how every childhood injury has its villain, its inflicter.

"Sure I'm sure. I was at the top rung of the slide and someone pushed me off. I landed on one of the cement pilings that the slide was anchored down with, cut my shoulder." She squirmed under my hand, as if the wound had reopened and was sensitive to my touch. It was then inevitable: we both spent hours describing childhood bruises, wounds, near-death calamities, and exhibiting the bumps and whitish disfigurements left even those many-odd years layer. Sandra had the most—fifteen—though they were smaller in most cases and not nearly as life-threatening as many of mine.

"But Caroline, I say, can't have a one," she said, murmuring to my palm where I had showed her the trail that five stitches had left after a broken car window.

"Mmmm?" I asked.

"Caroline. No scars. But she never had any fun. Got to get a few scars if you have any fun. Caroline always would stay indoors," Sandra said, lifting her eyes from the candle, turning her head in the nook of my arm, her eyes wetly luminescent. "She played piano, took sewing lessons, cooked dinner for Father—especially after Mother had left him. Poor Dad. Caroline tried to take Mother's place, I guess. Never went out. Never acted like a kid, not like the rest of us. On Sundays she made Dad drive us through Winnetka, the rich neighborhoods. And in that old Buick. I hid in the back seat, slumped down as we slipped up and down the blocks." She smiled to herself, lighting a cigarette.

"I don't know why I hid. Maybe I thought the rich people would come out of their houses and yell at us for being in their neighborhood. But Caroline, Christ!" She laughed, looking at me briefly. "Caroline would get dressed in her best clothes. Lace collar, mother-of-pearl barrettes, the works, and would sit bolt upright in the seat as if she had a back brace on. My poor father never took his eyes off the road. He looked as nervous as I was embarrassed. Tugging at his hat brim—he wore a hat, not many men still did—telling Caroline that it was foolish to drive around in those towns, that it was time to get back to Waukegan . . ."

I was staring vacantly out the blackness of her living-room window, imagining the three of them cruising down the shady, manicured lanes of Winnetka in a Buick with more dents than smooth spots. She poked me. I cupped one of her breasts, just to show that I had not forgotten that she was there. And it was great to be there with her again after so long.

"Yeah," she said, with a mouth of lazy smoke, "you'll go to Portugal all right. Go, find out what you have to, but get back in one piece. I just knew something was up when Toby didn't pick up his bag. Left it here, said he'd be back. Never showed. Vern, I need to tell you . . ." she trailed off.

"What? You mean Toby's bag is downstairs? Why didn't you *say* so?"

"I need to tell you . . ." she said again as she held my arm, pulling me back to bed as I tried to get up and look for the bag.

"I searched it. Nothing in it, really. Just clothes. I knew I shouldn't have, but . . ."

"You sure there's nothing?"

"Mmmm."

"I'll leave you some money for Toby's funeral," I said after a long moment, sitting back in bed beside her." There's a few people in New York who'll want to know." She nodded in agreement, exhaling through the candle flame, causing it to flicker. A good long time passed, one or two more cigarettes.

"So you're really going tomorrow," she said in a disappointed, girlish whisper in response to something I might have said minutes ago, responding the way people do when they've been up all night. When the first specks of dawn began to lighten the window, Sandra drifted off to sleep.

Sawtooth ribbons of jet trails crossed in the bluing sky while the building across from the window, a laundromat with apartments above, began to come awake. A couple in their sixties shuffled across a kitchen that had suddenly come ablaze. The man read his paper at a table just in front of the window. I slid from under Sandra's sleepy breath, making sure I didn't awaken her, and blew out the candle. I stood and stretched, naked and tired, watching traffic begin to venture down Devon.

I dressed in the kitchen and left Sandra a note about Toby's funeral, scribbling a few New York numbers. I slipped five hundred under the butter dish. I found Toby's suitcase downstairs, grabbed it, and tore it open. Clothes, clothes, and more gaudy, cheap clothes which I flung all over the back room. Nothing but *nothing* in the way of a clue. In the coat pocket of one exceptionally loud sports coat I found tissue credit-card receipts from restaurants in New York and Lisbon.

From more dinner receipts fell a wallet-size photo, bent at the corners, the emulsion cracked like an old, broken-looking glass: it was a picture of Toby and me standing outside the Hotel Camino Real in Mexico City, the night I won big at the tournament. Both of us were obviously drunk—Toby had a meaty hand on my shoulder and was in the process of grabbing my tux jacket to break his fall to the sidewalk. His cheeks were flushed with liquor. I had a hand over my head and clutched the winner's purse, an oversized cashier's check, in my teeth as if it were a flamenco dancer's rose. I was off balance and was about to fall with Toby. Both of us, laughing, gasping, did fall and flailed until our camera-tending sweetie—was her name Maxine, Dolores?—helped us up.

I ripped the photo—soft and easily rended—into smaller and smaller fragments of Kodak paper, cracked emulsion, and threw the whole mess off onto the storeroom floor. My stomach leaped. God damn. Just needed some breakfast. Yeah, there was no sense in waking Sandra, leaving the way I had was for the best. Why should she drive me downtown to pick up Gregory's package and then drive me all the way out to the airport? The last sight I had was of her sleeping peacefully, clutching at a pillow. Why would I want to spoil it in the plastic lounge at O'Hare, her mascara running, my heartburn rising, saying good-bye over and over again?

All I had to do at that point was to pick up Gregory's package and get the hell out of Chicago. It seemed as if everything that had been happening to me in the previous forty-eight hours was calculated to drive me into a corner; as if I were up against someone or something that knew all the moves and was patiently hemming me in. I had to stay in the game, on the board long enough to figure what I was up against.

——— FIVE ———

The night's feeble attempt at snow had melted off the cars, grass and tree limbs. The gutters and sidewalks were strewn with worms struggling up from underground to die on the water-logged cement. The air was damp and worm-scented and every bright, sunlit corner seemed to have a few extra pounds of wet newspaper stuck to its gutters. Faces that passed seemed to linger over me. I hunched under the weight of my suitcase and tux, wishing I could slink back into the comfort of night again, feeling oddly melancholy and vulnerable in the daylight. That melancholy, you can believe, hung tight on me. I blamed it on lack of sleep, the moments with Sandra, the fact that I had been driven around in the middle of the night by a couple of weird blacks who couldn't decide whether they wanted to intimidate me or befriend me, the odd couple at Zorine's. Toby, or what was left of him, kept coming back to me in flashes; yet each time I recalled him under that steely blue light, eyes wide and lidless, the mutilation-forced smile, I became less awed and shocked and angry. It was as if playing his corpse over and over in my mind was a way of accepting, recovering from the discovery. The sensation was not unlike the middle or end of a close tournament game when I felt drawn out of myself, my mind working over possibilities, odds, opportunities for moves.

I found myself in a diner near the El tracks, feeling safe in its shabbiness; the Formica-topped counter and bad coffee were reassuring. I glanced at the other customers: all seemed sleepy, innocuous, gray-faced.

Midway through my third cup, I picked up the morning *Trib* from the seat next to me where a commuter had abandoned it. Instinctively I turned to the features section; there I was, just below the "Ask Doctor Leonard" column. The waitress glided past, topping off my cup. Obviously Sid, my editor, had decided to go with my new column, at least in Chicago, where I ran biweekly.

> ". . . the game that's won with one attack can
> be lost with the next."

That damned last line jumped up at me from the page, it was so bad—didn't even make sense. I cringed, shuddered, felt like running out to the paper machine on the corner and ripping out every one of the columns. I recovered slowly, doing a slow burn with myself for being such a hack. But as I flipped through the remainder of the paper, I spotted a two-inch piece of copy:

> Responding to a routine complaint of a loud stereo at 1244 Albion, police discovered the body of Tobias Kale, 33. Detectives at the scene report that the victim had been shot from behind with a large caliber pistol. Said one officer, "This looks like revenge, a mob-related killing." Robbery was ruled out as a motive.

Mob-related. Hmm, right. I ripped the article out and slipped it into my wallet with the column he'd sent me and the bundle of receipts I'd pocketed from the suitcase he'd left at Sandra's. Short and sweet, not exactly an obituary. It was right across from another two-incher about a flood in India:

> . . . a large number of people remain trapped
> in remote villages. Reported one helicopter
> pilot, "It looks like a great foaming lake out
> there, where once were farms."

Toby dead. Flood in India. The stark simultaneity of it all struck me. As Toby was being killed, hundreds were flailing in the foam of an engorged river in India. The article appeared so fast, wasn't it only hours ago? It was, and yet here was the news of Toby. And of course the dead in India. And it occurred to me that as I was sweating and counting my last in the back seat with those ludicrous heavies the night before, a reporter must have been stamping his feet in the cold courtyard, rumpled spiral notebook in hand.

And as I was making love to Sandra in her kitchen, the death was going from phone line to typesetter. Letters punched into metal. I shivered, a street chill working itself in as patron after patron abandoned their coffee. I shuffled along in the crowd, boarded the El, taking a seat that faced the doors.

As I approached the Michigan Avenue building that housed DI-MIND, Inc., Gregory Massad's Chicago business office, I noticed that curb space was at a premium: moving vans, trailers, and rigs were standing two deep in the street and in the alley beyond. Movers were streaming out the revolving doors as they emptied the building. I caught an elevator to the eighth floor. A receptionist in a cheap, lacquered fall, a three-piece maroon pantsuit, and perfume that smelled as if it could only be tar-based, tapped her fingers on a bare desk top and glanced up at me.

"I'm here to pick up a package for Mr. Massad," I told her. She raised one of those idle fingers, putting me on hold, and turned to a mover who wheeled a file cabinet from behind the domain of her desk toward the elevator.

"Careful now, Mr. D. wants that handled with the *utmost*

care," she admonished, undoubtedly parroting her boss's exact words. "Sorry," she lied as she returned to me. "We're moving."

"I can see."

"Some college or night school bought the building. Everyone's moving, not just us. Personally, I'm glad. I've about had it with the restaurants around here. You eat in the same places for lunch every day for five years, you get bored, you know? Can I do something for you?"

"Mr. Massad sent me for a briefcase," I told her calmly. I believe I even smiled as I rested my suitcase on the worn carpet. I can be so polite at times.

"Mr. MASSAD!" She gulped. "Yes, of course." And she produced a handsome, light tan briefcase from under the desk. I really hadn't expected anything *but* a handsome briefcase; Gregory—if nothing else—did things with class.

"You actually *know* Mr. Massad?" she asked, all teeth and sincerely nervous in the presence of someone she suspected might have the power to stop her annual raise from going through. "I've worked for this company for five years and I've never even seen a picture of the guy. Is he a *nice* guy?" she asked, smiling wider.

"I don't really know him that well." I smiled back. "But I understand he likes to fire nosy secretaries."

It felt good to say that, taking hold of my old self again and giving back some of the accumulated crap that was being heaped in my direction. I began to realize that my only truly safe strategy toward the whole damned mess was for me to get on the offensive. It just so happened that the receptionist happened to be in the way when I felt my recovery, that awakening. I gave her a wink as I boarded the elevator. To her credit she kept that plastered-on smile, kept her vacuous cool. I loved her for it.

I grabbed a cab for the airport and tried to pry open the briefcase. Slim. Expensive. Very locked. I figured I'd take any edge at that point, and if the briefcase was going out of the country with me, I wanted in on what was inside. I fumbled with the latches and locks and chipped at the hinges and swore up a good sweat when the driver, stopping for a light, peered back and said, "You got troubles? Take this." And he tossed a red pocketknife into the back seat.

"Swiss Army," he went on. "My kid gave it to me for Christmas. If a Swiss Army can't get it open, it don't open." I went through the screwdriver, the nail file, the ice pick, and the hasp before the corkscrew finally managed to spring the latches. I don't know if it was worth the effort: all that was inside were blueprints and what appeared to be company deeds and leases from the Chicago office. Nothing much of value. I took a long look at the blueprints; there was no title or description on the margins. The sketch was of a roof segment that had been sectioned off in rectangular slices, in two separate layers. I gave up interpreting the sketches as we reached the airport.

I felt oddly comfortable as Chicago drifted off below. I slept all the way to New York, where I had time and a three-day growth to kill. I shaved in an airport john with one of those flimsy plastic razors, my face raw with nicks, and managed to find a pay phone and someone to give me enough change to make calls. I tried to call Toby's cousin, the dentist who'd done such a mail-order bad job on my bridgework, just to tell him about Toby. But the phone was disconnected and the operator had no new listing for him. Then something made me call Sid.

"And if you don't bring down a shit-load of gossip—you know what readers want: sex, scandal, sex, money, more sex—you can frame today's edition, because it'll be the last paper you're in. I have to sell, sell, sell. Punch up this trash or I've got replacements." He rambled on and on and on. I hadn't gotten in a word, although I'm not sure I would have had anything intelligent to say in my defense. I even dialed my father's number in Phoenix, but when his girlfriend answered I hung up and went over to the boarding area where I caught a few more Z's.

The flight overseas was more crowded than I had imagined; I sat next to an elderly Spanish man who was returning to Madrid—the stop beyond Lisbon—after visiting a son who had opened a small shop in New York. He was small but stockily built, and was eager to tell me everything about his visit; his face, deeply wrinkled and browned, was lit with pride as he explained how well his son's business was doing. I listened politely, finding the voice and the simple facts of the old gentleman's life nearly as comforting as the bourbon that my attentive stewardess brought me—miniature after miniature—without requiring me to flag her down for each round. Somewhere in the history of the man's experiences in World War II, I rudely fell asleep; my eyes, my ears, my nerves all shut down from sheer exhaustion.

I had a dream about Toby. The two of us were leaning over a huge, billiard-table-sized backgammon board, a harsh light hung low overhead. The length and breadth of the board was overwhelming, the backgammon pieces themselves as large as tea saucers yet thick and weighty. I was aware of other people watching, murmuring in the protective darkness beyond our game board. My wrists ached and I noticed they had become scratched by the rough onyx edges of the playing pieces. I looked across at Toby as if to say "Let's put an end to the game." I was tired and achy and I was having trouble seeing to the other end of the gameboard and the light—damn the light—was blurring the game pieces so that I could not tell how many of the white or the black were on any given point of the board.

Toby got pissed. He started to grunt out comments. "Roll the damn dice, roll them for chrissakes, Bradlusky!" When I looked over and squinted carefully at him, my eyes watering from the lamp glare and eyestrain, I could see that his lips seemed waxen and unmoving.

"Roll the fucking dice!" he screamed, and I could then plainly see that the lips did not move and the voice was muffled behind the mask of him: Toby was wearing a rubber impression of himself, and I knew it was to hide the slashed face beneath. His screams and jerks of the head tore the latex loose along the bottom, just above his collar, and fresh blood began to seep over his shirt and onto the yellow plaid jacket. He screeched again about the dice, and I held them out as if to throw them.

They had become too large to hold onto, and they nearly fell out of my hands. I gripped tightly at them and felt them give, as if I had broken an eggshell in my hand. I looked at the broken dice as they crumbled and seeped out of my fingers: bugs, hundreds of black, aphidlike bugs, crawled from inside the dice, scurrying rapidly over my hands, up and down my fingers, over my wrist and into the cuts there. The rest of the dice, the brittle eggshell exterior and the moist, brownish liquid it contained, dribbled between my fingers and plopped to the felt table. Toby was holding on to the table opposite me, gripping the edge for support, the mask was flapping open loosely off his neck, and a great pour of blood was making its way down his neck and soaking into his clothes. In fact the blood seemed to flow according to his bellows, as if forced out of his lacerated flesh even more freely by each burst of his voice.

"You stupid fucking moron! You chicken-shit bastard! I should count on you to fold! Can't play the game or the odds!" He went on and on. I wanted desperately to get those bugs off me; they were crawling higher onto my arm, into my scrapes and there now seemed to be thousands of them. I reached for a rag I could barely see in the dimness near my feet. I wiped and smeared the bugs and sappy liquid from each finger, and when I threw the rag into the darkness, I suddenly knew it was Toby's blood-soaked shirt that I had been cleaning my hands with. I looked across the table. Toby was laid out on the backgammon board, the mask removed. His face was just as I had seen it when I had found him dead. The light gleamed dully off the blood and I was trying to clear my mouth and nose because I couldn't breath with the smell: everything felt clogged, and I wiped at my nose with my blood-stained hands and fought for breath as I heard all those around the table shifting in their chairs, whispering and clearing their throats.

"*Señor, señor, señor!*" The Spanish gentleman shook me awake. My stewardess—eyes wide with alarm and concern—bent over me.

"Hold your head back, sir, hold this on your nose," she said, pressing a cold compress to my nostril.

"I don't understand," she stammered. "The cabin is pressurized."

"It's not the cabin's fault," I groaned from under the towel and ice cubes. "Just my nose's fault. It bleeds all the time. Bleeds when it rains. Bleeds when I get excited. Bleeds when it shines."

"What's that called?" she asked me, dabbing away blood that had made its way to my chin, neck. "When your nose bleeds like that?" A few other curious passengers craned their heads around to see what all the commotion was.

"What's the technical name?" I paused. The doctor had never given me a name for it. Just that one of the membranes in one nostril or the other was dangerously thin and could rupture at any time, for any reason. He warned that one time I might not be able to stop the bleeding entirely on my own. What I needed was an expensive and time-wasting operation that would reinforce that thin membrane. He'd never given me a Latin name for it, though.

"Pain in the ass," I said. "I just call it a pain in the ass." I could feel the flow lessen as the ice numbed the bridge of my nose. She handed me a paper napkin.

"Did you bring a change of clothes on board?" she asked.
"No."

She shook her head sadly, straightened up with the blood-soaked towel in her long, thin hands. "Your shirt is ruined," she said simply, before turning away and walking up the aisle.

My Spanish companion, who had wakened me and watched as the stewardess cleaned me up, turned suddenly toward the window and stared blankly at the ocean below.

"Thank you for calling the stewardess," I offered, pressing the napkin to my nose to relieve what little blood still trickled out. He mumbled something to me and I understood that he meant for me to leave him alone. My nosebleed had offended something in him: it had shocked him, convinced him that I was a bad omen or—at the very least—a very disagreeable and

vulgar person to share an eight-hour flight with. I couldn't exactly disagree with that.

—— SIX ——

Hours later, the plane banked suddenly, and I could look
directly past my companion out the window to the blue of the
Atlantic. The Spanish gentleman, I soon noticed, was clutching
at a small rosary, his anxious fingers worrying each bead as his
lips hissed prayer; we banked once more and suddenly off the tip
of our wing—Lisbon, the entire city reddish with its tile roofs.
Gray and brown flecks—trawlers and tankers—dotted the Atlantic waters and huddled up into the narrowing river.

Customs was no big deal after I convinced them that I had
no cigarettes and no color film. They eyed my shirt, however,
and I had to assure them in my rough Spanish, which they graciously understood, that I had not been involved in any violent
or antisocial behavior on the way over. A younger customs of-
ficial, in fact, offered me his handkerchief, which I politely—and
probably to his relief—refused.

I claimed my bag and Gregory's briefcase and grabbed a cab.
We glided through the avenues of Lisbon toward the hotel Sheraton, passing through what appeared to be an older section of
town: all the buildings—porticoes, ornate façades, and pitted
granite and marble walls—were swathed in layers of graffiti
amid the lush green and well-kept midways of the streets; it was
as if suddenly the buildings had fallen victim to some epidermic
fungus that touched nothing else. Banks were especially riddled
with the scabs of red lettering, initials, stars and sickles: PCP,
AUTONOMIA DO ALGARVE, and other slogans. But the red and
black spray paint was not all that defaced the architecture: be-

neath the new splashes of vandalism older, worn slogans were just barely visible, actually etched into the walls.

The cabbie accepted my greenbacks and disheveled appearance without questions; the hotel management was not so easily set at ease. There was some doubt as to the availability of any room whatsoever until I changed four hundred dollars in cash at the hotel's courtesy bank in plain view of the pinch-faced clerk. I waved off a mincing bellboy and took the elevator up to my room, wondering if, by some long shot, it was the same as Toby's, for he too had stayed at the Sheraton.

The first priority was to close the drapes: my room did have an incredible view of the city, but the city was, after my trip, painfully white, hot, and dizzyingly reflective in the light. I sprawled out on the bed, kicked my shoes off, and tried to place a call to Caroline; she and Gregory knew I'd be arriving, and as I had to spend a day or two in Lisbon I wanted them to know not to expect me right away. The tournament wasn't until the next week, so I felt I had plenty of time to check out my leads in the city before heading down to the southern coast. Neither Caroline nor Gregory was in, and I had to leave the message with a servant—a gruff-voiced guy who merely grunted hello but insisted, also with a grunt, that he had understood everything I told him. I had taken all the receipts Toby had rung up in Lisbon and was trying to separate his detritus from mine on the bed. I phoned the desk and asked them to send up someone for my suit. I slipped into my robe and turned the radio on at the nightstand. I was surprised to hear—loud and strong and definitely in English—Joan Baez. The radio turned from Baez to Pete Seeger; I was beginning to wonder if I were in a Greenwich Village time warp instead of Lisbon in the late seventies. The valet arrived, and I gave him my suit. Protest songs. I thought about the graffiti on the buildings, and I remembered that Portugal had had quite a bit of trouble a few years earlier: unrest, riots, a change in government or something that was not even clear enough in my memory to be called vague. I took a shower and fell quickly to sleep—that bed was like a warm, safe lap to doze in.

When I woke my suit was not ready at the valet shop, so I was forced to put on my tuxedo—a bit formal, but I had no choice. I stuffed all of Toby's receipts into the nightstand drawer and mine back into my wallet and headed for the one place in the hotel where I was sure that Toby had not remained a stranger—the rooftop bar.

I sat at the end of the bar closest to the outdoor patio that overlooked the city. I could see out and across to the Ritz, which glowed warmly over the park; far off in the distance, a brilliantly lit, spread-armed Christ towered above the city from a hill beyond.

The bartender, short, dark, with crisply trimmed sideburns and a mustache, came over.

"Irish whiskey?" I asked.

"No. Sorry," he answered.

"American?"

He shrugged helplessly. "I went out of American last week. I ordered, but the orders are slow. I have good brandy or a Scotch if you wish." I wondered if the absence of decent American whiskey or bourbon had anything to do with Toby's stay there. I was sure there had to be some connection. I asked for something local, and he poured a brandy.

"Another American," I began; the bar filled with a cool breeze that fluttered the awnings outside. "Did another American drink up all the whiskey?" The bartender righted a wisp of his black hair which the wind had displaced across his forehead. He looked up at me quizzically.

"Did you have another American in here nearly a week ago? Fat. Wearing very colorful coats."

He grinned in recognition. "Yes, yes," he laughed. "Mr. Kale. God is mighty, he could—" he motioned as if he downed a tankard in a split second. "Not the whiskey though. The whiskey the Germans drink down. Mr. Kale he drank the brandy. Mr. Kale was here all the time. Both times in Lisbon. Joao," he said, pointing to himself. "Joao made sure he had a good time. Party time, like Mr. Kale says." He laughed loudly, drawing the gaze of an elderly couple nestled at the other end of the bar. The wind picked up once again, and I even detected the faint smell of the ocean.

"What do you mean *two* trips to Lisbon?" I only had a receipt for Toby's one stay.

"Camille," he said plainly. "I introduced Mr. Kale to, how would you say, a woman with a short memory." He shrugged his shoulders again, nearly popping the brass buttons on his red jacket.

"A hooker?"

"What?"

"Prostitute. I think we understand each other. Go. How did you introduce them? When?" I downed the rest of the brandy, and helped myself to the bottle which Joao had left on the bar.

"When Mr. Kale came to the hotel. First of the month?" he turned to me as if I could confirm his arrival. "Somewhere in there, he stayed in the hotel. Spent time at the bar. Asked me if I knew where there was a party time. I keep the numbers of some ladies. Good ladies, you understand, who enjoy entertaining the international crowd. Camille"—he bent toward me conspiratorially and whispered—"I don't believe that's her real name. But Camille showed Mr. Kale a party time until he went south. When he came back up—last week, I'm sure, he and Camille were in the hotel together. They spent three nights. Mr. Kale went back to the U.S.A., and Camille . . ." his voice trailed off as he took up one of the bills I had placed on the bar.

"Hundred escudos," he sighed, making change.

"What about Camille?" I asked him once again. He shook his head with a sour expression, the wind mussing his hair. The couple at the other end of the bar moved closer as the woman made as if she were catching a chill.

"If you want a woman, you should pick someone else. I don't care what your Mr. Kale said about our Camille, she is— you would be much happier with another woman, mister?" He produced a small red leather book from the watchpocket of his bartender's jacket, asking my name.

"Mr. Bradlusky, but I—"

"There is Lucinda, Mr. Bradlusky," he interrupted as he thumbed slowly through the book. "She is blonde, if you like blondes. Perhaps it is the dye, but she does a natural job with it, Mr. Bradlusky. Or Louisa, fine girl. Family was killed in Mozambique. Very mannered."

"You don't understand," I said. He looked up.

"You want something more," he stage whispered. "More adventuresome?"

"No. I want to talk with Camille," I insisted.

He leaned against the bar and frowned. "Mr. Bradlusky, I have a reputation to uphold. If you do not have a good time, party time, then I look very, very bad and could lose business. I insist that you don't see this Camille." He stared at me a long time, determination steadying his gaze, set firmly in his jaw. I remained equally firm, finished my brandy in silence, and tucked my money away, all the while holding his stubborn glare. He swore quickly in Portuguese, tossed up his arms, and produced a piece of paper from his pocket. He scribbled something in pen and handed me the paper.

"Give this to a cab driver downstairs. She will be expecting you, I will call ahead," he said hurriedly, as if rushing me out before he changed his mind. I tucked the paper into my pocket without looking at the address and began to leave the bar.

"Mr. Bradlusky," he called as I neared the door, "you remember that I did not want to send you. You forced your way." He held an accusatory finger up and wagged it at me.

"I insisted," I agreed, and left.

The cab wound through street after busy street before it plunged into a section of the city that was only intermittently alive with a tavern, an open shop, or a corner grocery around which men and women congregated. The streets became narrower, and we made our way down toward the waterfront. The cab passed through an alleyway engulfed on either side by crumbling plaster walls and emerged into a small square. The driver stopped, got out, and opened my door.

"Y Rua Migual." He pointed to the paper that I held.

"Camille, 727 Rua Migual." I nodded, thanked him, and gave him a generous tip. I understood why he could take me no farther; the streets off this older section of Portugal were much too narrow for even his small Mercedes cab. No more than a few blocks down the hill, the bay lay flat, black, and pungent; the air was laced with must, oil, and rust. A winch on a trawler anchored just offshore screeched mournfully in the still air. I made my way up the inclined street, entering the canyon formed by the white-washed stucco that rose on either side and up in tiers, seemingly without a break, up and up the steep riverbank. I passed under an arch; a small boy stood underneath, looked up at me with shock and wide eyes; I was uncomfortable in the tux; it wasn't meant for such a climb. The street narrowed even more; above, laundry hung lifeless on lines strung between iron balcony bars. Splotches of light, radio music, the sounds of children echoed down from these open windows into the corridor.

I passed a closed grocery, its windows piled high with burlap grain bags. On the corner next to an empty wooden fish stall, I made the left the driver had instructed me to take. And this street was so narrow it was barely an alley. In the darkness ahead I heard laughter, loud voices. I approached a doorway; inside a blue-tiled porchway a group of men were huddled over a round table, busy with cards and beer. I peeked in, feeling timid in the sudden bright light.

"Rua Migual?" I asked. They grew silent and regarded me warily.

An older man, obviously drunk, staggered up from the table. He waved the bottle at me, perhaps offering me a drink. "Migual, Migual!" They waved me farther up the alley. I came to another corner, and found the house, which rose four or five uncertain stories. It had a few wrought-iron balconies, the windows and the front double doors were framed in blue Spanish tile. I knocked.

A girl, no more than ten, pulled the door open and stared up at me. She said nothing but bolted away toward the back when I asked for Camille. The foyer was dim, paneled, and carpeted. A coat rack stood near the ornately tiled staircase from which an elderly woman, face too white with powder, dressed in layers and layers of rose chiffon, descended to greet me.

"I am Camille's landlady," she said pleasantly, in perfect English, offering me her hand. "You are here to see Miss Camille," she told me rather than asked.

"Yes. An appointment," I said wondering how much her cut was.

"I will announce you, sir. And would you like wine? A meal perhaps? I have excellent *dobrada* tonight."

"Wine would be nice," I told her as she disappeared upstairs. She returned minutes later.

"Miss Camille will see you now. Room Five, second landing. Her English is quite good; ring if you need anything," and she flowed down the stairs past me and into the back of the house.

Camille was young, no older than seventeen, but I was not surprised; Toby always went for the younger girls. She was reclining on a small red love seat, her silky black hair displayed in a sprawl across the tufted back. She seemed not fully awake, her eyes half closed in the light of three candles placed on the dresser. There was a small fragile-looking nightstand, and a low coffee table that held perfume bottles, cosmetics, a magazine, and prescription bottles. She was topless and made no motion to cover herself. Her breasts, like her smooth, slim face, were olive in color and were slight enough to stand firmly away from her chest, her nipples a dark chocolate brown. She wore black satin pants that hugged her hips but blossomed loosely from her legs, which were propped up on the coffee table. She examined a nail in the weak light: it was chipped, cracked perhaps, and she frowned at it, her narrow penciled eyebrows puckering. She swore softly.

"Camille," I said, sitting down on the edge of her single bed, the springs squeaking. She looked up and swung her legs under her. Toby had good taste. I couldn't figure why Joao had been so stubborn about my seeing her. My eyes adjusted to the candlelight. She was smiling at me.

"You want a good time tonight?" She pursed her lips. I almost laughed, the affectation seemed so out of place on her.

"I came to talk," I said, trying to keep my attention on just her face.

She stood, walked around the coffee table, and wound her body around me as I sat motionless on the bed. The door flew open and the little girl entered, struggling with a bottle of wine and a battered tin bucket that was crudely welded to an iron stand. Camille ignored her. The girl hurried out as Camille licked at my ear, pressed her breasts to me. Her breath was hot, spicy-smelling. I tried to ignore her as she kissed at my neck, unbuttoned my shirt.

"I have a fast tongue," she whispered.

"Mr. Kale," I stammered simply, as if Toby's name were some incantation which could save me. I was in danger of losing sight of business. Mentioning his name had its effect; she faced me, her eyes questioning.

"What about Mr. Kale?" she asked, batting her heavily mascaraed eyelashes.

"I want to ask you some questions about Mr. Kale," I said, buttoning my shirt. She turned from me and drank from the wine bottle.

"You still pay. For talk I'll charge the same as if I suck off your nuts," she said in a cold, businesslike voice. She was no longer as enticing, as *seventeen*, if that were possible.

"Fine," I told her. She got up from the bed with the bottle of wine and sat back down on her love seat. She took a long drink and set it on the table.

"You know Toby, you stayed with Toby last week," I began. There was so much I didn't know I felt at a loss as to where to start.

"Toby and me had a lot of party times. Six days he paid me for. Three nights at the Sheraton," she answered, in a proud voice, her head cocked. "So what if he was a little *pesado*, too much in the stomach. He had a good cock and we went first class. So he sends you to get some of his money back or something? Tell him to be fucking off. I spent it," she said angrily. She opened one of the bottles on the table and downed two huge yellow capsules with a swig of wine.

"No, he didn't send me to get any money back from you," I assured her. "I just need to know a few things."

"*Guarda!* Policeman?" she asked. Much of her beauty had disappeared.

"No. Just a friend."

She relaxed a bit, uncovered a jar of cream from the table, and began to dab tiny dots of it along her breasts. She covered the jar tightly.

"So, friend, ask your questions, pay your money, and let me get on with my work," she said, rubbing the first drop of cream into her breast.

"So you know why Toby was here?"

She looked up with a foolish, immature grin on her face. "I would say Portugal is a good long way to fly to get a good fucking, but he put his mind on it, you know?" She winked. "But seriously, he was here because of something in the Algarve. He never told me, I never asked, but he was in the Algarve and when he came back he was wooden-faced, so serious." She mimicked Toby's mood by turning her lip inside out, dropping her jaw, and making a long, pouting face. "And it took a long, long night to get Toby back to himself again. At the Sheraton. First class," she reminded me, and rubbed the emollient into her breasts with her fingertips. They looked very taut, firm under her plying hands, and the cream made them glisten warmly in the candlelight.

I felt, even from the tough talk she spoke, that it wasn't just Toby's money she loved, but that there was something about Toby that she truly admired; he seemed, beneath the shoptalk she offered me, to have been more than another customer to her.

"You really liked Toby, huh?" I asked.

She looked up, her breasts properly tended to, giving them each one last, light slap. "Toby and I had a good time. He made me laugh. Why do you ask?"

"He's dead," I told her. "And I'm in Portugal to find out who killed him and why."

She examined my eyes, nodding her head when she was satisfied with what she saw. "You must be Merv Lusty. Toby talked of you. You two cheat backgammon together. Is that why he's dead? Cheating the wrong people, heh?" She tried to chuckle, but it caught hoarsely in her throat.

"Vern Bradlusky," I corrected her. "Yeah we were partners. I don't have a clue as to who killed him though. I was hoping you might know something. Anything." She got up from her chair and wrapped a black robe tightly around her, her head hung sadly, or possibly in thought.

"I'm sorry for being so crazy with you. Rude. I thought maybe Toby." Her eyes had filled with tears. "I thought you were a lawyer or a rough guy. That when Toby found out I had given him syphilis, he would try to get back at me. I didn't know until he left. I wouldn't have given him nothing like that on purpose."

"Syphilis," I repeated.

"But I had no idea it was something like this." She shook her head and wiped at her face with a corner of the robe. "If only I knew something," she shook her head. Syphilis, I thought. And I had been so tempted. That explained Joao's reluctance to recommend Camille; he didn't want to have the reputation of disease dealer to the jet set. He was right, Camille would have been—and I'm sure he thought she already *was*—bad for his business. As for Toby, it scarcely mattered what souvenirs he had taken home with him by then. Dead men don't get chancres.

"And if I had known you were Toby's friend, believe me I would never," she apologized.

"Sure." I calmed her. Her tears were real.

"In the closet," she told me.

"What?"

"In the closet. Toby's jacket."

I walked over to the far end of the room and opened the

closet door; it had a dog-eared poster of the Rolling Stones tacked to it. I rummaged through her wardrobe until I came upon one of Toby's plaid coats. She continued to rub at her eyes with her robe. Her voice had become soft, seventeen again.

"I stole it," she admitted. "I don't know why, I just stole it."

I sat on the bed, the coat draped across my lap. It was one of Toby's favorites: red and blue plaid that you could pick out of any crowd with no trouble. Toby did like to be noticed, and this coat always brought results. I went through the pockets carefully, Camille sitting beside me.

I found a pen from the Sheraton, two books of matches, and some stray American pennies in the outside pockets. The inside pockets were empty except for a wad of tissue; I carefully unwrapped it. Nothing.

"Maybe I was going to sell the jacket, but I never got around to it," she said. "It is an ugly coat, though. I could not get much for it. Take it back if you want it."

I felt a sharp prick at my leg, and I lifted the coat sleeve to find it was loaded with evergreen needles. I pulled a number of them out, showing one to Camille. Around the cuff of the sleeve I found a fine, chalky white powder.

"When did Toby wear this coat?" I asked her.

"I don't know—the first night we were together," she blurted. "It was the first night we went out on the town. Dinner. A fine dinner."

"And any other time? Did he wear it after the first night?"

"Not that I remember," she sniffled, her eyes puffy.

"Could he have picked up these at dinner, anywhere that night?" I held the pine needles out to her.

She told me she couldn't think of where. I wrapped the needles in my handkerchief and put them in my pocket. I laid twelve hundred escudos discreetly on her coffee table, and walked to the door.

"I want to know," she said.

"Hmmm?"

"I want to know who killed Toby. When you find out."

"*If* I find out, you'll be the first to know," I said. I meant it. She nodded quickly.

—— SEVEN

When the weather changes rapidly—from the cold and wet of Chicago, say, to the hot and dry of Portugal—my bridgework gives me fits. But that's what I get for having Toby's dentist cousin do the work so cheap, and through the mail. My whole jaw felt like aching, cold iron. I wandered the streets of Lisbon until I found a chemist who sold me a dozen or so painkillers and a pair of sunglasses. I found a tailor who fit me for some suits and assured me they'd be at the hotel in the morning.

And as I walked out of the shop I saw Josef, the wise-ass who'd taken me for that midnight ride back in Chicago. He was standing in the shade of a café parasol across the narrow street, sipping a drink and turning quickly away as he noticed me look his way: no mistaking that beaklike nose, that forehead, the wiry, bent-over frame. I took out toward him, walking fast, knowing he'd probably bolt. He did, taking off down the narrow sideway between the café and a jeweler's. I had to struggle past a gaggle of women who ambled into the narrow throughway. I elbowed between them rudely and ran up the cobblestones and back around to another corner. As I came around, running full out, Josef stood on the walk, hands on his hips, breathing heavily and smiling.

"What the hell are you doing?" I said, nearly overrunning him, not ready for him to give up so easily.

"No use, you saw me." His eyes were nervous, anxious. The fishseller whose stall we were directly in front of began to rinse out the wooden shelves and buckets, hosing off the leftover entrails. Josef nodded, and I followed him back to the café where Mobotiak was deep in the shade, drinking.

I took a seat and Josef ordered beers all around. I wiped my forehead with a napkin. My head was spinning. The rum and the painkillers. Mobotiak nodded to me, sweat marking dark rings under each arm of his shirt, his teeth bared from those drawn-back lips, the corners twitching. He took up the rope I had seen him with that night in the car. It was, seeing it now in daylight, not a rope. It was strand after strand of different-colored hair, intricately braided.

"So then, the whore had nothing to tell you?" Josef asked. But I couldn't take my eyes off the rope that Mobotiak worried with those stubby fingers. I froze, tried to keep the sudden shock from showing on my face; they'd been tailing me all along and this was the first time I'd noticed them. What else hadn't I been noticing?

"Why should she be any different?" I said, fixing him with a sudden and, I hoped, intimidating glare.

He tried to laugh but didn't convince me. The little amused grin he wore was wearing thin. I was very aware of the rope and the fingers that were twisting it. But I found myself saying, "Who killed my friend?" And the smile disappeared altogether.

"We do not know as of this time. No knowledge," he said quietly, shaking his head.

"What was he smuggling? I know he was smuggling."

"You are so sure of too many things," Josef said as the beer arrived.

"I am also sure Toby was doing some smuggling for you—"

"This is good beer. Made of bananas—smell the bananas." He held the beer bottle to his beaked nose.

"And it was that smuggling that got him killed."

Josef looked up at me once again. "We had nothing to do with Mr. Kale's death, and if he was involved with smuggling it was certainly not at our behest, no-no." He was angry, his nostrils twitching. "Mr. Kale was convinced to recover some property for us. Property that others might have wanted him to smuggle, but not we, no-no, Mr. Bradloozkey. His death is on other hands. Just as yours might be." He looked toward Mobotiak who silently, stoically sipped his beer, the bottle and his face both perspiring in the Portuguese heat.

"Who did he work for? Who wanted him to smuggle?"

"We can't say for sure and so I will not. But Mr. Kale was big help to us once we convinced him it would be in his interest," he continued, pulling a wad of bills from his coat pocket. "You see we Angolans find it difficult to enter certain sections of this society. Not all love us."

"Angolan?" I said with a start. I wasn't even used to the idea of being in Portugal and he was serving up another country. I finally tried a sip of beer.

Mobotiak spoke, his voice deep. "Troubles in our country. Wars. Property needed for the wars. Some people would like to see us cheated and they are doing well at this." He drank his beer, the hair rope lying on the table.

"How much cash would you need to be helping us?" Josef asked, his thin, nimble fingers already leafing through the bills.

"Who the hell said I was going to help you?"

"Do not be silly, Mr. Bradloozkey," he said, wearing that thin smile again. "You look for Mr. Kale's murderer, and you will also find our property. All will be happy. One stone for two birds, yes? So take the money, take the money for your worries and your trouble. For making you run so hard on such a hot, hot day. When you know something about our property you let us know." He stood and pushed a stack of money toward me. Mobotiak stood also.

"And how do I reach you?"

"We'll reach you. We will be close by." And they left. I looked at the money a good long time. The stack caught the eye of every person by the table but I didn't want to fondle it. To put it in my pocket was to be paid by those sonofabitches. And that was like being paid for looking for Toby's murderer. I shouldn't be paid for that, not that. But they had paid Toby. That was how he got mixed up in the whole affair. Maybe by taking their money I'd be doing as Toby had done, following his path, making the moves he had made. And then maybe I'd find the killer.

But hopefully not as he had. I drank and I drank, seeing how far the stack would go in the cafe. It would go a good long time, I reasoned. I ate there and then I took the wad with me to the hotel and up to the rooftop bar where I tried to drink an even larger dent in the pile. Joao, the bartender, was there to take it away from me. My bridgework was cutting me and I took it out for a rest.

"So you wouldn't tell me Camille had syphilis. Is that any way to do business?" I asked him. He stared at my teeth that sat demurely atop my cocktail napkin.

"You cannot leave them—" he began.

"You're the one for manners; what about Camille?"

"I told you not to be seeing her," he sniffed, tossing a bar rag over my bridgework. "But you insisted. You Americans are almost as bad as the Germans."

"Almost?" I asked. I had thought the Ugly American was immortal.

"At the least Americans tip," he said, refilling my glass.

"Not this American. A tip for more information though."

"No. I don't want to be the one responsible if you find fault with another of the girls."

"No girls," I told him. He fixed a drink for an elderly lady at the end of the bar and sauntered back.

"What kind of information?" He shrugged.

"Just anything else you can tell me about Toby when he was here. Anything at all you can remember."

Joao stood for a long time before I realized I had been rude. I laid a fresh stack of escudos on the bar. He charged me for the drinks and pocketed his "tip."

"Why are you so interested in Mr. Kale's visit here?" he asked, now obviously convinced that Toby had not merely recommended him as a dependable pimp.

"You mean I never told you why I'm asking about Mr. Kale?"

"No. You did not." He jerked his head decisively, proudly thinking he'd put me on the spot.

"Then it must not be any of your fucking business," I said. "I paid, so put up."

Joao lifted a hand and motioned for me to take it easy. "Listen up, I like you," he started. "Didn't I try to keep you from Camille? Even if you insisted on having a party time with her? I could send you to this good doctor. He does not charge but for the medicine. He is old, but—"

"Toby," I reminded him.

"All right, he was here with Camille. Twice. Each time he stayed at the hotel a few days. Then back to America, I imagine. Then this other American comes around asking questions and making trouble and not paying for his brandy."

"I paid for the damn brandy." I grinned, taking his bar rag off my bridgework, and prepared to go.

"And leaving teeth on my bar, not even Germans leave their teeth on the bar." I put the dental work in my pocket and finished my drink.

"And I should have known that Mr. Kale had bad friends when he had dinner with the Angolans."

"The what?" I said, sitting back in my chair.

"Yes. One night he and two Angolans had drinks and went down to dinner here in the hotel. I thought he had better taste than to hang out with the Angolans. They were properly dressed so I served them. They stink anyway," he sneered. I didn't pry into his prejudice.

"Who were they?" I said, pouring another drink from the bottle on the bar. He stepped back when he saw how intently I pursued him; he might have been calculating how much it was worth to me.

"No, I did not know the men. I would not be seen dead with them. They don't work, come back with what they stole back in Africa. Thieves. Killers. Things were just fine when they stayed where they were. Ruined the colony and coming to get Portugal now. That's what I think." His hatred was real, he resented me linking him to the two men.

"That's not the way I heard it. A skinny parrot-faced guy and a hulking sidekick with a mushed face?"

"Yes. Mixed-up *mestiços*," he said glumly. "Not Portuguese, not African. Messed-up hairs, so dark, they think crooked. Most don't know Portuguese and want to take all the jobs. But I'm not so good with faces. Especially these Angolans. They seem to come from everywhere at once. So many. They frighten me at times. How can anyone used to living in the jungle learn all about Lisbon? Live here in peace. Sometimes I believe they are still part animal. If you watch their eyes."

"You're superstitious and prejudiced," I told him.

"Prejudiced?" He wasn't sure of the English word.

"Hate for no reason," I explained. "You hate because you don't know them."

"You could be right," he agreed tentatively, wiping the bar in front of me. "But perhaps I am too frightened to know them any better. Most people are afraid of heights but I do not see them hanging from the roof here." He motioned to the edge of the patio. "They don't stand in line waiting to hang over the street. I am not anxious to know too much about the Angolans. A lot were killed there. A lot are still being killed. I have had enough of that kind of nonsense. We had it here in the streets of Lisbon; the riots, the killing. And for what? Put a communist in, throw a communist out. Put a socialist in, throw a socialist out. Free Mozambique after losing good soldiers. Free Angola after losing soldiers." He chuckled bitterly. "Free Angola. So Angola can come to Portugal? I don't understand politics too well. I don't understand Angolans too well. But I know that both have caused heartache here. That's all I need to know," he told me.

"Did you overhear anything they said? Did Toby mention them?"

"No. Not that I can recall. They were here for such a brief time, and then Mr. Kale came by the bar to ask if the 'chow' in the dining room was good. I told him it was. That's the last I saw of the Angolans and the last I thought of them until today. I wish I knew more. Important? Did they rob Mr. Kale?" he suddenly asked, his eyes hopeful.

"No. In fact it looks like it might be the other way around if you listen to their story," I said, as much to myself as to Joao. I put the change in my pocket and got up to leave.

"Be careful," he warned me. Indeed. I didn't like the way things were shaping up. I thought it was crazy enough that Toby was somehow involved with the Portuguese, and now I find him up to his neck with Angolans—if things continued along those lines much longer, I'd have the entire UN to deal with before getting any closer to who killed him. Angolans. Portuguese businessmen. Old girlfriends. Old backgammon boards and new tournaments. My old column. No, I did not like the way things were *refusing* to shape up. I decided to press on—when in doubt move forward, keep the dice warm. Besides, there was nothing else for me to check out in Lisbon; all my questions led to the Algarve, the southern coast.

I crossed the Salazar Bridge in a rented convertible Alfa Romeo and headed south toward the Algarve. It was another bright day, the sun warm and white on the chrome, the glass, my face. The highway tapered to two lanes as it meandered through Sagres, a small coastal town with roads narrow enough to predate the donkey.

The countryside was damned fine, but I grew impatient, anxious. Finally I came into a town—actually a house and shack across from a pock-marked local café—set off the road into a thicket of conifers and vines. I pulled in and stood to stretch and relax. A young boy, his arms hugging his own chest, sauntered out of the café door, looking over my car, my clothes, and the black, impersonal ovals of my sunglasses. I brushed past him and into the dirt-floored bar; a table with half-sprung cane-back chairs was pushed near a long pitted bar that two old men—one the proprietor—hunched over with glasses of wine. A mangy dog slept, snoring, in the far corner. I bought wine and took my glass with me to the open trough dug into the mushy clay behind the building. I drank and pissed at the same time, the wine tasting like stomach acid, gnats rising from the green, foamy puddle, the sun like steam, like breath on my neck. I went inside and sat at the table. The old men ignored me and each other, a polite and awkward silence. The boy leaned against the chipped stucco doorway, his face obliterated by the daylight that swam around him in the aperture; I knew he was sizing me up for begging, and it was something I wished he would hurry up and get over with so I could return to my wine and my thoughts. The comfort I had felt on the road and the impatience I had tried to rid myself of by pulling in had both vanished; I was plain uneasy and uncomfortable. I had another glass of wine in the shade of the red tile eaves, watching my car glare amid the dust and stones out front. One old man broke the truce and tried to bribe a sip of my wine with a half-smoked cigarette; I bought the house a drink and left. I was still more than an hour from the Algarve. I wouldn't even call ahead to Caroline.

The hills flattened out to sparsely grassed fields, gray and bluish rocks cutting through the soil; the cafés became cleaner, the roadside gas stations were rooted to the ground with familiar cement aprons and gazed out over the smoother highway with wide plate-glass windows. Traffic grew heavier as I passed through the seacoast town of Lagos: its houses and canneries formed cliffs that dropped straight into the sea; its wharves were tangled with fishing boats, sailing skiffs, and huge cabin cruisers—it was as if Lagos could not decide whether it would become a tourist marina or a quiet fishing village. The air was rank with the odor of sardines, the cannery spilling a steady vile stream into the bay. I sped east to Albufeira—a small resort town—to the fenced-in, secure resort complex that housed the villa of not only the Massads but many other wealthy Europeans and Portuguese. Apontarleve Praia, as it was called, straddled two ridges and encircled a perfect natural bay—there are few on the southern coast, and those that are navigable are usually the sites of old fishing towns such as Lagos, not a fashionable resort complex.

As I entered through the main gates, I could see the entire complex: fruit trees lined the ridge tops and gradually gave way to the golf course that suddenly groomed the hill. Below the course, cul-de-sacs burgeoned with red tile and white stucco houses whose grounds burst with trees, sculptured shrubs, and blue daubs of swimming pools. In the center of the valley a wide scrufty tract of land spread toward the twin gleaming glass towers of the Apontarleve Hotel. At the foot of the hotel, the docks and moorings of the marina spread out like serpentine rib cages in which boats, like white grubs, nestled in mooring or escaped out into the azure field of the Atlantic. To the left of the hotel and the gray, squat, windowless box of the casino, the jumbled walls of the city Quarteira intruded right up to the west gates. East of the marina, a sliver of ochre sand gradually swelled in width until it skirted a stand of tall red cliffs, jagged and rusting in the late afternoon sun. I turned into the gently curving side streets the villas were on and watched for the Massads' name. Nearly halfway up the hill and just at the very fringe of the golf course, I found it.

I ambled past a villa nearly obscured from the street by high hedges and eucalyptus trees; a central turret rose out of the vegetation, the black wrought-iron gate was open, a post outside it read: VILLA MASSAD, in hand-carved letters on a polished plaque. I pulled into the asphalt drive and parked behind the Citroen in the traffic circle. The front of the house was covered with vines, and the flower beds were filled with sparkling gravel, ornamental rocks, and a deep scarlet flower that grew from bushes. The windows of both floors were covered with black iron ornamental bars that bulged out like bird cages from the white stucco. The garage held a Porsche, obviously Caroline's: green—her favorite color. I was met at the door by a servant—a tall, thickly built man with a flat, lumpish nose that looked like a length of dough that had cooked into an oily, browned loaf; his hair poked out from his beret, which he had pulled down to waxen ears. His eyes were the black-brown of a mean horse, and he fixed them on me as he grunted for the car keys. I quickly dropped them to his pillow-sized palm, and he went about unloading my things.

I walked through the cool, marble-floored hallway; cactus and ferns lined the walls and funneled me toward the back of the house, which was a wall of three sliding doors, two partially closed off by metal shutters that were let down. I slid the remaining door open and walked out onto the back patio, which was shaded by the overhang of the second-floor balconies. On either side of the protected alcove stood an outdoor bar and fireplace. Beyond this, the grounds opened to a wide, skin-smooth expanse of lawn lined by gardens and sculptured hedges that fenced in the yard. Straight back, I could see the plastic of a lawn chair nearly blending with the hedges and tamed cypress bushes. I walked from the shaded porch into the sunlight of the lawn. Caroline glowed in the yard, lying at the far end of the property, tanning herself in a green bikini and a sheen of oil. I hated the brightness, the heat, but I was drawn out onto the stiff, too-green lawn, the heat rising from it, the air thick with sunlight, windless. I walked down past bush and tree to the spot where she lay on the canvas chaise, her body oiled and tanned. Her eyes were closed, arms limp to her sides and hanging from the chair, her bleached-blond hair pulled back so that the sun blazed on her cheekbones, her forehead. She was heavier than I remembered her. Yet it was a good piece of weight she'd added, right where I didn't mind a few extra pounds: along the inner thigh, the leg. I must have been squinting down on her for a few minutes, long enough for her to feel my gaze and open her eyes.

"Good God, you're here already? You should have called!" She squinted up at the tall, balding, yet moderately handsome backgammon player who found himself dizzy in the heat and swimming at the very sound of her voice. I was speechless, schoolboy again: it was her voice that sent the freeze into me. Crisp as her mind, the way she'd lash out, change the temperature in the room with one acidic comment. And only a word or two from her could thaw me out again.

"Thought it best to get right down here."

"You look like you could use a stiff drink and a soft shoulder," she said, picking up her sunglasses from the grass near the bestseller she'd left open. She whistled, a good, clean, baseball-park whistle, as I took the other chaise across from hers. The servant lumbered up and she rattled off her order. Even her Portuguese was crisp. She wheedled out a trapped droplet of oil from her navel with a finger. Her voice went soft and low.

"I was afraid," she said. Just that and no more.

"Afraid I wouldn't make it?" I asked, running a hand across the bald spot on the top of my head.

"Afraid you might not come."

"Yeah."

Desmiaou, the servant, appeared with the drinks, and she fell silent until the hulk had plodded back into the shade of the villa.

"Can't be too sure of him," she said almost to herself, sipping her drink. Perspiration or oil gleamed amid the darkened freckles that sprinkled into the hollow of her breasts. That night at the Waukegan Motel: "At least I've got good tits, Vernon," she'd said, holding both of them and giving me a wink. That had been the night that Sandra had mentioned. The night my wife had confronted us.

"What's the problem?" I asked.

"Gregory."

"Don't bullshit me this time, Caroline," I told her up front. When she had come to Chicago the year before, she had had a line as long as a campaign speech about how Gregory was mistreating her, beating her, doing everything to her except loving her. And that's how—after the line and the Irish whiskey—I'd ended up in her grasp, so to speak, in that dark back room atop half-a-dozen empty cases of Budweiser quarts. A dark back room until Sandra had come in to have a look, that is. "I'll lay everything in the open for you. There's only two reasons for my little trip here: the tournament and Toby . . . I'm here for Toby, you know. I'd say that dense clod has seen a lot more trouble than both of us put together. Dead is more trouble than you've seen."

"I'm very sorry about Toby," she said and started to sit up in the recliner. I didn't like her hair blond, I decided. She did look sorry about Toby, though.

"It's just—I'm in a fix over this," she stammered. She took off her sunglasses. She was crying, her blue eyes tired, awash, her lip trembling. I must have put an arm out because she came right to me, and I found myself straddling the chair with Caroline in my arms, her legs draped across my one leg and onto the lawn where they kicked over my brandy.

"Caroline," I said, almost to myself, as I held her, unfastened the barrette, and fluffed out her long, thick hair across her smooth back.

"Where the hell have you been? Where the hell have *I* been," she sobbed, wiping at her eyes, looking up at me with a weak smile. God, she looked tired. Used up. "What's happening to everything?" she went on, untangling herself from me, leaving the smell of her tanning oil heavy in the air.

"I wish I knew . . ." I offered lamely. But that's about how I felt just then: lame and numb in that oppressive sun and heat. She offered me a taste of what was left of her drink.

"It's this business with Gregory that has me all tied up in knots. I wanted to get away from him last year, but I didn't."

"When you stopped in to see me?" I asked.

She nodded. "And things weren't half as bad as they are now."

"So leave him. You're unhappy, your life takes a bad turn, try to make it right. Get on a plane and leave."

"It's not that easy. If I leave *him*, I lose everything."

"Big deal. So you get used to eating cheeseburgers again. And going without green Porsches. You'll live." I was getting annoyed.

"Damn it, that's not the point. I should get something out of all this, shouldn't I? I put in my time with the bastard. I put up with his craziness, his bullshit. Shouldn't that count for something?" She polished off her drink, then whistled again for Desmiaou.

"You sound like you want a commission."

"Maybe I do," she said hollowly. Desmiaou obediently made his way across the lawn toward us in long, heavy strides. A trickle of perspiration made its way out from under the beret as he took up my spilled glass and Caroline's emptied one.

"I mean the bastard is crazy, Vernon," she went on, looking me square in the eye with an I-dare-you glare.

She told me how everything that had happened to Gregory—his reclusive habits, his losses in the business that forced the shutting of offices—all went back to his brother's death over a year earlier, at the height of the war in Angola. There was Angola again. I said nothing but nodded for her to continue. The last partner, one Addidam Sitizar, was pressing to take over what remained of the business, and with Gregory in such a state Caroline was sure the partner was going to succeed in screwing Gregory—and naturally her—out of every last escudo.

"That's why this tournament surprised me. Shocked me," she continued, shaking her hair across her shoulders and the brown leather chair back. "This tournament, of all things, is the most lucid, active thing he has attempted to do in nearly a year. A *tournament, games,* while his fat partner is pulling the plug on him." She shook her head in anger.

"How?" I asked.

She pointed up at the second story of the white villa. "See that side?" she went on, getting up from the chair. I got up also, turned to look up at the house. The whole north wing of the villa—perhaps three of four rooms with a half-a-dozen windows—was shut off with massive metal shutters. "Never comes out anymore. Not during the day, at least. At night you can hear him prowling around, leaving the villa, and returning before dawn. Like some Dracula character. He talks to me through the door, if at all. I haven't really laid eyes on him for months. Once, late at night, I saw him pass through the hall. Not more than a shadow really." Her voice trailed off, her eyes fixed on those shutters.

"And he doesn't see anyone?" I asked.

"Not lately, no. Up until a few weeks ago Sitizar and a few lawyers could go up. But now they're not even allowed. That's why Sitizar is so nervous. No one knows what goes on up there anymore. No one knows what goes on with the business."

"And he sees no one, not a goddamned soul?" I couldn't believe it.

"Oh, Desmiaou. And whoever he sees late at night. If he does see anyone when he goes out."

"Follow him, that's my advice. Follow him and get a good lawyer yourself." I took an ice cube from my drink and tossed it squarely at one of the metal shutters where it splattered with a hollow thunk.

"Christ, what are you doing!" she hissed at me, grabbing my arm.

We went inside, ate lunch, and drank. I felt uneasy in the house and with her. And not just the usual awkwardness one feels upon seeing an old lover and friend after a long separation. That had passed. The awkwardness I felt then wouldn't evaporate as we talked—even laughed—over our drinks that afternoon. And I found myself saying in my mind that it was the jet lag, the paranoia, the weird and gruesome events of the past three days that made me regard Caroline with such a clinical and skeptical eye. I kept saying it, but I didn't believe it. I found myself looking at that blond hair that used to be a gentle reddish brown. And at those blue-gray eyes that were as tired as old denim. Her voice had lost its crispness, its sureness, and seemed buoyed up on only the brandy. I excused myself. I needed rest.

"Vernon," she said, straightening one strap of her bathing suit. "I need you at dinner tonight. Sitizar will be here. I think he means to discuss his taking over Gregory's share of the business. I need you to help me hold him off."

"I'm not a businessman. I don't know a thing about—"

"You don't have to know anything. Follow my lead. Back me up. I'm just trying to buy time."

"All right, fine," I told her, just wanting some rest.

"I'll call you," she said. Desmiaou, glassy-eyed and smiling just a bit, showed me to my room.

And it was Desmiaou who woke me later. By that time he was obviously drunk, stumbling over the dressing table on his way to my bedroom shutters, which he rolled up noisily, mumbling to himself in a gruff, saliva-fuzzed voice. The late afternoon sun struck at me as I lay in the bed. Desmiaou laughed, wiping his mouth on his coat sleeve, tucking stray hairs under his beret. He made a wide, sloppy sweep of his hand to the corridor and then shuffled out. I got up, drew my robe around me, and stepped out of my room onto the outdoor balcony. A tiny metal chair and table: a fine place to write my backgammon column, I thought. I sat down and looked over the stucco wall of the balcony. The late sunlight was a deep, almost greenish gold as it fell steeply over the grass and lawn below and across the wide, perfectly manicured apron of the golf course that lay beyond. Birds chirped throatily, surprisingly loud in the dusk, and a welcome breeze blew in the scent of the eucalyptus that cut jagged, striped shadows across the lawn from the border of the Massad property. I heard a shower. The master bedroom was just to the left of my room, behind the stairwell between the short wing my room was situated in and the massive, longer wing that Gregory occupied. I went in and across the hall and knocked on a door. Caroline answered.

"Come in," she yelled from the shower. I walked in and sat on the toilet, rested a foot on the bidet. The steam from her shower filled the room. She stepped out, grabbing a towel and ruffling it through her hair, her breasts jiggling.

"I could have been Gregory or Desmiaou," I said, looking at her more closely than I had in the yard, seeing that her ass locked as firm as in those days at Northwestern.

"Desmiaou never knocks, and I told you Gregory never leaves the rooms until after dark. I've got to get dressed," she went on, nudging my foot from the bidet.

A door slammed. Caroline dropped her towel and ran into the hall. "Gregory?" she yelled. She approached the closed door at the end of the corridor, yelling his name. "Gregory!" She pounded, rattled the knob. No answer. She turned quickly from the door, brushing past me roughly. I stood staring at Gregory's door and heard a rustling within the room. Caroline's voice cut at me as she screamed, her face scarlet with anger. "We've got to get dressed! Go on!" I did as I was told, but not without one more glance at that door.

─── EIGHT ───

I'd had two or three brandies in the living room before Gregory's partner arrived. He crossed the room, jerking a thumb back over his shoulder to Desmiaou.

"Butler thinks he's a beatnik? Or what? The silly beret!" He began to laugh, "*Hih-hih-hih-hih,*" like a string of hiccups, and he offered me his hand, a flabby, slack-skinned hand, which I reluctantly shook. He settled into a chair and recovered from his tittering fit. Desmiaou brought him a frothy, blenderized-looking drink, which he sipped through a straw.

"Sitizar. Addidam Sitizar," he said after a long sip, setting his cataract-fogged eye on me, the other eye less opaqued and more its natural brown. He had a wide circumference, that much was sure. Only the navy-colored coat that hung limply over him and the baggy, oversized pants of the same color hid the entire extent of his weight. His chin hung over a black ascot fastened with a diamond pin, and he seemed much paler than most Portuguese, even paler than most Europeans. If it was the laugh or the sheer weight of him I'll never know, but I instantly disliked the sonofabitch. He was bad news, I could feel that. Sort of an after-the-fact bad news, though. Parasitic bad news, as if he merely followed trouble, sniffed it out, and picked its half-eaten and abandoned carcass.

"And you must be one of Caroline's lovers?" He arched an eyebrow to its fullest, dark arch and went *hih-hih-hih-hih* again.

"Vern Bradlusky," I offered, and whistled as Caroline had for Desmiaou.

"The backgammon columnist? But I thought your name was Vernon *Stewart*? Isn't that the name of the columnist in the *Herald*? You two are one and the same?" he asked.

"Yeah, but—"

"I understand. That other name is perhaps a bit too ethnic for backgammon advice columns, mmm?"

Caroline came in with her drink and mine. Sitizar did not get up; it would've been an all-day project. Caroline looked damn fine in a simple wraparound dress. White. White against her tan.

"Caroline, dear," Sitizar purred up from his crater in the couch, shifting his weight a bit to show that he really meant to get up but it was a bother, and a nicety that all could forget.

We went in to dinner, which Desmiaou had announced in brandy-slurred Portuguese. We ate in silence, cutlery scraping. Sitizar was an audible eater, however, huffing, snuffling, and even humming as he ate three, maybe four helpings of pork and clams in a thick, aromatic gravy. It wasn't until he patted his fleshy lips with the napkin that had lain folded beside his plate through the meal that he finally spoke.

"I have the papers ready," he said to Caroline. She did not look up from her plate.

"Papers?" I asked.

Sitizar did not answer me but continued to eye Caroline, the milky white of his cataract pointed to her.

"No one is signing any papers," she said to her plate.

"I'm losing thousands of dollars a day, dear. You are losing money also. Get him to sign or I'll be forced—" His voice trailed off. He grabbed a crust of bread and circled it about the brown-red gravy on his plate, knocking a stray clam shell onto the white tablecloth.

"We are not signing a damn thing. The company stays in his name."

Sitizar thought this last remark was funny. "*Hih-hih-hih-hih-hih-hih,*" he went on for an interminable time. I was about to throw a fork at him when he stopped and sighed wistfully to himself.

"Old fat Sitizar," he began. "I thought this was truly a partnership. The three of us. I had no idea after all these years that things were not equal. They should have been. This whole affair started with one *fuck-een* sardine boat. One boat," he said to me, holding up one, chublike finger.

"And years later, lots of sardine boats and factories and farms and more sardine boats later, it comes to this." He shook his head and stuffed the sopping bread into his mouth.

"You don't deserve the company. It was Gregory and his brother that built it. You tagged along, you sucked up the crumbs they left for you. Take a look at you." Caroline finally raised her eyes to his, pointed her fork angrily across the table. "What was the last work *you* did? Sitting in that office at the casino. Not a damn day of work."

"Moreno and I, not your husband." Sitizar raised his voice, his long teeth bared now, his jowl quivering over the black ascot. "Moreno and I did the work. Me. Your husband and his gambling. And now this craziness. Me. Me and Moreno made this company." He jabbed himself in his chest a few assertive, authoritative times with his thumb.

"Who? Who and Gregory?" I asked, hearing a familiar name. Moreno. The weirdo at Zorine's. The weirdo I'd hustled back in Chicago?

"It wasn't you and Moreno, and you damned well know it," she hissed, not hearing me, getting up from her place at the table.

Sitizar started up, gripping the table and pulling at the tablecloth as he struggled to his feet.

"Moreno?" I nearly shouted to get heard. They had their eyes locked, were rising to get at each other.

"Gregory's brother," Caroline said, answering me but still looking at Sitizar who had reached into his coat pocket.

"His craziness. No wonder," he said, taking his eyes off her for only a second as he pulled the papers from his inside pocket and slapped them on the table. "No wonder her husband goes crazy." He glared back at Caroline who took up the papers and began to rip them, tossing the pieces at Sitizar. They hit his coat and shirt and fluttered to the floor, piece by piece. "Crazy from having a slut wife. Fucking with the immigrants. Fucking the stinking immigrants," he hissed. "The same people that killed

Moreno. The slime that killed his brother, she sleeps with." And with that she was at him, beating at the blubbery, dark shape of him, taking a rip at his face with her nails. I stood there. The fat slug didn't lift a finger to protect himself, and I felt he had a few of her licks coming. He ducked her nails a few times but she caught him a few good, long scratches, arms flailing. She called him a faggot, a bastard, a eunuch, a rat-fucker. Desmiaou had staggered in to watch, the fat man getting red, huffing. He squirmed then to hold her hands away, backed out of the dining room toward the hall. She took a good kick at him as he slipped from her and made his way through the hallway. She stood glowering, tucking back her hair and listening for the slam of the front door. I poured us both some brandy on ice and offered her the glass. A long silence. Desmiaou shuffled into the kitchen.

"Talk?" I said. She finally smiled, taking the snifter in both hands. We went into the backyard. It was dark; the moon had not yet risen. We took chairs on the back patio. She caught her breath and I sipped. A bright dusting of stars arched in the night sky.

"You said Moreno was Gregory's brother's name?" I asked.

She sighed. "It's not really a bad night. Kind of like a North-western night. Atop the music building, you remember?" she asked me, ignoring my question. "Remember we used to sneak up to the roof of the building."

"I had Purfoy's keys—the night maintenance man," I re-called. It *was* one of those kinds of nights. I too tilted my head up to the Portuguese sky, a warm breeze in the air, remembering the two of us up on that graveled roof back then, an Indian blanket spread out, a six-pack of beer—usually warm—at our feet. Lake Michigan would be just below, breaking on the rocks, and Chicago would be south, its lights a brilliant flood of gold and white and silver that attempted to thrust out into the black-ness of the empty night and lake beyond. We'd drink beer and talk. Just talk. Somehow the spot seemed good for talk but not making love.

"And you told me you were going to marry rich, hook a rich

one," I reminded her, "one of our last nights on top of the building."

"Did I?" she laughed, schoolgirlish, flouncing her hair, the
ice of her drink chiming musically in her glass.

"And I guess you did."

"I really told you I'd marry a rich husband?"

"Sure did. Spring. Can even tell you what beer we were
drinking." I stopped, feeling foolish. I got up, found the patio
bar, and fumbled through the top bottle rack in the dim light
cast from the parlor out through the patio doors. I poured one
and returned to my chair.

"But you were right about yourself. Rich husband and all," I
said, waving my drink at the villa, the yard, in a careful-not-to-
spill-a-drop sweep of my hand.

"What kind?" she asked after a long pause in which I could
see her original red-brown hair, see it back then atop the music
building, the city lights sparking smooth, metallic highlights in
its lengths.

"What do you mean what kind?" I asked.

"You said you could remember the beer. Come on, smartass, what kind of beer were we drinking?"

"Meister Brau," I answered, remembering how we had left
the empties that night scattered on the gravel roof. We both
turned in our chairs as the light from the parlor disappeared. It
had vanished behind Desmiaou who stood blocking the doorway. He said something in Portuguese to Caroline. She thanked
him, then nodded before he returned inside and allowed the
house light to spill out toward us once more.

"Gregory," she said, puzzled, "wants to see you. Now."

"Now?"

"Yes. You're to go up right now." She took a meditative sip
from the brandy, the tinkling ice setting two notes onto the
warm night air. "I'll be waiting," she called after me.

Desmiaou led me up the spiral stairs to Gregory's door, where he hammered on the thick oak with his fist. A weak voice told me to enter.

The room was long and dark, lit only by candlelight. Coming in from the patio, I still had to adjust to this fainter, more diffuse glow. Along both walls were bookcases from floor to ceiling. At the far end, a massive four-poster bed with veil curtains took up the entire far wall. Between me and this bed were perhaps half-a-dozen bishop's tables, each set with a backgammon board. And just before the bed, in a very high-backed chair, sat Gregory, his legs propped up on a mushroomlike hassock. I walked past the backgammon sets until I was just a few yards from his chair. From the shadow cast by its shell-like back came his arm, thrust out at me, a finger pointed sharply.

"Hold it!" he managed to say. He sounded remarkably calm in contrast to the gesture, his voice steady and sure and agreeable. I paused, one board between us and the hassock on which I could make out the forms of his feet. They were pale in even that light and the knobs of each ankle joint were clearly visible. The thin legs gradually disappeared into the much thicker dimness cast by the chair. The finger wavered in the air; it, too, was thin, much thinner than I remembered Gregory Massad. I strained to see his face in the deep shadow.

"It's good to have you with us, Vernon. Good to have you at this tournament I am arranging. Most important games, most important. As you can see, I'm ready. Playing, replaying five or six games at a time. All the time. I must be ready, ready for the games," he said. It was Gregory's voice all right, but it didn't have the husk, the meat to it. Not like when I had met him in the Bahamas. There was a hollowness, like the room we were in. I cleared my throat, maybe to see if I was capable of making a sound in that place. And I was beginning to make out his face—smooth, thinned, the Gregory Massad in that chair had lost nearly fifty pounds of himself since I'd seen him at the gaming tables at the Nassau tournaments where he'd first met Caroline.

"Yeah, but as you're up here honing your skills there's a lot going on in the outside world," I said to him, looking down at the board on the low table. Odd-looking slab of rock, really, not much of a playing board.

"To hell with the outside world!" he said in a rasp. His voice had not risen but his tone had, his temper had. "I've broken my back and nearly my life for others; now they can worry about me, about what I might be up to. You wouldn't believe how my brother and I fought our way up to get where we are now. Fought our way up only to have some half-brained revolutionaries and confidence tricksters . . . to hell with the outside world and to hell with their way of doing things. I have precious few people I can trust anymore and precious fewer things I can depend on. In this game I have found both, Mr. Bradlusky. And in this game I hope to get my revenge and my survival and a new life. It may be too late for me to get everything back, but I may get enough to be free of it all."

"Free of your wife? Free of the company? While you hole up in this room a lot is passing by. People are out to get in your pockets. In more ways than one. And whatever else is going on, my best friend has lost his life."

"Lost life? I am not directly responsible for that, I'm sure. But I have enemies who might. And as to my wife and pockets, I think she knows where all of yours are at and what's kept in them, eh?"

"So that's why I'm down here? To take Caroline off your hands?"

"You, like all others I invited, are here to play backgammon, Mr. Bradlusky. The game will see to you. And I'm afraid Caroline is gone from me no matter how I'd like it to be otherwise."

"Then get out of this fucking room. Get out and go downstairs and take control of things!" I reached into the shadow of the chair and gripped at his wrist, to pull him up. He stiffened and I let go.

"I *am* taking control, damn you! That's why I'm in this room, that's why I can't face the people I know. I had to give myself up to keep control! I had to give up Caroline to keep control. That's why I've asked you up here tonight. You must do me one favor. No, do it for yourself or for her, but take care of her. Take care *for* her!" I saw his face for the first time in the candlelight as he leaned foreward in the chair, his eyes gleaming, his face incredibly thin, smooth, and taut as a drum skin. He reminded me of a starving child, a nearly dead child. He slipped quickly back into the shadows of the chair.

"All right, all right!" I backed off, standing to leave. "Play it your way. But these game boards and that tournament aren't the whole world, and no matter what you think, squirreled away in this little room of yours, the tournament isn't what's important. Things are falling down around your ears!"

"This tournament *is* more important. The game is most important. Tidy," he repeated. The repetition, the coldness to his voice unnerved me a bit. "And the game is so old. And that antiquity is part of it, of the tidiness. Of what I'm trying to do." His voice grew even more lifeless, ebbing. "The board right there. Roman. Unearthed in this very compound, out near the marina. Roman soldiers or sailors or merchants playing on that board, that slab of granite."

I examined the gray rock again, noting the faint lines etched into the stone face.

"Only seven markers found on the site. Amazing there was even a one." As I counted what would be points and checked the boundaries, it became clear that this wasn't the backgammon board I had been accustomed to.

"See there, in the middle?" He pointed, then retracted the arm into the shadow. I noticed an etched inscription along the middle where a bar would be in a modern board.

"Reads IDIOTA RECEDE. A player's prayer? A good one for

you." I shrugged. "So here you are for an old game, Vernon. A very old game. I only hope you are up to the tradition. I hope you are an asset to the games. Go entertain my wife," he said then. I left after a long silence.

"So?" Caroline asked, standing in the slant of light on the patio, drink in hand.

"So you're right. He's nuts," I said, not knowing then what else to say.

"What did he want?" She tangled her arm about my waist and pressed lightly to me, her cheap, rummy cologne engulfing me. Good old Caroline, still in her gardenia despite the opulence around her. She probably still thought it the best scent on her.

"We talked about the games," I told her.

"The games," she said bitterly and snuggled against me, her drink at the small of my back.

"Moreno," I said slowly, playing the name over as she kissed me lightly on the neck. "Sitizar mentioned Moreno being Gregory's brother. Is this Moreno skinny? Tanned? Pits and scars all over his face?"

"*Was.* Moreno is dead. Pits on his face from the first few times someone hadn't quite gotten the job done. But they finally got him in Africa. Zaire. Some shady double-cross with the company or something. Moreno wasn't even his name, vain sonofabitch. Liked to think he was Italian or Spanish. Thought that gave him the edge when he was in a deal or . . . vile bastard. It's a good thing that snake's dead. Except for what the scum left behind . . ." Her voice trailed off. She started to kiss me once again. The man I had been playing backgammon with in Chicago was Gregory's brother? The night of Toby's murder. I couldn't make it out; it was all a senseless jumble.

"You sure, you absolutely sure he's dead?" I asked her, turning her toward me to look me in the eye. A shudder ran up me, even in that warm evening air. She looked up at me, frightened and suspicious.

"Yeah. He's dead. What of it?" she said slowly, watching me

with great care. I let go of her. Damn! I couldn't trust her, couldn't say another word, could I?

"I need to know. I just need to know," I said.

"Yeah, he's dead, long dead. I told you in the letter. And so is tonight, I guess," she said, pushing past me, dropping her brandy glass on the patio where it broke with an expensive, musical splash. She rushed into the house, slamming the patio door with a rattle of the metal shutters.

"Take care of her," Gregory had asked me. What could he possibly mean? Only hell could take care of that woman.

I got good and drunk out there on the patio, watching the stars, mulling over the game with the man named Moreno in Chicago. It was a coincidence that chilled me to the bone and pissed the hell out of me; it was as if the game in Chicago were continuing; I hadn't left the table at all.

The brandy finally got me to the point where I was more pissed off than scared, and I made my way up the spiral stairs to the corridor and Gregory's door.

"Come out, ya spook! Come out and answer a few questions about your brother! Come out and answer a few questions about my partner!" The room, the hallway were silent. I began to beat on the door with both fists until they ached.

"He's not even in his rooms, you ass." I heard Caroline behind me, her head poking from her room. "He often leaves. Late at night like this. Go to bed, Vernon, you're drunk."

"Yeah, I'm drunk, and I'm not passing out till I get answers, some goddamned answers!" She slammed her door and I put my back into trying to smash Gregory's door open, lunging again and again at the thick, unforgiving teak until I felt Desmiaou's hand on my shoulder, holding me back from one last desperate attempt.

He didn't have to say a word to me and didn't, leading me to my room with a stranglehold that mercifully helped me to pass out cold.

TEN

The next morning Caroline was chipper and bubbly and overly sweet as she plied me with rolls and jams and two kinds of coffee at breakfast. She wanted us both to forget the night before, and I guess marmalade and currants were a good beginning. I know I needed to forget that night—the only way I'd get those answers was to hold on, stay cool.

"Damned Algarve is alive with red ants." She frowned, brushing one from her roll and feeling about her lip for another that she trapped between thumb and forefinger. "And about last night." She caught my eye timidly, brushing at her forehead. "It's just what with the reminiscing about the old music building, the two of us, and the row at dinner and in the hall and everything."

"And the brandy," I offered with a jab of my roll, spying an ant careening on the white linen tablecloth between us. I set my saucer over it.

"Yes, the brandy," she took up. "But today I want you to meet, well, my lover. I don't want Sitizar to give you the wrong impression. What with Gregory the way he's been, I just, well, he's really such a nice guy. So strong, what I need right now. I'm stuck on him bad, Vernon." She roughed up her bleached hair, a faint underbrush of dark roots showing in the stiff light of the dining room. She looked embarrassed, her nose scrunching the way it always did when she was explaining an awkward situation. "Let's go see him, I really want you to meet him. Get out of this spooky place. It's so damned quiet. Let Desmiaou drink his brandy in peace."

"Mmmm," I disagreed, roll in mouth.

"Why?"

"Things to take care of."

"Such as?"

"Such as where did you say you saw Toby when he was here?"

"I didn't say. It might not have been him, but—"

"You were pretty damn sure when I talked to you over the phone."

"I was scared. That's quite a line to just drop on a girl over the phone. And I really had thought it was Toby," she went on, giving a practiced pout.

"So, where?"

"Casino. Walking into the back offices."

"And when he left?"

"Listen." She stopped me short, getting up to clear the plates. "I only saw him a second or two. He didn't even see me."

"You weren't even curious? You didn't follow him, say hello, ask what the hell he was doing in the Algarve?" I followed her into the kitchen where Desmiaou, slumped in a straight-back chair at the kitchen table, watched us.

"No, no!" she snapped, her back to me, throwing the dishes into the sink with a rattle and clunk. "I was busy, I had other things on my mind. If he was in Sitizar's office, I must have thought it had something to do with the casino or the tournament or I don't know what the fuck I was thinking." She glared at me. "What do you want from me?" She looked up, trying to make me believe I'd upset her, that she was on the verge of tears: this was a favorite number of hers that I could tell wasn't getting much use lately. It wasn't nearly as convincing as it had been in the past, years ago.

"I want you to give me something to go on. I need a good lead on him down here if I have any chance of following what went down with him, move by move. I find it a little hard to believe that you couldn't check up on him."

"Like I say"—she gave me a shrug of those tanned shoulders, puckering her blouse front—"it might not have been him."

"I *know* he was down here," I told her. Desmiaou wiped his

leathery nose on the back of one of his crooked paws, watching me between slow, slow blinks.

"So you know, then go ask Sitizar. Like I said, if it was him—" She stomped her bare foot down on the gray marble floor. "Fucking ants. Do something about the fucking ants," she said to Desmiaou, pointing to her foot where she'd smashed a few, a trail of live ones making their way from the sink cabinet. He pivoted his head in her direction, taking his beret off in a sign of respect. Getting off the chair and staggering over, he proceeded to shuffle his big, loaflike shoes over the ants.

"Oh, for chrissakes!" she said, and went out of the room.

The casino was down the hill and toward the marina, a square of white stucco and black shutters with enormous conifers that stood on each of its four corners and to either side of the canvas awning entrance. Stucco and pines. I laughed at myself as I pulled up in the parking lot, thinking about the pine needles I'd pulled from Toby's coat pocket back at the whore's apartment: the whole damned Algarve was nothing but pines and white stucco. Some clue. What was I going to ask? And what if, in all likelihood, Sitizar wouldn't cooperate? Hell, I really didn't know. That was my problem: no strategy, no approach. I had the right attitude: stay cool, taking easy steps, not thinking too far ahead, the way you would open any good game. But I still had little idea who I was up against. Gregory? Possibly. *Was* Moreno dead? Not likely, not that night at Zorine's.

Between the tellers' cages and the bar entrance was a long, low hall that slanted down into a basement. One door. I went in without knocking. I was blinded by a sudden shaft of light.

"*Hih-hih-hih,* get out of the way! Be getting out of the *gotdamn* way, American!" Sitizar's voice called from the abrupt darkness behind the light of the movie projector. I closed the door, which had been doubling as a screen, and slid over toward him, fumbling for a chair on the other side of the projector. He was slumped into a great hand of a chair, popping candies into his mouth, jowls working, his flaccid cheek striped with Caroline's three red gouges.

"And what is it I can do for you Mr. Stewart?" he said, still watching the screen.

"Bradlusky, and I have a few questions. You left so abruptly last night." I finally looked up at the screen, hearing just the flutter of the projector. It was a bit of a surprise. On the screen a tired, sleepy-looking woman was being licked by two Latin boys. She held her breasts out for them.

"Better with the sound off. I don't like to hear my voice too often. I just finished dubbing this one," he said, popping another candy, crunching down on it. He ran a finger lightly over the scratches. "Bitch. Truly a bitch."

"You mentioned Gregory's brother." One boy left a breast to start a southern journey.

"Moreno, yes. Now if he were alive," he sighed.

"He is," I ventured. Sitizar stopped in midcrunch and turned from the screen.

"What?"

"If he's the guy, I played a game of backgammon with him in Chicago. Right before I left."

"Impossible, *hih-hih-hih*," he tittered, and returned to the screen once more. "Impossible. Moreno never played backgammon."

I interrupted him. "Skinny guy, white hair and mustache, deep pits, scars along one side of the face. Thick glasses. Thick as my wrist, the lenses in those glasses."

"But—" Sitizar gagged, turned to me once again. The first boy had found his way to the triangular, downy mound of the woman's vagina; a clumsy close-up showed his tongue part the curly hair. Sitizar fumbled for the sound button and the woman's moans emanated from a speaker somewhere behind us. She swore in Spanish.

"I do a good job, you'll agree?" he asked, changing the subject, trying on a weird, awkward smile. "I dubbed a lot into Spanish. These are very big now that Franco is gone. Seems Seville, Madrid, can't buy enough of these now. But they come to *me* in English."

"Moreno is alive," I said. He shook his head, looked up at the screen and then back at me.

"If he is alive, then something very funny must be going on. And I choose not to believe you until I see for myself. Besides, who are you? Why should I trust you?" He leaned back into the chair, returning to the movie with a sudden retrieval of his confidence. The woman continued to moan and swear. It *was* Sitizar's voice but an octave higher. The first boy stroked his penis through the woman's hair as the other continued to part her legs with his face. I nearly laughed hearing Sitizar's voice come from her wetted lips. Sitizar abruptly switched off the projector and turned up the lights.

"It is money. I didn't always dub the blue ones. I helped to dub *Gone With the Wind, Bonnie and Clyde*, and many others," he said defensively, getting up from his chair, only to sit down behind the desk that held the projector. The walls of the small office were covered in movie posters. Behind his chair was one for *On the Waterfront*.

"If Moreno is alive then it is because the Angolans are up to something. It simply can't be him. The Angolans killed him, I know. And for him to be alive would mean . . ."

"I don't give a shit about the politics. I've got other reasons, my own reasons for asking. This guy was in town when a good friend of mine was killed—a friend that was seen down here, in the Algarve, just before he was killed. Seen in your office, in this damn casino as a matter of fact," I told him, picking up a piece of candy from the dish. I waited for all that to sink in on him.

"I have no doubt Moreno could have killed your friend," Sitizar said. "He could kill without thinking twice of it. I saw him shoot six men in Zaire. Six, a bullet for each. I was trembling so badly I nearly urinated on myself. The noise, the thunder of the gun in that hotel room, the plaster flying in my eyes and the stink of the blood. He could kill, Moreno could kill, yes. But he cannot be alive. He himself was killed in Zaire last year. Shady dealings. He was taken care of by the people he crossed."

"Who?"

"Does it matter? One side or the other. Since the revolution Moreno was playing all sides. Making so much money I found it very difficult to make use of it all, but I did." He held a hand mirror up, and, reaching into a desk drawer, he took out a jar. "I am the best accountant in South Europe, I can do with numbers what Moreno could do with deals and what Gregory could do with dice," he went on, unscrewing the lid and daubing a finger into the makeup. He applied a fingertip to his forehead where his true, darker skin tone was coming through. It was remarkable; the paint had looked so natural before, I wouldn't have guessed. I watched, fascinated, as he continued to touch up his face. "So we three made a very, very lucrative partnership until—" He broke off, cleared his throat, and returned the jar to his desk. "And so what is this about your friend?"

"I heard he was here. In the casino. A big guy, wore loud sports coats, backgammon player," I said, watching him, watching for a reaction.

"American?"

"Very."

"No. He wasn't here. I dislike Americans, and I would have remembered him then." He stared at me, then stood to begin to rewind the film.

"Caroline said she saw him here," I said firmly.

"*Hih-hih-hih-hih*, that stinking whore? Of course she told you, who else? She lies the first thing in the morning and the last thing at night. Especially night." He turned on the projector, holding a hand lightly over the fast-spinning take-up reel. "She probably had something to do with your friend's death, think on that. Her and the Angolan slug she shacks up with. Things were just fine around here until she made her appearance. Just fine. She has been the trouble. The slut."

"And Moreno's girl?" I asked him, the leader running free, slap, slap slapping against his soft white palm. He stared incredulously at me, as if by mentioning the girl I had proved Moreno had not died. He would have gone stone white if he hadn't already painted himself that color.

"J—Ju—Justine?" he stammered.

"Yeah, what about her?" I stood.

"Nothing, nothing. Fine woman. So you've met?" he said, collecting himself with a shrug and placing the film back into its case. "But if you'll excuse me." He tried on another type of smile that hardly fit. "I have work to do. Arrangements. Things I must see to."

"Of course," I said, leaving him.

I drove down to the water, distracted by what I'd found out. Or rather by what I hadn't found out. I parked near the docks, walked into the hotel, and checked out the marina bar. Wide picture windows looked out over the one arm of the vast marina, boats wobbling back and forth on the flotation pier. The windows were tinted, yet the water still blazed in the near-noon sun. I gulped a few brandies and ordered lunch. Things were getting curiouser and curiouser, all right . . . Justine swept in, long, tall, a slit beach skirt revealing a cool length of her leg, body swaying, hair as dark and pure as I'd remembered.

"You must have followed me. Wasn't it enough that we lost so much money to you, Mr. Bradlusky?" she said, taking a seat across from me and my grilled swordfish.

"Why don't I feel surprised to see you?" I found myself saying aloud, something I should have just thought.

She took up a tomato slice in marvelously long nails, nibbled it sensuously, deliberately. "I'm sorry I'm not a surprise. I'd love to be a surprise."

I watched her eat the hell out of that slice. Damn. Who would pop up next and how? Toby or Toby's corpse? I felt as though an incredible play were being acted out in front of me, and I was powerless to affect anything. Just sit back and watch. Sit and listen. Sit and listen.

"What brings you to the Algarve?" I asked her.

"The tournament, of course," she answered. "And you also, I expect."

"Yes," I agreed, taking a bit of fish, nodding. Did I look careful? Calm? I hoped I didn't look as though I were suspicious of her.

"Such a coincidence," she dared me, staring into me with those stone-cold eyes.

"Not really," I said smoothly, an unconcerned wave of my fork, then a sip of my drink.

"No?" She helped herself to an olive and told the waiter her order without looking away from me.

"No. We're both excellent players and we both know the Massad family, correct?"

"Do we? I had no idea." She popped the olive into her mouth, turning it languidly about.

"Yes. I know Gregory and—"

"And I'm his brother's mistress," she finished for me. "But it seems everyone thinks he's dead. Moreno, that is." I looked up from my fish to watch her. She cast her head back sharply and laughed. "Yes, yes, they're so foolish, aren't they? To think such a thing? My goodness." She shook her head.

"Foolish, yes, foolish," I agreed.

"Of course the situation would have it no other way. It is good publicity for him to be dead. Highly convenient."

"I don't understand why. But I've told a few people that he's alive. I'll probably tell quite a few other people before I get to the bottom of all this." An even temperament. An even keel. A smooth surface was essential.

"And none of them believed you, I would imagine. They don't want to believe you. If he's alive it spoils too many plans for too many people. He could prove very dangerous to a great many interests."

"Whose interests?"

"A lot of people profit from his death."

"Gregory?"

"Or . . ." She trailed off, gazing suddenly outside, down the corridor that led into the restaurant. And at the end of the hallway I saw Caroline, a straw purse slung over her arm, her kaftan open to the black swimsuit she was wearing; she looked startled as she focused on Justine and me at the table inside. Justine took a long drink.

"Caroline?" I asked.

Justine chuckled wickedly. "How do you think *you* ended up here?"

"I see you have company." Caroline was instantly at our table, glaring. I reached across my swordfish to hold Justine by the wrist; she was half standing. She did not squirm free of me. Her skin felt warm in my hand, her pulse beating against my fingers. "I really have to go," she said.

"Let her go," Caroline nearly spat, eyeing Justine.

"You two know each other, of course?" I asked stupidly.

"You could say that." Caroline smiled wryly, giving Justine the once-over before taking the chair she had occupied.

"I hope to see you before the tournament," Justine was saying to me, ignoring Caroline.

"Justine was just telling me about Moreno," I said to Caroline.

"Seems Mr. Bradlusky is under the impression that Moreno is alive, Mrs. Massad," Justine said, finally acknowledging her, yet keeping that cool eye on me.

"Yeah, well I'm sure you'll do your best to spread that rumor, won't you?" Caroline said bitterly.

"If only it were true," Justine said with a quick wink to me. "Things would be much different, eh?" She left.

"Bitch," Caroline said. "Greedy bitch had the bull by the balls when Moreno was alive. Still don't trust her, she's so much like him." Her eyes were vacant, unfocused. I noticed a slur in her speech. I watched her knock back a good slug of my drink. Did she swallow something, a pill? I wasn't sure. I played over what Justine had just intimated: that Caroline stood to profit from Moreno's being dead. But how? The business was in Gregory's hands. At least for now. Unless Caroline meant to have Gregory committed. And that still left Sitizar. How could she profit? And I thought of Toby. She couldn't have been responsible for Toby's death.

"Quit staring at me, damn it."

"Sorry, just thinking." I pushed my plate away, not hungry and feeling restless. For some reason I wished I had left with

Justine. And it wasn't just her good looks. I liked the way she handled Caroline; few people could. Caroline snapped her fingers in front of me, shattering the daydream.

"Hey, I said let's go over to Dalva's."

"Who?"

"Dalva's," she said. "I want to show you my boyfriend, if you promise not to get jealous."

ELEVEN

We took that green Porsche of hers up to the coastal road that rose above the ocean on the cliffs. Villas, manors, and any number of restaurants and private castles perched on the rock, which overlooked the water. From those heights we circled down into the town of Albufeira, through its narrow, steep streets, until we climbed once more up into hills streaked with smudges of almond, olive, and cypress gone wild. We climbed until we came to a short driveway; the house—its stucco stained and crumbling—looked deserted. The yard had a fine collection of rusted machine parts, a junk Mercedes. Chicken wire and the remains of what might have been a stockpile of pottery lay stacked against the exterior walls, dissolving into the gravel; wooden shutters, slats missing, were drawn shut; a few chickens bobbed and weaved at the far corner of the house, where a cypress provided some shade. A brilliant green flowery weed crawled over the cracks in the stucco and into the window shutters. It was a wicked, run-down-looking joint, to be sure, and I almost preferred sitting in the car, but I followed Caroline to the back door.

She walked right in: the interior was the flip side—not a rusted machine part or cracked pot to be seen. The walls were covered in African masks and string and percussion instruments: dark woods, heavy material, all richly polished and gleaming. I noticed the floor in particular, the only wood floor I'd encountered in the country. The furniture was leather and teak and the air was sweet with the smell of . . . it wasn't until I took a seat with Caroline I noticed the smoldering hash pipe in the ashtray. The air was definitely hash-sweet. She took a long toke and offered it to me. I declined.

"Dalva!" she suddenly yelled. I jumped. She giggled, and I heard a grunt from down the hall. In walked a muscular man, light on his feet, his eyes darting quickly around the room, to the pipe, to me, and then to Caroline. I felt I knew him, might have seen him before. He was very black, in fact that was his most striking feature, despite his eyes and the tight, oiled afro he wore.

"We're making ourselves at home." Caroline smiled up at him, her eyes already heavy. I shook hands with him, still trying to place him. Where had I seen him? His handshake was solid, hands rough and thick with callus. His eyes darted quickly between Caroline and me. He sat down across from the couch where Caroline and I were seated and took up the hash pipe. I realized he was trying to size me up.

"This is strange, but we haven't met, have we?" I asked.

"I hardly think this is so," he said, his accent heavy, his voice rough. He didn't look at me, passing the pipe to Caroline. But we had. And it came to me. He was the guy that nearly ran down old scarface's woman in Zorine's. It had to be! Justine had turned to him and was chewing him out; I remember her yelling at him, and him disappearing—I'd thought little of it at the time. But what in the hell was he doing in Chicago last week? I found myself watching Caroline very carefully. Watching Dalva very carefully. I couldn't help replaying that seemingly small incident in my mind while looking at him, making comparison after comparison. I kept coming up with the same answer, and I didn't like it. I told myself that the bar had been dark and the whole scene swift. I was even out of earshot—couldn't there be room for a mistake? I wished there was.

It was like finding and refinding only unpleasant moves

open to you on the board. Think and rethink it as you may, your ass is only going a few directions; the dice thrown, the paths known. I decided to sit tight on this one for now. Perhaps he didn't recognize me from that night and maybe that would be an edge—but an edge on what I didn't know.

And like an ass, I kept watching him. His skin seemed less black here in the light of the villa than in the cavelike atmosphere of Zorine's, yet the shade of blackness from that night was still there deep under the oiled sheen of the afternoon, like the rich wood grain of a fine piece of furniture lost behind its finish. His face glowed in that light, but the deeper color of him was just beneath that glow. It was him, the guy who had trampled Justine in Chicago, there was no doubt. What *could* I say? The talk went around as absently as the pipe. He didn't seem to recognize me, or at least was doing an admirable job of pretending not to.

"So, you're the old flame," he said, blinking a grin, taking the pipe from Caroline.

"Let's *do* something," she moaned, her leg swinging. "The damned villa and Gregory are about to drive me over the edge. He's getting worse," she said to Dalva with a sorrowful shake of her head. Dalva leaned forward in his chair to look more closely at me, the wood floor creaked under him. Caroline sipped in the smoke.

"What about it, old flame?" He grinned at me, his quick eyes glassy with smoke. "Let's have a good time today, yes?"

"I'm afraid Vernon's too uptight to have a good time today. He'll have to be *persuaded*," Caroline told him. Dalva nodded, went to the pocket of his T-shirt, and opened a palmful of red capsules toward me.

"I'm out," Caroline said and plucked five or six from his hand before he could even say to me:

"This may persuade you to *re-lax.*"

"No thanks," I said, and sat back uneasily as I watched Caroline knock back the half dozen with water.

After the pipe went out for the last time we piled back into the car and into town where we wolfed down some greasy ham-and-cheese tostadas that had the consistency of fried tar on pizza crust. Dalva led us down the narrow streets to the hotel Balaia-Pents, through its white, sunny-domed lobby and up to the bar for whiskey and Coke, which sat in my insides like nettles, each sip driving tiny spikes deeper into my insides. They danced. I watched. I watched Caroline playfully hike up her beach kaftan. I watched Dalva laugh. It was a damnably long afternoon before we left. It was getting near sunset, the ocean a mellow blue-green as we staggered down the buoy-floated pier to Dalva's boat, the *Embora*, a fine old cabin cruiser, long and high in the water. We tossed off the lines, kept the wake down until well past the last arm of the marina, and then Dalva gave her more and more throttle. We skipped out into the Atlantic, headed east, away from the sun, the red, wind-and-salt-eroded cliffs around Albufeira to our right. Dalva drew in close to some of the towering spires serrated with black caries of grottoes and caves. He took an abrupt turn toward the ocean at one particularly craggy point that seemed to be the very gate to Albufeira's deep cove. We pulled away from shore until the cliffs became a red smear on the horizon. The air on the ocean was cold, and the spray that leaped up onto the back deck drenched Caroline and me; yet she didn't seem to notice. The running lights along the back deck suddenly came on, and Dalva let the throttle down, spinning the boat around into its own wake.

"Grab it!" He yelled to us over the chortling of the idling motors, pointing down from the bridge into the darkening green of the water. Caroline got up woozily with an aluminum pole, a hook at its tip. She tried to lean overboard without falling into the drink, but I could see it was nearly impossible in her state. I got up to help and could see that she was trying to latch on to an orange buoy—about the size and shape of a football—that floated along on the port side. She finally hooked it, my arms around her waist for support, and Dalva took up the rope. Caroline slumped into a deck chair and opened the cooler next to her. I wiped off my wet hands on a nearby towel.

"Squid pots," she said, motioning at Dalva with the wine she'd pulled from the chest. "He's pulling in squid pots." I watched as Dalva pulled in yard after yard of nylon rope, which looped every which way onto the deck until, at last, the first pot appeared—a bucket of woven slats with wire mesh across the top. But Dalva did not stop to open it. He continued to roll up line until all the pots—sixteen of them—were on deck. He took a drink from Caroline's bottle and rested a moment in a deck chair, catching his breath, wiping salt water off his arms.

"When I was a boy, we could bring in nearly a hundred or so a day. My father was very good at this. Good," he breathed. "Lobster or giant octopus. And we didn't have boats like this in Angola."

"Angola, huh?" I heard myself ask, the words rising out of me like air bubbles. I shivered. There is a strategy in the game of backgammon—used at times on the unsuspecting, the brash and overconfident player—that I refer to as the "free lunch." The player purposefully leaves one of his men open, exposed on a point of the board so that the strutting opponent can easily re- move it from the board with his own piece. But the beauty of such a move is that the man you expose to such a quick, un- thinking attack is in a decidedly unstrategic position, and its removal to the bar where it must reenter the board is actually an advantage: by recovering the board you can often pick your op- ponent apart from behind. Dalva seemed to be offering me just such a "free lunch," casting out the delicious information that he was Angolan, and it floated there atop a long, lazy lull in the conversation for me to strike at. When I didn't, he cleared his throat and took the bottle from Caroline's hand. Her arms had gone to gooseflesh but she was too stoned to complain, shiver, or ask for a coat. Dalva got up from the chair, handed me the bottle, and knelt on the deck at the row of squidpots.

"Vernon has been very curious about Angola these days," Caroline said to him. "You could say it's been his hobby." He unhooked the pots from the line and began to coil the rope from his fist to his arm.

"Well, I *was* Angolan," he said, dropping the coiled rope and opening the first pot. "My father was big in the government, a Portuguese. My mother, pure Angolan. Both killed in the war. Me, I took what I could and came to Port-u-gal . . . Opened a restaurant outside of town, outside the bullring, for tourists." He replaced the salt-eaten old bait with a fresh pink prawn from his bait bucket and closed the lid and checked the mesh door.

"Pizza," Caroline giggled, sitting up and reaching for the bottle impatiently.

"Pizza?" I asked.

"Yes. I run a pizza parlor," he said, turning fully toward me as he slid the next pot across to open.

A pizza parlor in Portugal.

"And it does quite well." He beamed, as proud of pizza as of his boat. "I'm fortunate-fortunate. Most Angolans here dig ditches or work the sardine-canning factories, even if they are with luck." He shrugged. "After the revolution nearly a million from Angola came here." The next pot held a healthy squid, nearly as thick and long as his muscular forearm. He removed it with a quick jerk to the bait line, slopping the gray-blue fish into a plastic tub. "Nearly a million at one time is a lot. If you have no money or influence, naturally you run into obstacles." He smiled up at me, his words still well chosen, slow in coming. "So why are you so curious about Angola?"

"I have reason to believe that a friend of mine was killed by an Angolan. A prostitute in Lisbon saw him with two Angolans before he returned to the States. Seems everywhere I turn there's another Angolan popping out of the woodwork. Like in Chicago."

"Chicago?"

"Chicago is in the United States, hon." Caroline provided the answer. I'm not so sure he was asking a question.

"Very impossible," he shook his head, turned down his lower lip. "I wanted to go to the United States myself," he said, looking me right in the eye. "No visa, no visa for Angolans. The war. The revolution." He finished and unwound the leathery-looking tentacles of another squid which was tangled in the slats of the pot. "No visa," he repeated like a song lyric.

"I said it was just a hunch. Maybe these Angolans just know what happened to Toby—my partner." I took a slug of the wine and hunched over in the chair to hand it to him. "And maybe they just don't want to get involved in a killing." Dalva reared his head back and laughed up into the graying sky, his mouth a sudden pink in the very blackness of him.

"These Angolans go crazy for killing lately. They nothing but involved in killing. Revolution means you have to kill." He looked in three more buckets but all were empty except for the bait. "And with all the revolutionaries you got all manner of ways to kill."

"More than one kind of revolutionary in Angola?"

"Many flavors of revolution. You have the communists that say they are in control, the socialists that hide in Zaire, the democrats who hold onto the south and northeast." He checked them off on his fingers. "And many, many more who wander around the land, switching sides according to the food supplies, the quality of liquor, and the omens they read in the cracks of the earth."

"So the communists or some other wacked-out group could have killed Toby? In Chicago?" I asked, searching those evasive eyes of his for only a second. Caroline sighed, either from the sleep of the barbs and wine or from exasperation at the conversation.

"I didn't say any such thing. You let my words around that corner," he said carefully, as if his slowness was a difficulty of picking the precise English words rather than caution on his part. "I didn't say your friend was killed by anyone." He looked across at me, checking out my jeans, the Banlon shirt. "You Americans I love. Black hats and white hats, communists and anticommunists. In the real world it is harder to tell a man's motives from his politics. Perhaps your friend was killed by communists, perhaps UNITA, the FNLA or MPLA, who knows? Or more probably your Mafia or a jealous girlfriend or some maniac man loose on the streets." He sneered at me; at least I felt it was a sneer. And a chill ran over me, a lightheadedness, as if I were on the outside watching all this rather than pitching to and fro, seated on deck. "But no Angolan would bother your friend in Chicago if he hadn't done something to them. Angola has enough problems of its own than to go around shooting up Americans for sport."

"Your Angola's halfway around the world from Chicago. What could Toby possibly have to do with a revolution in Angola?" I looked at both of them trying to sound sincere. "What the fuck does any of this have to do with Toby?"

Caroline spoke with her drowsy, lolling voice. "You brought this Toby bullshit up. We're sorry the sonofabitch is dead, Vernon, but you brought up all this crap about Toby and Angola. And it's silly. If you ask me, the slob got hit by a loan shark, a poor bastard you and he cheated at the tables."

"Then why was he in Portugal?" I asked. Dalva finished emptying the pots and began to clip them back onto the line, lowering them into the water. The brandy and wine and the day swirled in my stomach.

"It must be the games," he offered in that careful, sure-footed tone.

"The games?" I asked. This might be what I wanted to hear.

"To fix them?" Caroline shrugged. "Maybe he was working some—something on the games. What with Gregory *incapacitated.*" She winked at me, having a little trouble with the last word. Justine's accusations about her ran through me like a quick shock.

"Makes more sense than revolutionaries in Chicago," Dalva laughed. When I stopped and thought about it, it *was* a pretty absurd notion. I cracked a smile and took another drink.

"After all," I went on, feeling a wave of relief, feeling that, yes, that tired-ass Toby had gotten himself mixed in with some gambling scam, something plain and easy and right up Toby's alley. "After all, why the hell would Angolans kill Toby gangster style, slicing his face?"

I took a good, cold draft of sea air, which was sweeter-smelling than that afternoon's hash. I realized then that Dalva, and especially Caroline, seemed stricken, both their faces pointed to me.

"What do you mean slicing his face?" Dalva asked, his voice low, softer than the waves that licked at the hull.

"Whoever killed him sliced his face," I explained, flashing a quick image of the corpse: the steel-blue light, the strips of flesh.

"I'm afraid, old flame, that your friend was indeed killed by revolutionaries. So very bad." He lowered his eyes, ran his hand across his forehead and through the oily afro. "That is their way." He took quick strides up the stepladder to the bridge. Caroline seemed to be holding her breath. I felt the wind pick up at my back. Dalva gunned the engines, and we turned into the west, leaving a foamy green wake.

"I'm sorry," Caroline said soberly, perhaps fully aware for the first time that Toby was dead, that it was no joke or game that would disappear. The wake splashed her, but she merely pulled her soaked kaftan more tightly around her black bikini.

I sat in the back of the car on the way into town, the squids sloshing on the floor, Caroline and Dalva silent in the front seat. This silence, along with the deliberate words of Dalva, was making me retreat more into myself, risk less with each word I spoke.

On the road back to town, he came dangerously close to the cliff edge, swerving, a slop of the squid's water lapping over the plastic bucket onto my canvas shoes. I was chilled, the flesh tightening between my shoulder blades, my scalp growing taut under the baby-fine, salt-stiffened mat of my hair. "*Hey-hey,*" he chortled as the car sped out of the curve. "Sorry *ay-bout* the ride." And he shot me a glance in the rearview.

——— TWELVE ———

We went around the town to where the bullring rises: clusters of shops, petrol stations, souvenir stands gathered about narrow streets. It was a weekday, and no events were scheduled. A drunk slouched against the metal bars that closed off a flimsy cavelike stand just out from Dalva's ITALIANO ROMA PIE. It had modern chrome-casement windows, a tile interior. Small Formica-topped tables with Cinzano bottles and plastic flowers topped off the chintzy decor. It was a sudden, garish eruption on the otherwise brown-cobbled, stucco-faced street. The menu, painted on the wall, was in blue and pink letters that the fluorescent lights hyped to painful clarity. The only touch of class was a seven-foot cylindrical brass bird cage, which dominated the middle of the sterile room like some artful, gilded rocket. Inside, two white cockatoos fluttered, stretched, and cooed. Dalva led us past their cage slowly.

"A large sum of money for these birds," he nodded, his hands locked in a hug around the squid bucket. We went into the back room, where Caroline pulled off her drenched kaftan and slung it over the gooseneck temperature gauge of the greasy, smudged pizza oven along one wall. She flopped into a chair beside a cardboard drum of flour and lay her head on the table where a nonplussed cook in jeans and a torn, tomato-splotched T-shirt was rolling out a pie crust. He took one glance at Caroline, head on arms, hair wet and astray, and continued his work. Dalva said something to him in Portuguese. He left in a hurry. I took it Dalva was closing the place. I stood against a bare stretch of wall opposite the oven, as alert and upright as the menu outside on the wall. Dalva set the squid bucket next to a claw-footed bathtub just to my right. He scooted over to a case of empty bottles to sit on.

"God," Caroline moaned. I scarcely knew her, or so it seemed then. The back room made me feel claustrophobic. Caroline grew stranger, even more high and spacey, so that there was no longer a firm, easy, reliable place to rest my eyes. Flour splotched her tanned forearm; it was smeared along one side of her face, where she had laid her head, and in her now straggly hair. Her eyes stared ahead blankly, as dead and unfocused as the squid eyes that sloshed around in Dalva's bathtub.

Dalva had the squids in the chipped bathtub, the plastic bucket atop a wooden beer crate. He fished in the bucket until he found a likely candidate, which he spread out on a piece of wood spanning the corner of the tub.

"God," she went on, her eyes focused somewhere else, "what was it like to find him? Toby?" She did not look up for me to respond. Dalva turned on a small spigot in the wall, and it began to splash into the tub at the far end. He took out a pocketknife from his pants, standing to do so, turning off the water when he saw that there was enough.

"So you say Toby was killed by revolutionaries?" I said to him. Caroline was looking through a star-shaped hole in the back window, as if staring into her own eye. He straightened the squid, spreading the tentacles out like thick tresses of hair, his knife ready.

"Had to be. That type of murder . . ." He left off, shrugging. I looked down. A splash of pizza sauce, fresh on the browned floor, was alive with red ants, just near my shoe. My head ached in that deep hollow behind the eyes. Dalva sliced down the body of the squid—it was a gray-purple under the harsh light of the kitchen. I scuffed away the ants with the heel of the other shoe. He peeled back the flesh of the sac-ish body, searched it carefully with his thin fingers and the point of the knife, and with a few quick slices of the blade, he cut loose the bulblike eyes, the bleeding organs, and other mucuslike innards. He plucked the ink sac, a thumbnail-sized, veined black kidney, and placed it into a small bowl at his feet outside the tub. With another flick of the knife he loosened a blue-white cartilage, the flat cuttlebone.

"For the birds?" he said, tapping it against his teeth. "Sharpen their beaks?" And he tossed it into the bowl with the ink sacs. I could see I'd have to ask again; he was volunteering nothing.

"How are you sure Toby was killed by revolutionaries?"

"A particular revolutionary. And it saddens me," he said. Caroline got up and took a beer from the crates that leaned against the back wall, opened one, and threw the cap out the hole in the cracked window. She stood there, her black bathing suit flour-splotched. Dalva shifted on the beer case. "Tribalists. Counterrevolutionaries. Tribal ways. Some of the old ways, the primitive ways."

"Primitive?" I asked, watching as he deftly sliced tentacles into thin, fresh-cut wedges: they reminded me of green beans. Pink beans.

"Your friend, old flame, was killed by tribalists. Want the old ways back. Not progressive enough. Traitors to the tribes are slashed. The nature of the treason indicates the nature of the mutilation. Faces are a person's identity. A man is his face. Remove a man's face and he becomes homeless. It is like cutting him off forever from the world of the spirits. He cannot take his place in heaven because the spirits do not know who he is. Not without a face."

The sliced squid made it into another bowl. He reached for another squid in the bucket.

"So they took his life and his identity. He must have really fucked someone around," I said. Caroline was watching her kaftan drip onto the floor. "So how do you know so much?" I went on, somehow bolder, peering over his shoulder into the tub water, now milky with entrails. Caroline wiped beer from her chin with the back of her hand and walked back to the seat, collapsed into it, her legs apart, the stubble on her thighs clear in the light.

"I know so much," Dalva answered me, "because I used to be Angolan; remember my telling all this?"

"But about the tribes, the mutilation?"

"One hears. One reads. One can keep in some sort of contact."

"But Toby," I said, watching Caroline finger the strap of her suit. "Toby is from New York. The farthest he's been—all I know is he was here. What does that have to do with Angola? With revolutionaries?"

"Caroline? Caroline?" Dalva said to her, as if waking her from a deep sleep.

"Honey?" she asked.

"Old flame here wants to know what does revolution have to do with here. This Algarve and his Toby friend."

She cleared her throat. "Vernon," she sighed, as if I were an annoyance. I probably was. "Toby probably had business with the wrong people. My husband's kind of people."

"What do you mean?"

"The people who used to rip off Angola. Those kind of people. That's why the revolution in the first place. Gregory lost, you can see that in him. Maybe Toby lost too."

"I don't understand," I said.

"I think Caroline is trying to say, that there are men still ripping off the country, its people, even after the Cubans and the courageous people regain control."

Revolutions. What the hell could Toby ever have to do with that? And in Chicago, no less? "But I thought Gregory," I began. He stood, wiping his hands on his jeans, pinning me against the wall with a hateful glare.

"Yes, old flame, maybe Gregory is no longer the businessman. The big man, the commander, but maybe the company be like some beast, some shark, still eating even after the head gone. The people once work for Gregory perhaps stronger than any revolution, keep eating and eating away. Or maybe Gregory feigns his madness, feigns this weakness while he controls such forces, so very bad forces."

Both ideas fit, at least from that night I had an "audience" with Gregory.

"And Toby was involved?" I said. Dalva laughed horribly, a thick, bass laugh.

"I'd say dead is no more involved than one man can get, yes?" He glared up at me, helping the slop along under the door with his shoe heel and broom handle. Splashing it wetly into the alley.

"But how?"

"Pigs. Capitalist pigs everywhere. No telling how a sucker as your friend, old flame, could get involved. Even Gregory may not be behind all the theft in Angola. Maybe bigger pigs, yes?"

"I never trusted Moreno, that's for sure," Caroline said suddenly, and I went a bit weak, if not from that remark, then from the sight of all those squid entrails, guts oozing out the door, dripping wetly into the alley below. "Before he died he owned Gregory. He'd tell Gregory to shit and Gregory would ask what color. Moreno was behind most of it. He was the shark, Gregory just a fish, a triggerfish."

"Killed in Zaire. Nearly a year ago," Dalva told me, wiping his hands on a rag.

"But Chicago?" I asked, seeing Dalva once again as I had in the bar, at Zorine's, running into Justine, him yelling at her, his muscles taut in his neck.

"Chicago?" he asked me, but I saw him hesitate, as if his hand had lingered too long over a key game piece. He hesitated perhaps to make a different move, one less obvious, one more subtle.

"That night you were in Chicago I played a game of backgammon with a Moreno. The night of Toby's murder," I said firmly, each word a buttress for the next. I was feeling more confident, as if I suddenly had gained some leverage, as if the dice, the circumstances were fresh. Dalva stood still and stared as Caroline launched into a frenzy of drugged babble.

"Impossible. Not possible. No," she said, twirling the empty beer bottle on the floured table. And then she let loose. "He's dead. He's fucking dead, how many times do we have to tell you!" she screeched, saliva speckling her words, her head weaving in the sudden rage. "Are you trying to drive us crazy? Is that what you want? He's dead, what are you trying to prove?"

"Caroline!" Dalva yelled, and gave her a thick stare. She calmed gradually and took a long drink of the beer. It got quiet for a time. There was a guaranteed reaction when anyone mentioned Moreno, but I wasn't anywhere near prepared for that outburst: it was all the more impressive in light of the drugs and booze. Her eyes watered, she looked away from us, out the hole in the window once again.

"I heard he once had workers, native workers beaten with rifle butts for taking a long break while loading trucks. He owned a few whorehouses in Zaire." Dalva said. "It's a good thing the bastard was killed."

"How was he killed?" I still wasn't buying the oft-repeated fact that I'd played three games of backgammon with a dead man. I was beginning to toss out every wild story the two of them had been feeding me. There was no telling what would come next. I knew only that I was on to something whenever I brought up Moreno. His name was gunpowder.

"Shot in his whorehouse." Dalva picked carefully through his words. "There was a party. Moreno had one girl of each color—like he liked them. A yellow, a black, a tawny girl. He was in his suite, there was a lot of drinking and they say a lot of drugs. One of Moreno's trading partners came in and saw that Moreno had all these women in his bed, had some tied and some so very high. One in *par-tick-u-lar* was the very partner's wife. He shot Moreno in the head and cut off the manhood. Just cut the thing off like cane and left it lying on the floor."

Caroline was wriggling into her kaftan, pushing the matted strands of her hair back out of her face, perhaps finally feeling the dried patches of flour on her.

"And you know this about Moreno? You know so much, Dalva," I said, prodding him. "And Chicago?"

"I've never been to your Chicago." He gazed at me coolly, broom in hand. Caroline went to his side, slipping an arm around him. She was trembling.

"And you know all the right people, I'll bet," I said.

"I know what I need to know. And sometimes you need people to look after you." He held her tightly to him. "Can we drop you somewhere?" he asked, running a thumb across the waistband of Caroline's suit. She nuzzled at his neck.

"No." I raised a hand, backed toward the door. "I'll get a cab or something."

I left the pizzeria with a queasy, dizzy feeling. I was acutely aware then, perhaps for the first time, of being had. Dalva was without a doubt using his foreignness, his heavy accent and expertise with a knife, to get me spooked. At the same time he had been heaping on the crap about the revolution and big business and any other smokescreen you could imagine. I knew a few things for certain: he was in Chicago the night of the murder, the same night I played Gregory's "dead" brother, Moreno. Toby had been to the Algarve, all right. No one was denying that—from the hooker in Lisbon to the Angolans to Caroline to Dalva himself—they had all admitted to Toby's being in the Algarve. Trouble was, all of them were disagreeing on everything else. It was obvious Caroline and Dalva wanted me to suspect Gregory and his partner, Sitizar. And of course she had her motives: if the crazy hubby were put away, she and Dalva would never again have to fry up another pseudo-pizza for the tourists. Despite what everyone had been telling me about Gregory's business failings, I had the distinct impression that there were still more than a few lonely escudos tucked away here and there. And Dalva . . . he could afford to look suspicious, to get me rankled—we both knew I had nothing on him. Yet. And Caroline . . . I no longer knew her or thought about trusting her.

I made my way to the main boulevard that fronted the stadium and found a cab parked, its driver outside, leaning on the trunk, passing a beer with a friend. I nodded to him and got in the back as he scurried to the wheel. I was in a strange country in the company of strangers waiting, supposedly, for a backgammon tournament. I was really waiting for a murderer to reveal himself, make himself clear with a quick, greedy move.

"*Villa Massad, Apontarleve, por favor,*" I said, and sank back, thinking about what I wanted from the murderer, and then I realized why Dalva, although decidedly shady and definitely dishonest, did not *feel* like Toby's murderer: I was expecting one certain, deft stroke from the murderer—an attempt on my own life. In fact I knew then, with a chill and with elation perhaps, that my own jeopardy was the cutting edge, the only edge I had over whoever had killed my partner. I was moving through another player's board, another player's strategy, another player's mind, moving through like hands folded into hands, yet I was blind. My only sight would come if I edged myself closer to the danger—real or imagined. If Dalva and Caroline wanted me to believe Gregory and his business were behind some plot, then all right. I'd pursue it, regardless of their motives. For I felt that even Dalva was not entirely his own man. A hand manipulated his hand.

—— THIRTEEN ——

I paid the driver to drop me off well before the Massad villa so that I could sneak up to the house along the gravel road.

Gregory's rooms were open and I went in cautiously, even looking behind the door I had opened. The tables set with back-gammon boards were still scattered throughout the room, candles set burning beside them. The bookshelves and cases stood in the shadows along the walls, and the bed and high-back chair, as I approached, were empty. No Gregory. I fumbled along walls feeling for a light switch, but the one I found did not work. He had disconnected the lights entirely. I went to one bookcase, most of the titles in Portuguese, when I decided it would be worthwhile to search the room by that crazy candlelight. I began to empty the shelves, piling armload after heaping armload onto the floor. I felt the shelves: nothing. I stood on the pile of books, aware that I would not hear anyone approach because of my own heavy breaths. I tried to gulp them back, but I still heard no one, not a sound in that too quiet night. I found the briefcase I'd brought over for Gregory opened on the bed in plain view, and I was surprised to see that not only the blueprints but a passport were inside. My chest was tight with alertness. I sat cross-legged on the made bed, briefcase drawn into my lap: the passport on top. Marteno Massad, Apontarleve, Algarve, Portugal. And the picture in the damned thing was definitely the guy I saw in the bar in Chicago, the guy that Justine had told me earlier that day was indeed alive, despite the fact that everyone else was determined to keep him dead. Here in my hand I held his passport,

the gaunt-faced, thick-lensed, silver-haired and mustachioed
man with the ulcerated, deeply scarred face. He had entered the
city of New York from Lisboa on March 16. Quite a trick for
someone who's dead. Or wanted most people to think he's dead.
Moreno, or as his passport read "Marteno," would be a likely
candidate for Toby's murderer and anyone else's: he looked the
part, no doubt about that.

As I rummaged around the case, beneath the blueprints and
tucked into the corner lining I found a remarkable envelope: it
held eight color photographs, which I held toward the candlelight. I shuddered and couldn't believe what I was seeing: in
each picture Caroline was posed in the nude: each shot had her
legs spread, dark pubic hair separated by her own painted nails,
her breasts rouged and full, fuller than I'd seen them in years. It
dawned on me how old the photos were; she was wearing the
slight bouffant, the waterfall bangs that she had worn back at
Northwestern. That baby-blue choker with the cameo on it. The
pictures had to have been taken years and years ago, but here
they were in Gregory's briefcase. Taken when she and I were
supposed to be so tight, so on the verge of becoming a permanent thing . . . She looked up at me from these pictures, eyes
glazed with beer, her legs spread on that unfamiliar motel-style
bed, her fingers probing her own vagina for the photographer. In
one shot she was astraddle the hotel chair, ass thrust up, taking
a man from behind, his face cropped out of the photo. I clutched
the pictures and tossed them in my coat pocket. I took them out
and looked again. Hadn't Sandra said something about a photographer? But that was something about pictures of *Sandra*. Here
was Caroline. I put them in my pocket again, feeling breathless.
My arms were heavy as I let the blueprints fall back into the
case. Was she being blackmailed? Or Gregory? I shifted the case
on my lap and found in the loose pockets four syringes still in
their plastic packets, and a sealed vial. As I replaced them I
glanced at the blueprints again. The architectural drawings had
been marked in white ink; junctions in what appeared to be the
overhead heating ducts of the casino were circled and corre-
sponding numbers—dimensions, I imagined—were scribbled in

larger figures in the margins. I looked through the whole group of blueprints. Only the casino plans had been marked up in such a fashion. I was rifling hurriedly through the case looking for more when I heard noise—sudden and crisp as a gunshot, yet it wasn't a gunshot. I scrambled to the side of the bed, spilling the briefcase from my lap, my heart racing. I stood all ears and stock still there in the room for what seemed to be a dreadfully long time until I heard the sound again.

Swunk, abrupt and disturbing, coming from beyond the shuttered windows in the yard below. Had someone heard me tumbling those books onto the floor? As I was about to step toward the shutter I heard it again: the measured, even *swunk* that was neither closer nor farther away. I relaxed, sensing the noise had little to do with me, and found myself squeezing at the pictures of Caroline in my pocket as if they were a black-jack. I tried to straighten the room but gave up: who would know it was *me* snooping? I stepped downstairs, down the cor-ridor, and, lightly and without a whisper of my own breathing, toward the open patio doors that allowed the faintest wisps of a night breeze to trickle in from the yard. I stood in that boundary of stuffy indoor air and the gentle night and saw, with amaze-ment, a long line of glowing green orbs laid out on the dark lawn. Perhaps a dozen were there, glowing a cool, chemical green as they lay in the moonlit grass.

Golf balls!

I saw a slender figure waggle at the nearest glow, draw back in an easy swing, and a *swunk* filled the night. The green golf ball arced high over the back hedges, up and up, only to angle down into the darkness of the golf course beyond. It was Greg-ory practicing chip shots over the back hedges, in the middle of the night with glow-in-the-dark golf balls. I shook my head, went to the bar where there was a bottle left open and his own snifter of brandy. I walked toward him, the bottle and his glass in hand.

"Groove your grip. Steady swing," he said to me, club held high and pointed to where the ball had disappeared. He did not turn around; it was almost as if he'd spoken to himself; yet even

I could hear my footsteps on that brittle grass. "Groove your stroke, but you would only know backgammon, Mr. Bradlusky. Backgammon and perhaps other men's wives." He waggled at the next ball, practicing a backswing slowly before *swunk*, another ball launched onto the golf course beyond. His hair was wet from a shower or perspiration, and his face, in that moonlight, seemed even smoother, nearly porcelain smooth and unwrinkled. He kept his back to me for the most part and I saw that he was considerably thinner than the time in the Bahamas when Caroline had first run off to be Mrs. Massad. Thinner and more nervous, for even his golf swing seemed to tremble. He scratched his ears, his face, turned into the shadows as though to avoid me when I drew near with his drink. A shaking hand reached out and took it, but he turned to the hedges to empty the snifter with one long gulp and then threw the bubblelike glass over the hedges with a quick toss.

"So you may know about grooving strokes, yes. Are you ready for the games?" he asked. I had moved away from the next practice swing of his club, sitting in a lawn chair with the bottle.

"Ready?" I asked, the tournament all but forgotten. How had I forgotten?

"Haven't given it much thought, have you? The sun, the drinks, the women here in the Algarve . . . makes one forget one's calling." *Swunk*. Another shot, following the same precise arc of the others, went over to the course.

"I've been doing my own calling," I began, shifting in the seat.

"I'm sure you have."

"And the things I've found out disturb me," I said more boldly, setting the bottle down. I looked steadily at the back of his head.

"Are you easily disturbed? Do you upset easily? I would hope so . . . I have you down as an easy first-round loser in the tournament. You will probably go down in straight games . . ." He continued to talk the tournament, avoiding my eyes and the direction I needed to take the conversation. *Swunk*. Another green-glowing parabola in the night sky.

"Disturbing to find that your company is involved in some shady deals. Ripping off some revolutionary movement or whatever. Is that why you're going bankrupt? Closing the Chicago office? And Toby, did you recruit Toby through that office?"

"Toby, Toby . . . sounds like a child's imaginary friend. The kind one talks to on rainy, lonely days." Each word was like the *clunk* of an ice cube into an empty glass. He set up another shot.

"What do you have planned for the casino?" I asked, thinking of the blueprints upstairs, the white marks. "What do you have planned for the tournament, what's up, damn it, you must have a few answers." I got up from the chair, stepping up to him, the smooth backswing rising up before I could stop myself, the club face shishing past my nose.

"I look for answers myself, Mr. Bradlusky. Look and look to get frustrated once more. I've looked until I've found—we've found—the only solution: the game itself. It was so simple," he went on, holding his follow-through position. "The game itself is objective, clean. Without guilt or remonstrance." He turned to face me, his jaw working barely at all, as if he were a ventriloquist, his face bright and smooth in the full moonlight. I thought of the syringes and the medicine vial in the briefcase. Gregory, one severely gone individual, either from drugs or disease, was playing out of a different time zone, a different set of board rules in that silent, windless Portuguese night. He laughed: a thick, wicked sound in that still air. And that laugh probably covered miles; it seemed to roll far out into the night. He turned to walk toward the hedges, a golf bag hung over his arm. I stood frozen to the spot, and he picked a seam in the shadowy hedges and slithered through to the other side, leaving me behind.

I fought through the tangle of hedges. The golf balls sat like so many jewels on black velvet, all had landed under a protective bower of cypress, shielding them from even the dim silver of the moonlight. Gregory stood amid them, lazily swinging his club.

"The game is objective. Play the game, the dice, the probabilities. Do not play the hunches, the information given to you. Play the black and white of it. The tournament will tell me all I want to know. Objective. Then it will be time to settle sides, to settle angers."

I picked a twig out of my hair and brushed myself off with my free hand.

"And what do you have to settle? Did you settle with my friend?" I asked.

"I wish you knew how trivial your concerns were, Mr. Bradlusky. You see so very little of the entire board. Yes," he snickered, as if someone had just whispered an important and satisfying comment to him. "Yes, of course . . . you see so little of the board, but just enough to make you concerned. Just enough to make you a part of the board, just enough to make you a member of the solution. But don't get a larger view, keep to your own meager space. A larger view is dangerous; I am one who knows." He fell silent as he set up and hit one, two, three, four of the glowing golf balls to the ridge of the fairway, each rising, bouncing and rolling to a stop high up the crest which narrowed toward what I assumed must be the green. He bent to retrieve the remaining shots and strode off toward the four which dotted the ridge, barely luminescent in the moonlight. I fell in behind him, thinking I'd get little from him besides this ass-backward crazy talk. Who knows what chemicals were buzzing in his brain? But I felt that he *was* making some crazy sense of everything he could tell me, perhaps even in his own oblique way, something that would begin to tie up all loose ends.

"Why not just cut the talk. You're so smart, what *am* I up against, if you think you know it all?" I huffed up behind him, both of us rising along the slope toward the crest, a triangle of greened moonlight dusting the evenly clipped carpet of the fairway. "What are you after? How is some fucking backgammon tournament going to straighten things out for you? How the hell are you using us?" He continued to stride toward the crest, ignoring me. "Hey, I feel for you. I understand," I tried to soften my approach, my legs burning as I tried to keep up: I was out of shape and this fairway was damned steep. Gregory moved steadily up ahead; I swayed as I stopped, getting my balance, looking back at the soft slope that descended below to the tee and the bright white of the villa, the cloudlike clumps of trees and hedges. I nearly shouted: "After all, your wife getting caught up with the Dalva guy, and your brother getting killed, or so everyone says, and . . ." I saw Gregory stop walking. Abruptly. I clambered up after him, both of us then at the crest. He had halted nearly ten yards from the four perfectly placed golf balls: whatever I had said had stopped him cold.

"You don't understand a thing, Mr. Bradlusky. The destruction that they can cause."

"Who, who, damn it!" I waved the bottle at him, his face a moonlit slab of smooth flesh despite the terse, angry words that hissed out of him.

"Caroline does not know what she does; they've used her, they'll use her again, and you could save her but you will probably use her also. You could save her, don't you realize? Get her away . . ." He choked with a sob as he turned around.

"You're a chump!" I said. "You think Dalva is using her or something? For what? She's no damned saint, buddy. I just had squid and wine and a fine little boat ride with your darling bride, and it looks to me like they want to frame you. At least they want me to be suspicious of you. And I figure, why not? But Caroline's no ripe virgin, no innocent by any yardstick. But you already know that. I don't have to refresh your memory." I found myself getting angry at him. I clutched the photos in my pocket, he walked up to the top of the crest. He bent over a golf ball, shaking, shivering with anger.

"I mean who the hell do we think she is?" I was telling myself just then as well as him. "She's no angel, she's shacked up with this other guy, this fucking Angolan, on her own free will. You know her . . . you know what she can do . . . Shit, Gregory you know what she's like, but don't expect me to believe she's some damned innocent victim. I'm beginning to think she never spent an innocent day in her life. She wasn't born yesterday. And not the day these precious pics were taken either." I tossed the whole packet of her photographs at the golf ball he was bent over, her photographed bare limbs shimmering in the dim light, arms and spread legs like wisps of smoke thrown down at his feet.

"Who is blackmailing her? Or is it you that's being black-mailed? And Toby's death? She could just as well be involved, she's no fucking saint. I think we both know that by now." I gagged on my own words, fumbling for the bottle cork with my teeth, when what I thought was his backswing, suddenly be-came his stepping over to me, pitching wedge held over his head. A tight snarl came out of his gritted teeth like rocks being ground under enormous pressure, and that club came down. I tried weakly, too late, to block it with my arm.

What remained of the blow struck the bottle I'd been cling-ing to, and it broke in my hand, booze spilling over my legs, glass splattering over the grass. I cowered, then jumped to one side, trying to grab his arm as he tried to swing it back again. "You overstepped, you went astray, you imbecile," he growled. "Black stays black, white stays white. Stay!" He came at me again; this time the club face struck my shoulder, and as I went down to my knees, grasping at him, clawing at him, my fingers suddenly gripped and ripped at the very flesh of his face. I looked down, confused. I was clutching a flap of flesh! I looked up, wincing into the sky at him looming over me, a splash of moon-light showing the sudden ugly scars under what I had ripped free: it was Moreno under that flap of latex, it was Moreno's scarred and pitted face! And then the thick shadow of his arms went down and I caught the iron in the forehead, the metal slic-ing at the skin and thrashing at the bone with the familiar *swunk*. The pain leaped through my head down to my toes, and I felt other blows—to my mouth, my ribs and legs—but they were far off and getting farther until only the sound *swunk*, *swunk* was hitting me. I went numb all over and felt—like a warm, fresh breeze—a tingling that enveloped my entire body. A tingling like thousands of bubbles bursting inside me.

─── FOURTEEN ───────────

I woke looking up a long black line that tugged at my forehead, a line that jerked and jerked at the skin as if tugging the flesh off. As I followed the black line I saw it end in brown fingers that held a needle which flashed with each taut tug. I said, "Shit," real loud, right to Josef's face, and he jerked back a bit, needle still in hand.

"Quiet *ya-self*, Mr. Bradloozkey. Quiet now. You feel the pain of the needle?"

I didn't. But aches. Aches and pains as though giant scoops of me, big raw forkfuls of me had been ripped out of my chest, legs, one arm and my entire face. I flinched as Josef came down with the needle once more. But I felt only the gentle tug of steel pushing through the deadened flap of skin. No needle pain; the ache beneath, deep under, was so much greater that it must have blotted out the tiny pricks as the needle continued to stitch me up. Quickly, expertly, beak-nosed nostrils flared in concentration, yellowed eyes a slit of intent, Josef bent over me. I counted ten strokes of the needle, ten passes of his hand. How many had he put into me before I had come to?

"I tried to stop the bleeding. Had to do this." He shrugged, clipping the end of the thread close to my face. I sank down into a mattress, seemed to sink as if released by the thread, and I moaned roughly through the mucus in my throat that I didn't dare try to clear.

"I tried too, me too," I heard Mobotiak's voice off to the side of me, wherever I was. I smelled charcoal and a tang of fish.

Mobotiak shuffled in one corner as Josef looked down at me, winding what was left of the black suture onto its aluminum spindle.

"A lot of blood, Mr. Bradloozkey. Good thing we had been watching. Good thing I had followed out to the golf course. You took a beating, yessir. Whack-whack." And he gently chortled after golfing at the air with a few swings.

"So why didn't you step in, you fucking bastard." I creaked up from the bedding in fits and starts as if hauled up with stiff block and tackle, each pause and stutter bringing a fresh wrack of pain in my ribs, face, arm, legs. Josef propped a pillow behind me, I could see Mobotiak standing in a doorway that emptied onto a dawn-dim street.

"Not any way for that. No, no. If I had even been caught on the premises of such a place as Apontarleve without work orders, a job, a villa of my own. No, no. The best of things I could do was to wait out the crazy man, then see what was left behind of you." Josef finished, getting up from the stool he'd been sitting at, and went to a basin of water near the bed where he washed his hands. More light poured in from the doorway, where Mobotiak stooped over a small grill, poking at fish. Color-splashed posters covered the cracked walls of the small room; I sensed a doorway in the wall behind me and to the left, which went deeper into the house. I smelled my blood, alcohol. I was thirsty and Josef brought me a ceramic mug of wine. I guzzled it as he protested and Mobotiak laughed. I heard a horse or donkey snort on the street outside and knew the door opened onto a narrow alley; the animal noise was close, as if it were inside the room.

"Where is this?" I asked, my mouth mushy-sounding and my lips loose and oddly slack. I felt my jaw, though to raise my hand was like lifting weights. "Fuck," I moaned, as I realized my bridgework was gone, probably knocked clean out of my head when I'd been smacked with one of those iron shots.

"Wait, wait," Mobotiak said, and came up from the grill and fumbled in his coat pocket and held out a jumble of my partial plate in his palm. "Josef say to hold onto." I took the chunks of loose false teeth, like so many chipped-up dice, and the gold-wire frame that had held them but was now a useless S-shaped twist of metal. I rolled them from palm to palm, my tongue probing the gaps along the gums, which seemed the only spots on my body that were calm. I poked around the false teeth in my palm until Josef said, "So you must be making progress to finding a murderer; you were almost killed yourself." He snickered as he took the stool near my bed again, drying his hands on a blood-spotted rag.

"Very close. A man named Moreno, really Gregory Massad's brother, older brother, is responsible," I managed to slur. I felt the corner of my lip was tight, discovered a discrete stitch with my fingertip.

"Responsible for what? Do you even know what there is to be responsible for?" he asked.

"Toby's murder. Must be. Look at this, look," I said fumbling at my pockets, searching for the latex that had covered the side of the face. I found nothing in the pockets but dried patches of my own blood here and there . . . nothing.

"Look at what?" Josef seemed to mock me, his yellowed eyes getting incredibly wide.

"Face. Covered-over face. Gregory Massad must be dead because his brother is masquerading as him, covered the scars with the latex, I ripped off the latex and saw the scars below, Moreno, it was Moreno."

"It was not Moreno," Josef slowly answered, a smile, a thin, satisfied smile spreading over his lips. Mobotiak got up from the smoldering sardines and walked over to peer at me, his own eyes wide with fear.

"What if?" he said to Josef.

Josef's smile broke up into a snarl, and he spat a few harsh words in Portuguese. Mobotiak answered, pointed down at me, argued with Josef and finally retreated to the doorway and to the fish on the grill, mumbling to himself in a mixture of Portuguese, English, and his native dialect.

"Seems there is disagreement on that point. I know other people who know that Moreno is alive. I can prove it. No one but *no* one owns a face like that. You can't possibly believe I could mistake it." I pulled the cover off my legs, untangling myself from the bedclothes. A flash of two, three children moved across the doorway as they scooted down the alley, laughing. A fresh wisp of smoke rose from the grill.

"I'm sure you saw what you say that you saw. It is just that my own experience tells me otherwise, Mr. Bradloozkey."

"Your experience?"

"Yes. You see, I killed Moreno, as he calls himself, in Zaire last year. I shot him many times in the head." Josef indicated the shots by poking a long brown finger at a spot above the nose, one above the right eyebrow, the middle of the forehead, and finally at the cheekbone. He was precise about this demonstration, his finger spotting each point with care. "I checked his pulse. I put the gun in my pocket, and I walked out of the hotel before the flies in his room even had a chance to settle once more." He said this calmly, looking me dead in the eye. "And now you tell me that Moreno is alive. One of us is wrong. Either I did not kill Moreno that afternoon in Zaire, or you did not nearly get clubbed to death by him on the golf course. Perhaps we have mistaken similar individuals for the same man." He raised an eyebrow, shrugged. I shook my head; it was a painful and nauseating thing to do.

"I saw a passport in Gregory Massad's room: *Marteno Massad*. The picture on the passport was the man I played backgammon with in Chicago. It was the man who Justine says she went to Chicago with. She *knows* who he is. I pulled the mask off him. It *was* Moreno, don't you see? He's probably killed his own brother." I was desperate to convince him just then. And I can't really say why except that I was sure that the man on the golf course that night was responsible for a whole lot, and to have him be Moreno was a neat and satisfying solution.

"And then the man I shot in Zaire?" Josef asked, standing. The grill hissed as Mobotiak began to remove the fish, tiny pieces falling through the grate to the coals below.

"Why the hell should I trust you?" I suddenly thought aloud.

"Because the people you are with are slime, Mr. Bradloozkey. Because we may be the only, just now, the only people that you can trust. We don't want anything from you but cooperation. Paid cooperation if we must! And the slime in that compound, that rich man's garrison, will keep you alive only as long as it suits them. Only as long as it takes to do their bidding and then I am sure that they will kill you. And not because you'll talk, no! You could talk and no one would care. Not the authorities, not the police. No, they'd kill you because you'd become a nuisance, a pest." He began to bluster, waving his arms, pointing toward the resort, pointing to me, the stone floor, the doorway. He was mad as hell.

"Then for chrissakes tell me what it is everyone is after. Tell me, you righteous sonofabitch! If you're *really* out to save my neck, if you think you're such a sweetie pie, why don't you fuckin' spill it once and for all. I'm damned tired of being in the dark!" I had stood also and was gripping his shirt, talking a long, even stream of pissed off. I was trembling when I finished, still gripping that shirt, my breath breaking on his face, which flinched slightly with each new burst. He took a good, long while to answer, giving me a cold glower with those yellowed eyes of his. Gently, he took his shirt out of my clenched fist.

"We've gone through this before Mr. Bradlusky," he said slowly, pronouncing my name correctly. "If I tell you what the product was, you are able to do some very dangerous things while you are here. You are liable to ask the wrong questions and look in the wrong places and get yourself unnecessarily killed. But if you determine the product and its whereabouts on your own, I'm sure the discovery will be one reached most naturally and without the neck in the noose to endanger yourself." He sat once again, crossing his thin legs.

"I'd say I've already been pretty endangered!" I wiped at the stitches in my head with my swollen hand, sitting heavily back on the bed, still mad enough to take him on, but obviously less than able. "Or just maybe you don't want me or Caroline or anyone else getting their hands on the product, huh? Maybe you're scamming me like you scammed Toby. After all, he got himself killed taking your side. And I'm coming pretty damn close myself."

"It's either us or them, Mr. Bradlusky. Us or them. Mobotiak, come here." Josef waved him over. "Take a good look at that face, Mr. Bradlusky." He pointed a bony finger at the quivering face, standing so that Mobotiak could take the stool directly in front of me. The muscles jerked in tense, scrunched tightness, teeth bared, nose and cheeks wrinkled. He breathed through those bared teeth, rasping. All the muscles in his face had some twitch, some spasm.

"The peoples you and I are up against, are responsible for this face and for Mr. Kale's death. Tell Mr. Bradlusky what happened to your face," Josef said, his hand still holding Mobotiak toward me, fingers splayed across Mobotiak's broad afro.

"Nails," he said in that boom of a voice.

"Nails?" I asked, and he glanced up toward Josef without moving his head.

"Moreno's men tied Mobotiak down when he refused to pass along another shipment without prepayment. Moreno was getting in the habit of paying us far less than the product was worth. They tied down Mobotiak," he went on, letting up his hand. Mobotiak sprang up from the chair and went out the door. Josef looked after him, shaking his head, then taking the stool with a sigh.

"The men took lumber nails," he said, watching the doorway. "Lumber nails about so long." He showed me his long pinky finger. "And they hammered these nails up into Mobotiak's upper jaw, his head strapped down, jaw forced open. Stuck them between the back teeth to guide the nails, one at a time up into the serus cavity."

"You mean sinus cavity," I corrected. He looked over to me finally, turning on the stool.

"Yes, the cavity." He tapped at his cheekbones. "They pounded them up through the jaw until he talked. Oh yes, he talked. And the wounds infected the nerves in the face. The nerves rotted, fevered. It still pulls at the muscles, makes the face dance as it does, you know. And pull back like that dog growl or something. But this is from the nerves being fevered by the nails pounded so deep." He sighed. "And they got the product. Almost all we had to trade for. All we had at the time to buy supplies, an advance on supplies." His voice had become quite low, his eyes bright with anger. "The nerves to the face, as you can see. Five nails. Five he suffered through before he talked." The story seemed designed to get my sympathy. Somehow I just grew more impatient.

"I said I want to know what it is, what killed Toby! I want to know!" I struggled up to my feet again, grabbed him around the throat, holding myself up more than I was doing him any real harm.

"You're starting to bleed again." He pried my fingers loose.

"I'll bleed all over the fucking town, I'll bleed all over this fucking country if you don't tell me. Now!" And I wiped a fresh splotch of blood from my forehead, flicking it in his direction. Josef forced me to sit down.

"Enough, enough. You need to know so badly? Diamonds." He said it so softly I wasn't sure I'd heard. He repeated it. It was diamonds then. Cold, cool rocks causing all this grief. "Yes, diamonds. And there are more than what Mr. Kale carried. I'm afraid there is more diamonds than what Mr. Kale brought to the States. But he carried a significant portion. And he had agreed, for a large fee, you understand, to turn the diamonds over to us rather than his original employers. Yet it seems they might have them after all. Who knows. I do know there are more diamonds within that compound. Your friend did not carry all of our product, I'm sure. And the original shipment, Mr. Moreno stole them rather than pay fair price as we had agreed. Moreno's men. No one else knew we were smuggling the diamonds out of Angola just then." He took out a handkerchief and blew his nose. "We'd been using the Massad brothers to smuggle for us ever since the revolution began. They had the contacts here in Portugal, the United States, England. So when I was tipped off that Moreno was in Zaire, I was told he was there and went to kill him. You must be wrong about Moreno. I pray you are wrong. And then nearly a year later I am also told that the product is still here in

Portugal, that it was never moved from the country. Moreno had all the contacts for disposing of them. And when he was killed, well. Naturally we wanted to recover it." He shrugged, getting up from the stool as Mobotiak came in, a bottle of wine in his hand.

"Needed wine," he said, holding it up awkwardly. Josef took the bottle and went for a corkscrew in the other room, coming back with the open bottle and three clean mugs. I thought about what he had just said and recalled Justine and Moreno in Zorine's back in Chicago. Justine just didn't seem to figure. Hadn't she sat there with me at lunch the day before, at the marina, telling me Moreno was alive?

"But the guy on the golf course?" I asked again. My head started to spin; it felt like a branch in a stiff breeze, swaying under the influence of the painkillers that were beginning to kick in.

"I told you we must pray that you are wrong. Because if I didn't kill him back there in Zaire . . . Mobotiak, come here." He walked over and Josef took the hair rope from Mobotiak's belt where it was fastened by a piece of rawhide. Josef ran the rope through his fingers, separating strands until he came to a thick, black braided section in the middle. "See this?" he asked, holding it close to me. "This I cut from his head. For Mobotiak. But I left the girl alone. I killed him and took my proof for Mobotiak. But that is all; I left the girl," he said, seeing that the strands of hair shocked me, and he needed to prove there was a good, civilized reason for their existence.

"You mean the whores? You left the whores? I've heard about the whores," I said, remembering Dalva's version of Moreno's death. And here was the man who had supposedly done Moreno in. "And I heard the hair wasn't all you chopped off." Who else had contributed to that revenge rope? There were a few more locks than Moreno's.

"I cut off the hair, that is all. Who knows what the crazy white woman did when I left."

Justine? I had heard from Dalva that there were whores, three at least. And now this account.

Mobotiak cleared his throat and began to dig into his plate of food.

"But how in the hell would Toby get mixed in with all this? Was it that trip he took to New York?"

"Eat." Josef's voice was quick and wakened me from the dizziness that I was becoming aware of, a dizziness that had been so pervasive, so much a part of my waking, that I actually had to come up a little from it, peak up over its edge to even be aware of its gauzy swirl. I found a plate in my lap and put the false teeth that I had been holding in the blood-stiffened pocket of my coat before I picked up what looked like a very small doll fork in my stiff fingers. I pushed the sardines around the plate; they were hard to the touch, like crust. I wasn't hungry but felt good about pushing the little grilled sonofabitches around the plate, back and forth, two of my fingers ballooned as if a few too many breaths had been pumped into them.

"Do you need more of the pain relievers?" Josef asked, and I looked up to see him and Mobotiak perched over the plates of sardines which rested in their laps.

"Pain relievers? How many did I—?"

Mobotiak held up four fingers. He chomped away. More light; it was way past daybreak. I could see the tiredness in both their eyes.

"None now," I said and finally pulled the shirt away from my chest where it had dried to the hair.

"Why don't you shower. Out back." Josef pointed through the door behind the bed with his fork.

I stood, groaning, and made my way through another sleeping room, shuttered and dark, to the battered wooden stall that sat outside, resting against the stucco walls. Nailed to the one side was a mirror in a small metal frame that I had to stoop down in front of to examine the jagged, diagonal slash that bisected my forehead. Josef had done a good job stitching it; there were rips and angles to the wound that he had bound neatly. My face was caked with blood. I stripped off my clothes, amazed at how stiff they were with blood (how could I lose that much?), and turned on the faucet that fed a bucket to my feet. I splashed the lukewarm water over me, flecks of dried blood drifting to the concrete and into the narrow alleyway, down the crazy zigzag gutters of cobblestone. I stood up straight as possible, dripping wet, in only my briefs, and laughed as I felt my smooth, unbloodied upper lip and nostrils in my cold, wet fingers. Laughed and laughed dizzily, shivering, not tasting blood in the nostril, not a drop of blood, fresh or dried. I laughed until Josef opened the door of the stall, looking in anxiously.

"You all right, Mr. Bradloozkey?"

"My nose. You realize my fucking nose didn't bleed!"

"Why don't you come in with your clothes. Come in and dry off, you'll feel better."

When they had me cleaned up, Mobotiak and Josef led me outside, the sun like knives thrust into my eyes. I cowered behind my arm, a wide-eyed Portuguese on the street looking at the poorly dressed foreigner, probably thinking I was ashamed. They led me to a battered VW, ushering me into the back seat. Josef ducked into a *mercado* just down the block for some dark glasses, but not before a few Portuguese boys, curious, peered in at the American with his face stitched up. I winced at them or at the harsh sunlight. I sighed as I put on the glasses.

"Don't even stop for my clothes, just right to the airport," I said, and found myself fumbling through my pockets for another pain reliever: they felt good, made me pleasantly numb.

"What do you mean?"

"The airport, how long to the airport?"

"Why would you want to get to the airport? You have unfinished business, Mr. Bradloozkey. Your friend's murderer is no doubt in that complex." The VW churned up bone-colored dust in the narrow street that opened up onto the highway toward the gates of Apontarleve. I swallowed a pain pill dry, the taste of it and road dust like chalk in my mouth.

"You are going back to that place to end things up. Once and for all. It is your place. None of us has a choice."

"I do. I can leave. I can get on the damned plane and leave," I said, my voice small in the cramped back seat, fighting to be heard over the clacking engine. Josef reached over the seat and grabbed a good hunk of my shirt in his hand, his yellowed eyes wide open in a rage.

"You are going back, you stinking coward. You are going to finish this off. It was started and must be finished."

"And get my ass killed!" I said.

"If you must, yes. Get your ass killed . . . But you may be the only person to get the property back and the people responsible for your friend's death brought to justice. When you know for sure who has killed your friend, Mr. Bradluskey, when you find that person we—Mobotiak and I—will kill the son-of-a-bitch. But you must continue. You must go on."

I grabbed his wrist, pulled his hand loose from my shirt. "I—I don't know where to go from here. Diamonds, shit, I know nothing about diamonds." The painkillers and the pain and the events of the day spun in my head like some whirlpool of sludge and silt.

"Tell us what you know," Josef ordered, almost barked. I wasn't used to him using that tone of voice with me; the sugar-coated tongue-in-cheek wisecracks had fallen away. Mobotiak had pulled up just shy of the Apontarleve gates.

"What do you know!" he demanded, pounding the back of his seat as if to smash it down so he could get at me easier. I began to babble, hoping I could calm him down. They were my only sources, my only friends.

"Caroline is making it with Dalva. Is this guy with you? He's Angolan too: and he's making it with Caroline and both of them suspect Gregory of ripping off people, but you know that don't you? You told me about Gregory's brother, but you say he's dead and I say and Justine says that he's—"

"What do you know for a fact. Stop the blubbering," Josef insisted.

"I know I was almost killed by Moreno. Moreno dressed like Gregory Massad. I know Toby is dead. I know the two of you saved my life. I know Caroline is . . ." I shook my head and felt sorry I'd done that, my stomach taking a sour, wrenching leap.

"You know very little . . . Don't you see why you have to continue?" Josef said calmly, his dulcet, wise-ass tones resuming. "You have some people to pay back, some questions of your own to answer. Could you really get on a plane and fly back to your America and carry on with so many questions left in your own life? There are questions back in America, too. And you have no answers for the authorities at home either. Answers are all inside that gate." He pointed a finger at the entrance, and as if on cue, a blue Mercedes erupted onto the highway past us. "Everything will work itself out in there," he said with a sad purse of his lips, and pushed up his seat so that I could painfully climb out. The sentry wanted I.D. and a call to the casino to verify that I was a guest at the Massads'. He let me pass and I trudged through the heat along the hot asphalt.

I made it back to the villa and found Desmiaou passed out on the living-room couch, snoring, an empty bottle glinting on the carpet amid a splash of sunshine from the window. I went upstairs and found Gregory's room as I had left it: books spilled onto the floor, backgammon sets scattered about. The briefcase was missing though. And Caroline. And so was Moreno. I was disappointed. I wanted to get that S.O.B. alone. I changed and shaved, admiring the jagged, stitched cut that ran along my forehead. What a scar that would leave, ugly enough to be an improvement.

I searched Caroline's room downstairs and found nothing of interest: some business papers in Portuguese which bore Sitizar's, Moreno's, and Gregory's signatures; a picture of Dalva, leaning against a cliff face, a smile bigger and more cheerful than I thought him capable of. She had very few clothes in her room. Most were probably at Dalva's.

I found a hunk of bread in the kitchen that I had to brush ants off of before carefully chewing on the good side of my mouth. That was when the messenger arrived with the telegram for me. I pulled out a blood-splotched wallet to tip the boy and went into the kitchen again to read the damned thing. It was from the States. From Sid.

COLUMN? STOP. MUST NOT NEED WORK STOP.
KEEP IT LIGHT AND GOSSIPY IF YOU DECIDE TO
SEND STOP. NO MECHANICS STOP. LAST CHANCE
STOP.

Light as air, eh? I stuffed the telegram in my shirt pocket and trudged back up to the balcony and set up a typewriter on the rickety metal there. I ditched the sunglasses Josef had bought me for the darker ones I had gotten in Lisbon and sat down to the empty page, taking a few more painkillers with a swig of brandy. I shivered in that sunlight. Damn the fucking Portuguese days. Every one of them had been sunny, moronically, narcotically sunny. A few cottony clouds hung on the horizon over the sea, but they seemed powerless against the deep blue that vaulted overhead. Dizzying. The paper flapped in the carriage and I felt a breeze off the ocean. A breeze at least. And the smell of eucalyptus. Gossip is what he wanted. What gossip did I have? I snickered to myself, lightheaded. One ear cocked toward the downstairs, waiting for the bastard to show again. But I started to type:

> Gregory Massad, tournament organizer, seems heavily involved in international smuggling ring which traffics in Angolan diamonds. After cheating counter-revolutionaries of their war chest, Marteno aka Moreno Massad was killed in revenge. Or was he? This reporter had a narrow scrape with the Grim Reaper and it looked as if Moreno was holding the scythe. Nevertheless, Mrs. Massad provides thrills for the gallery by humping around with yet another Angolan that operates—of all things—a pizza parlor. Meanwhile, Mrs. Massad may be tit-deep in blackmail as porno shots of her, circa 1965, have surfaced in the mits of one drug-crazed and/or razed Gregory and/or Moreno Massad. Tournament two days away yet and your fearless reporter wades through thieves, murders, and would-be murderers, whores, porno-dubbers, and intriguers of every sort.

There may be a backgammon aficionado or
two prowling the port also, but most moves
have been made against yours truly. And this
one's literally from a very inside source: things
will come to a head at the Southern Europe
Invitational tournament. Keep you posted:
your rooting correspondent, Vernon Stewart.

I laughed and tore the column out of the typewriter. Fuck
Sid. I hoped that was gossipy enough for him. I folded it and set
it aside, reaching for more paper. I began, as if it had already
been written in my head, a straight column:

Often it is wise to keep an opponent off balance. Especially an opponent who has had the
opportunity to play and observe your type of
game in the past. He may know your strategies—even those habitual moves and quirks
of positioning that many of us repeat but
never fully realize how much of a rut our
game has gotten into. The best but perhaps
most dangerous *habit breaker* is the use of a
back game.

The *back game* is risky in that you allow one,
two, or three of your men to become open
and free for your opponent to hit. Sounds like
bad strategy doesn't it, letting up to three of
your men get hit, removed from the board
and forced to start from the very beginning?
But wait . . . doesn't your opponent have to
bring his men back into his home court—just
where your blots must reenter the board? Of
course. And even if your opponent is careful,
the dice may provide him no alternative but
to leave one of his men open and then . . . I
think you get the picture; your opponent—secure in his knowledge of how you *usually*
play your game—has decided to run home
and try for a gammon. But you've been sly,
right? While those blots have hung back in
your opponent's home court, you have been
rearranging the rest of your pieces to provide
formidable obstacles—a solid block from the
board—in *your* home court. Your opponent
runs into his home court carelessly, trying to

get that gammon. He miscalculates, leaves a
man open. Blot. You hit him from your position in his home court. He sits on the bar, no
chance of getting on board because you've
frozen him out, blocked every point he could
enter on. His game is at a standstill. You roll
one turn after another, leisurely skipping
home.

The odds are against you on a *back game.*
Some say as high as four to one against. Still,
you can improve those odds with practice.
The *back game* is a difficult one to play, and
you just may improve your overall backgammon skills as you try—and probably lose—a
few games in the learning process. But it is a
useful tool in keeping your opponent honest.
One good *back game* against a complacent
opponent will win you newfound respect.
Stuff legends are made of. Well, back to the
tables here in the sunspot of southern Europe—the beautiful Algarve.

"What are you doing?" Caroline asked, squinting up at me,
the dark roots of her hair obvious from up on the balcony. She
wavered as though very drunk. Her loose kaftan was partially
open, her naked left breast hanging out, stark white in the
daylight, and she seemed oblivious to that. I mentally flashed on
one of the photographs I had seen the night before and instinctively looked at the golf course where I had thrown the pictures
at Gregory. A man and woman swacked in the rough along the
crest.

"I said, what are you doing?" she asked again, tucking her
tit back in. She did seem drunk.

"Burning a bridge," I said, taking both columns and folding
them into an envelope.

"Come on down." She waved and disappeared into the
house. So I did, just as she was waking Desmiaou. He stood,
shaking that great head of his, smoothing down a woolly tuft of
his hair before putting his beret on again. I handed him the columns and Caroline helped me explain that I needed them sent
by telegraph to the address I had carefully penned on the envelope. I gave him some money and he went off to the hotel.

He left and she was all over me, twisting her arms around me, and pressing tightly to my chest. She looked up at me, her voice thick, her eyes wildly dilated: you could drive a truck through those pupils they were so wide. Putting the make on me after her brother-in-law had tried to snuff me: I couldn't help feeling skittish.

"Poor Vernon," she began, finally taking some note of the stitches. "Poor dear, did you fall?"

"Your fucking husband did it. Or Moreno posing as your husband!"

"What do you mean, poor, poor, Vernon?" she went on.

"Cut the crap, Caroline!" I said, sweeping her arms off me and stepping back. She *had* to know. "Moreno! The bastard is alive, and I'm not buying the bullshit you and Dalva are laying out, so hold it, just hold it!" I yelled at her. "The bastard is alive and I know it, he nearly took me off, nearly got me! I don't know what all of you are up to—Dalva, you, that fucking scar-faced maniac . . . did you kill him?"

"Kill him?" she asked. This was no act. Either she really didn't know anything or she was too wasted to tell me anything. It looked like both.

"Kill Gregory . . . your husband. The guy you claim hasn't made an appearance in months. Is it because he's dead, Caroline? Dead, and his brother is taking his place?" She looked at me, arms limp at her side, expressionless. "What are you on now?" I asked her, taking hold of her. She looked about to swoon. She grabbed hold of me again, nestling into my arms. I was pissed at her for being sloppy stoned, pissed off at her for those photos taken so long ago, but I smelled the clean, sun-warmed hair of hers as I held her and thought of making love to her despite the anger.

"Just a little potion. Just a little love potion from Dalva to me," she cooed again and kissed my neck dryly. I shifted my weight from one foot to another, nervous, listening into the house, listening for him.

"Let's go out in the yard and fuck. Let's go fuck in the sun," she said in that same teasing, stoned-to-coyness voice. She tugged at my arm and I winced; she kissed the bruises on my hand. "Poor-poor Vernon. Let's go out in the sun. I'm so cold. Let's go out on the lawn." And I followed her out.

I hadn't brought sunglasses. The damn sun. She laughed and flounced awkwardly onto the lawn. Lying down, head propped on elbow, she stroked a patch of grass in front of her. "Come to bed, come on to bed." I hated the tone of that voice. I'd started to perspire, feeling the heat from the sun radiate up from the lawn.

"Caroline."

"But, Vernon." She pouted.

"Can't you see I was almost killed, don't you even want to know what happened?" I said, standing over her; she lay flat on her back, closing her dilated eyes to the sun.

"I just want to lie in the sun. Lie in the sun and fuck." She reached up my pant leg with her hand, tickling at my ankle, her eyes still closed. "Let's just forget about all those other things today. Maybe every day." I couldn't forget. The stitches wouldn't let me. The stitches, and those pictures of her.

"Its so cold, take me out in the sun." I watched goose bumps suddenly pepper her arms. A shiver ran through her. "Let's forget about the diamonds." She knew. She'd known all along.

"You *are* in the sun. Are you being blackmailed, Caroline?"

"I *am* in the sun?" She opened her eyes, blinking.

"Listen to me," I said, fed up with her stoned inattention. I kicked her hand out from my pant leg.

"I am. Listening to drivel. No one wants to have fun anymore. Just this serious stuff." She pouted, lay back, and opened her kaftan, her bare, untanned breasts an aching white. She was nude underneath that robe.

"Who has the rest of the diamonds?"

"You know about the diamonds." She giggled. Just giggled away like some goofy schoolgirl.

"Who has the diamonds?" I repeated.

"I don't want to talk about diamonds. Trouble. Diamonds

and trouble," she said, and her giggles went into hysterical laughter which doubled her up. And that's where I left her.

So I was the last to know about the diamonds! But knowing about the diamonds hadn't done Toby any good. I took my car over to the hotel. Moreno was the answer: a lot of people were in love with the idea, and even more scared shitless, that he might be alive. I made my way through the crowded lobby and began to spot familiar faces: Brady Palt, some champion from Florida. Why were all the players checking in early? A lot of unfamiliar faces, too. I avoided people, and with my stitches most folks reciprocated.

——— FIFTEEN ———

I finally wheedled Justine's room number from the clerk; I didn't have her last name, but her description was more than adequate to jog his memory. There was no answer at her room and I broke the door down. For such a classy-acting hotel they had cheap doors. I buzzed around the suite. The table was positively loaded with jars and boxes. I looked through the jumble. Liquid latex? This was not all Justine's. And on the bed was the briefcase I had found in Gregory's shuttered room. Passport, the business papers, blueprints for the hotel, the vials of drugs. I pocketed one of the vials. The blueprint for the casino was missing. The blueprint with all the notches, marks . . . I took the passport to the balcony and threw open the curtains. *Was* this the same person who nearly clubbed open my brainpan? Older-looking, I decided. If that could be. And the scars, the scars were there, but in the passport picture they were . . . shit, how are you supposed to tell anything from a passport photo? But I found one thing. Entrance to New York. No exit from New York or entrance stamped to Portugal. He hadn't left New York and I was holding his passport in a Portuguese hotel room?

When I got to the casino the staff was hustling around, trying to get the place set for the tournament the next day. My head was spinning with painkillers and the pain they were merely taking the sharper edges off. But I waltzed right into Sitizar's office, half hoping to find Moreno, and then half relieved when I didn't.

It was just old, fat Sitizar, slumped over his makeup kit, applying a fresh coat of powder into his hairline, around the temple.

"Americans," he humphed, commenting on my manners, then raising an eye to get a look at the fancy needlepoint across my face.

"Where is he?" I asked, standing in front of his desk.

"Who?" He was fascinated by the stitches, couldn't take his eyes off them.

"Moreno! Cut the shit, I want to see him. Now!" I was feeling more and more numb, the drugs finally taking hold. I loomed over him; that's what it felt like: looking down on him from two stories above, his beady eyes even beadier from that height.

"You are not looking for Moreno," he said softly, and took up a makeup brush and went back to business in the mirror.

"Don't tell me who I'm looking for," I said, and with a swat I sent the mirror to the wall where it bounced off the poster of Brando.

Sitizar, brush poised, continued to gaze at the spot where the mirror had just been.

"You say he did that to you?" He finally looked up. I nodded. "Good God. I knew things were going rough, but . . ." He leaned back in his chair, the leather creaking.

"But what, come on."

"But it was Gregory who did that to you. How?" His eyes trailed over the wounds once again. It gave me the creeps the way he sized them up, as though he were planning how he'd cover them, with what shade . . .

He gestured for me to take a seat, and I did. It was a sudden relief to be seated. My head felt light.

"After Moreno was murdered in Zaire we found that we had no way of moving the diamonds . . . no way of fencing them. You see, Moreno knew all the contacts in the States and England for selling such stones. I take it you know about . . . ?"

"The diamonds? Yeah, go on."

"In fact we knew the people to contact but also knew they would not deal with Gregory or myself. And there was also the matter of getting the diamonds into the States. Moreno would never say how he managed that. We knew the only way to get things moving once more was to convince these people that they *were* dealing with Moreno. So I offered my makeup services to Gregory. I wanted to make him look exactly like his brother. It could be done."

"But that was Moreno under the makeup of Gregory. I held the latex in my hand, damn it! It was Moreno underneath."

"Listen to me and shut up for once, Mr. Bradlusky," he said loudly, glaring at me. "But Gregory said it must be real. More real than makeup. He began to mutilate himself, re-create his brother's face in his own."

"He did that to himself?"

Sitizar stared down my disbelief, my shock, an intense purse to his lips as he spoke. "I know he had other reasons as well. He sat there in the hotel, injecting his face with morphine. Cutting. Burning with acid. I helped when I saw what a terrible job he was doing, as high as he was. And of course he didn't have my touch." He smiled a proud, sick smile. "I took over and did the job right."

"He mutilated himself to look like his brother just over some diamonds?" I asked, flashing momentarily on the moonlit scars I'd seen: the same tortured face in Zorine's. The pain he must have gone through, and for what? Some gems, some pressed rock?

"There were other reasons for his actions." Sitizar shook his head slowly, sighed.

"Such as?"

"You know Moreno was the one who led the whole company, the three of us, to the success we have had. Even when he became involved in this very sordid business, it was Moreno who held the machinery together. Gregory wanted to be so like his brother. He worshiped the man, you know this?"

"That's no reason to take a knife to your face."

Sitizar shifted uncomfortably in his chair. I was sure by the sorry-looking droop to his flaccid cheeks, and the way he pushed a piece of candy along his desk top with a porky finger, that he wished he'd never started to tell me a damned thing.

"You are correct. There is more reason for his actions. The craziness that came over him. The mutilation. There are times now that he really believes he is his brother, as if the mutilation would give him his brother's face, his brother's power . . ." His voice trailed off like a string of those red Portuguese ants, and he swiveled his chair around to the wall, looking at the poster of *On the Waterfront*. "But even that . . . he says that he now wants revenge, that the tournament will provide revenge for his brother's death."

"How?"

"Investors that abandoned the company when we lost our interests in Angola, the local bankers that called in our loans, the creditors that wanted full payment. They made it necessary to go into the whole business of smuggling in the first place. Made it necessary for Moreno to double-cross the rebels."

"Bullshit. From what I understand Moreno was never a prince to begin with." I remembered what Josef and Mobotiak had said about him.

"Perhaps not, but he never would have taken such risks if it weren't for the collapse. And you must remember that Gregory believes this. That is what makes it true, true in his mind and others'."

"What others?"

"It is true in Gregory's mind because he refuses to confess it was really his own fault that his brother was found and killed that night."

"I've heard about the night he was killed already. By the people that killed him," I let drop.

He swiveled back from the wall, his face sadder than I thought possible. "You have made contact with the rebels too, then? Did they tell you how they came to know where to find Moreno that night in Zaire? Gregory . . . It was his own brother that told them and that is something that Gregory cannot live with now. He wants revenge at the tournament; in his twisted mind he wants to blame the creditors. God, how I wish I could wash my hands of this. But I've been with them since the beginning." He sobbed just then, and took to the makeup kit the way most people might go for a drink or a cigarette, dabbing on the makeup, checking his face in a compact mirror, his eyes dewy.

"What does he have planned for the tournament?"

"The people he blames have been invited. They plan to rip off the creditors. Why don't you leave me the hell alone." He swiveled away again.

"They?"

"Yes, they. Justine and Gregory. Go talk to them, Mr. Bradlusky. And please leave me be."

I caught up with Justine just outside the marina bar. She didn't try to duck me; she looked cool and ready when I walked up. But I could see that she was taken back by the remodeling my face had undergone. I told her who and when, and she sighed, put out a hand as if to smooth down the swollen flesh.

"He is dangerous now, Mr. Bradlusky. You are lucky," she said, and I found myself walking with her down the marina concourse. The sun was setting rose-colored on the water, the air blustery and heady with the smell of the sea and eucalyptus that lined the walkway of shops, cafés, and little boutiques. She teased me about the stitches in my face and my lip, calling me Frankenstein. We settled into wicker chairs at a dockside restaurant, the umbrella of our table flapping in a stiff breeze. I must have looked as washed-out green as the sea beyond the concourse which was kicked up by the wind. I took painkillers from my pocket, and they dissolved in my mouth, their metallic aftertaste lodging like moss at the back of my throat.

Justine looked warm, warm skin and eyes against the wintergreen sea and sky, her hair rising and falling like twining fingers in the wind. I was trying to act casual in the way one does when drugged and clumsy. I managed to pour us some house wine the waiter had thoughtfully brought, but my hand wavered and the wine missed her glass. The wind took it up and flung it back in droplets across my wrist; and she laughed, a full, throaty laugh that blended with the wind. I finally managed a glass of wine for each of us.

"Clumsy Frankenstein," she teased. "You'll be all the rage in the tournament tomorrow."

We drank and looked over the menu.

"Order something heavy," I suggested.

"Heavy?"

"Something that won't blow away." I slid my chair over to block her from the wind. A waiter appeared and recommended the swordfish, for such a manly fish would surely bind my wounds in no time at all. Justine ordered prawns in garlic sauce. The sun set. I collapsed the umbrella at our table before it could carry us to the pier's edge and into the water.

"Mmmm!" Justine suddenly giggled, as prawn and her hair became tangled. I reached across the table and tried to sort them out. She laughed, wiped her sauce-dripping lips, and retouched her gold lipstick.

"Dinner, I think, is a disaster. A walk?"

"Sure," I agreed, and signaled the waiter for the check and a bottle of champagne to go. He admonished me for not finishing my swordfish.

"Your wounds need the fish. Now you'll have big scars," he said gravely. Justine and I disappeared off the pier and out onto the dark beach, arm in arm.

We took off our shoes and rolled up our jeans, just as you're supposed to do on such strolls, and walked in the skirt of the surf, the cold Atlantic water rushing over our feet. The half moon was coming out and cast an arc of greened light across the whitecaps and waves. The town of Albufeira twinkled in the cliff face just three miles down the coast, the hotels, the brightest and tallest, hovering over the glowing water. The sandstone backing the beach at the pier was merely a collection of jagged, half-buried boulders. We set off into the growing darkness between Albufeira and the marina. The wind howled down on the unprotected beach, setting Justine's hair straight back from her face in ripples. Her features were remarkably clear, and for that reason, I thought, her beauty was nearly a disadvantage; beauty like hers was always a captive to such clarity of features—in her anger you watched her eyes, in her disgust you saw only her smooth cheek, in her fatigue you, well, you saw her beauty no matter her mood, and that made her incredibly opaque. I watched her turn in the wind, her eyes focused on the lights of Albufeira, and I wanted to know what she felt but realized that a long look into her face, even her eyes, would never even give me a clue to such questions. Pedigrees are like that, I mused suddenly, and caught myself laughing aloud.

"What's so funny?" she asked, turning to me.

"I was just thinking. You remind me of something."

"Such as what?" She caught a wisp of hair that blew across her face; her eyes were nearly tearing from the force of the stiff wind.

"I really don't know what the hell to make of you."

"I hope you never do. That takes all the fun out of it, doesn't it?"

I thought of Caroline. "Someone else reminded me of that very thing once. Long time ago."

"Did you listen—to this person?"

"Of course not."

"A shame." She mock-pouted and rested her head in the hollow of my shoulder. We wandered in and out of the cold surf and finally into drier sand.

"It's just that in Chicago, if you were with Moreno—" I

began tentatively, trying to steer our conversation back on course.

"You mean Gregory acting as Moreno," she corrected.

"You know what I mean," I said.

"But there's a big difference. Between the two, I mean. I was acting, just as Gregory was acting, when we played the games at the bar. And the real Moreno, I loved the real Moreno."

"What were you doing in Chicago in the first place?"

"Hustling you. But not at backgammon. You thought Gregory was Moreno, you thought I was his girl, you thought you hustled us—everything we set out to have you believe," she said in quick, clipped words, as if listing my sins.

"You mean—"

"Right," she said, her eyes motionless but those lips screwed into the smile. "You were supposed to meet Moreno—but as a team."

"A team? I don't understand." I held her lightly by the shoulders.

"We followed Toby from the Algarve, to Lisbon and finally to New York and Chicago. We wanted to know, naturally, where the intercepted diamonds might be headed. He'd spent a few days on the *Embora*, so we knew he had the shipment."

"Dalva's boat?" I asked.

"Yes, Dalva's boat. Caroline's lover. We could only get that shipment across to the States with Moreno's help or a Moreno look-alike. But the diamonds in the villa disappeared before we could get them to New York. And then your friend arrived. Somehow Dalva got them. I'm sure Caroline . . ." Her voice snarled, yet her face remained smooth, impassive, her eyes focused into the sea, the blackness between Portugal and Morocco. "But they won't get the best bundle. The best shipment."

"But in Chicago?" I asked her again.

"We followed Toby to Chicago. When we discovered he was the one who was taking them across. He went to a bar—"

"Murphy's," I said.

"Yes, Murphy's, and then to his apartment. He stayed in his

apartment. He didn't answer the phone. We thought the only way to get him out of the apartment was by greed. We went to Zorine's and lost enough money to attract attention—and hopefully Toby. But you showed up, alone."

I took her by the waist and we walked along the sand in silence. Things were making sense; finally, someone was making sense. The sandstone boulders had grown into cliffs; black arches of grottoes gaped in the sinewy-looking stone faces. The moon disappeared completely behind the clouds that covered the entire sky. The wind became cooler. We sat on a slab of rock. She leaned into my chest, into my arms.

"We had to talk to Toby. To convince him that he was wrong, to give him a better cut of the profits than they did, if necessary," she told me quietly.

"They? Caroline and Dalva?"

"But of course, they are lovers, right?"

There she went, accusing Caroline again. Caroline, it seemed, was on everyone's shit list. "But Toby got too greedy and kept the stones for himself," I continued for her.

"And now they have Toby's shipment," she went on. "I'm sure it was them."

"Wait a minute, what makes you think they have the diamonds Toby smuggled over?" I asked her. She sat up and faced me, shivering a bit in the cold.

"They killed him, didn't they?"

"You weren't the only ones tailing Toby," I told her, thinking of Josef and Mobotiak. Why would Toby send me such a cryptic little treasure-hunting clue? And why would my apartment get torn to shreds *after* he was killed?

"You see, all Gregory and I knew was that Toby was dead. We saw the police cars, the ambulance, the paper the next day. We knew you were his partner, the bartender—"

"That bastard Ted," I started, and then realized he'd set me up to be hustled into *winning*. Crazy. Hustled into winning.

"Caroline is responsible for much, Vernon. Much, believe me. She and her lover intercepted the diamonds even as we were prepared to get rid of them, contact the people Moreno trusted in New York. We would have been successful. But they didn't get all, not all the diamonds. We have some left and will no doubt get rid of them after the tournament."

"There's more?" She was only confirming what Josef and Mobotiak had said, and I needed to hear her say it.

"She and her lover didn't get them all. There were only some in the villa, the rest were in the casino."

"What do you have planned for this tournament, what else is up, dear heart?" I remembered what Sitizar had said to me. The bankers, the creditors.

"You have been speaking to Sitizar? It's all right. Yes. We will cheat some of those vain bastards. We'll get some of the money they owe. But they should pay in blood." She looked up at me and planted a kiss over the stitches in my lip. "And maybe show Caroline for what she really is." She kissed me again, licking lightly at my wound: it seemed to excite her. "Has she told you where the diamonds went? What she did with them?"

"I just can't believe it was her . . . that she got Toby to . . ."

"She has destroyed everything. But we can salvage a bit of what my Moreno left behind once she is found out, put away where she belongs. And we are going to see that you do well at the tournament tomorrow."

"What?" I took her by the shoulders and held her where I could get a good look at her.

"You'll play a banker or two, they are really quite bad. But they feel honored to be with the professionals. You should advance easily. It's on the level, no crookedness at all. But you should find them easy."

"Don't do me any favors. I don't want any part in this bullshit." I was just thinking of Caroline. Caroline and Dalva. I knew that it was only Caroline's stupidity that had gotten her involved with ripping off her own husband and getting Toby to mule the diamonds back to the States and try to fence them. I could believe Caroline's stupidity but not her being responsible for Toby's death. Greed and stupidity would hang on Caroline like that bleach job of hers, but not murder.

"We insist. But get Caroline to turn herself in, get her to talk about what she's done."

"It just can't be, she couldn't." But I knew Caroline had to have had a hand in somewhere. Who else would have gotten Toby to do the dirty work? These people couldn't have even known Toby existed. Yeah, it was Caroline who'd gotten him involved. I couldn't deny it, couldn't stop it from being so. I covered my face with both hands, my stitches stiff and numb as leather seams under my touch. I saw Toby again as I'd found him; I saw Caroline's face as I remembered it, years ago, atop that fucking band building on campus, softly lit, smiling, laughing; and I finally recalled her face from that very afternoon at the villa: stoned, slobbering, used up. I found myself on my knees, nearly crying like some silly, heartsick kid and hating the sound of it in my own throat. "The bitch, the stupid bitch," I kept saying, pounding back those sickening sobs with each word. I felt Justine's arms around me, she kneeled in the sand beside me, her face pressing to my hands. She kissed my fingers as they clutched at my face. "The stupid bitch!"

"I know, I know." She took my hands in hers, and I finally got back on my feet, dusted myself off.

"Fucking painkillers, make you do funny things," I mumbled, looking away. We walked arm in arm along the beach. We smelled the rain before it actually began to fall and found a fairly deep niche in the rock face and opened the bottle of champagne. The rain was heavy and lightning bloomed over the dark water. I wrapped my coat over her shoulders and she lay down, her head on my lap. We passed the bottle and watched the rain, which walled us into the grotto. "I'll talk to Caroline. I have to. But don't ask me to get involved in anything else. Please."

"If that's how you want it," she said after a long pause. The rain began to come down even harder, slapping, riffling at the beach and grotto entrance almost as thickly as waves from the ocean itself.

"We'll never get out." She shuddered, curling under the coat.

"Such a goddamned shame," I said, suprised at how loud, how close my voice sounded in the shelter.

She turned to face me, looking up from the cozy nest of my coat and lap. I could scarcely see her eyes in the darkness, or the dimly lustrous halo of her hair as it spread out across my lap.

"Vern," she whispered, and it sounded nice to hear my name in her voice.

"Mmmm."

"We might spend the night here. The rain." Her voice trailed away.

"That would be, that could be what we'll have to do," I felt her arm circle my waist and I placed my hand on what I felt to be her shoulder. She murmured something as her lips brushed across my arm; I wanted her; every sound we made was amplified in the grotto. I drew her up to me, felt her breath burst across my neck. Her fingers winnowed between the buttons of my shirt.

"I guess we have everything we need," she said against my cheek.

"Wine, dry place," I checked off our assets.

"No wine," she corrected, then kissed me lightly on the chin, my shirt nearly unbuttoned. I lifted the folds of her knit blouse, bunching it around her chest, my hands working beneath the fabric to her cool and firm breasts.

"I just kicked the wine over. It's spilling out into the rain," she confided. Her voice seeming to hover in the closeness of the cave.

"Why'd you throw out the wine?" I muttered, feeling the warmth of her face near mine in the darkness, waiting for her lips to return.

"I said we had everything we needed," she repeated with mock exasperation. I took the coat from her shoulders, lay it on the sand beside us, and guided her to it. She pulled off her top, shivering under my touch. I took off my shirt, folded her into my arms, and searched the blackness for her lips.

She screeched as if I'd cut her deeply with a knife. But her screech quickly became screams, compounding in the narrow cave. She scuttled from under me and pressed against the other wall. I moved toward her, trying to feel for her arm, a leg, asking her all the while what was wrong.

"Something warm! Wet, dripping on me!" she cried. I instinctively felt for my nose. Sure enough, I was bleeding, dripping down into the sand between the two of us. I crawled hands and knees to her.

"Justine," I said, trying to calm her. "It's me, just me, my nose is bleeding."

"Your nose is what?" she said with a tinge of disgust.

"My nose. It bleeds at odd moments. Sometimes. Always at the wrong times."

"Good God, from the golf course," she said, the disgust just faintly tinted with sympathy. Yet still she pressed against the far wall.

I dropped and found her arms crossed against her breasts.

"God, its all over me." As I held her wrist she brushed at the blood I'd left on her breasts, across her shoulder. I took a handkerchief from my coat and held it in the rain, wrung it out and brought it to her. She swore softly and I heard her get dressed.

"Are you all right?" she asked. She paused at the opening of the grotto, the rain heavy as ever.

"What do you mean, all right?"

"Have you stopped bleeding?"

"No," I said, slumped in the farthest corner, feeling a trickle of blood make its way down through my chest hairs.

"I'm sorry," she said, still perched at the entrance, sitting on her haunches as if to lurch suddenly into the rain. "It's just that it startled me and then—"

"I know, I know," I told her. "Not too romantic."

"Yeah," she laughed feebly and ran out into the downpour. I saw her form glide through the rain and mist toward the pier, and suddenly her lithe figure appeared in the yellow light of the café windows, my coat held over her head, another figure approaching. I thrust my face out into the rain, holding my nose to the downpour, feeling the cold water numb my lips, my eyes, and wash away the blood. I pulled on my shirt and took a good long walk across the beach and behind the marina. I headed across the weedy, undeveloped tract of land toward the hill and the villas, finding myself in the Roman ruins that Gregory had mentioned. I sat atop a large marble block; similar blocks were strewn about where they'd been unearthed. My nosebleed had stopped; the rain had begun to abate.

The tournament was tomorrow. The tournament. I was going to play in the tournament. Regardless of Toby's death, the fucking revolution in Angola, Caroline, and the diamond business on either side of the Atlantic, I was a backgammon player and there was a tournament to snuggle up to. I could win. I could walk away from the games with a win. I needed a win of any kind, and backgammon was all I had left. At any rate, I was there to play. *Play backgammon, play backgammon,* I chanted to myself, slogging and staggering through the soggy field, a light drizzle blurring the honeyed houselights of the villas that clustered the hill. "Play backgammon," I said aloud. Play the tournament.

───── SIXTEEN ─────

That morning I had Mobotiak run the vial to a chemist as Josef and I hunched over the business papers I had lifted from the briefcase in Justine's room. He translated them for me carefully.

"It is just corporation nonsense. Stating who gets what part of the business in case of dissolution or sale."

"Who does get what?"

"Wives. If partners dissolve their interests or die."

"Mrs. Massad?"

"Absolutely right." Mobotiak returned with a breakdown

the druggist had scribbled for him on a piece of paper: nearly pure morphine, but another chemical was present; the chemist couldn't find out what it was. I headed to the villa to get ready for the tournament. The rest could wait.

I walked into the casino after three. There was already a healthy gallery forming along the one side of the casino and across the back of the betting windows—when Justine had mentioned getting the bankers' money, this is what she meant; there would be more money flowing on the gallery bets than the paltry $160,000 pot. There were people in the gallery, I knew from experience, who would bet an individual player or combination of players as high as six or seven thousand.

The center of the room was split—game tables to each side of a long, low dais that displayed the standings. I counted the pairs of tables to each side of the dais that cut the room in half. A table for each point on a backgammon board. This was the "game board," the marks on that blueprint.

Each linen-covered table was set with six backgammon boards. One side of the scoreboard on the dais listed the thirty-two players with a grouping on the next column for the sixteen winners of that round, and space available for the eight winners of that round, and so on in eliminations until the scoreboard had just the two skinny, empty lines left for the final, the last pair.

The other side of the scoreboard, the side facing the gallery and betting cages, kept a constant point count on the individual games for the benefit of the bettors in the gallery. This way, the crowd could bet on individual games in any round and the actual scores of games if they wanted. The casino could clean up. I checked in with the refs at the registration table, went through the game arena, and exited into the bar. Brady Palt, that year's international champion, was holding court at one end, a characteristic champagne cocktail in one hand and a trademark blonde at the other. He bristled with laughter, and, I knew, nervous energy. Aside from Brady I could only pick out two other celebrity-rank players: Lord Alfred Lingon, a lush who amused the gallery between rounds with cheap magic tricks (scarves from the sleeve, disappearing water in a cone), whose game had been slipping of late, I'd heard, but who still insisted on paying for the privilege of losing in the most expensive tournaments; and Jim Tunnis, a Fort Lauderdale gambler who played—and won—everything from the nickel slots at Vegas to a 100,000-dollar-a-seat poker game in London last winter—he was one dangerous dude and looked it in a burgundy-detailed tux, rings with rocks the size of grapes, and a build like a nightclub bouncer. I got a drink and wandered around the bar until I found Justine tucked into a corner booth with Sitizar.

"Have yourself a seat!" Sitizar pointed out an empty spot on the bench seat with a wave of hand and wobble of goiter, trying for a friendly tone. It wasn't right.

"So today the tournament." He blinked at the full bar, the bustling crowd, the tuxes, the gowns, and the smell of tobacco and money as thick as cream in the air. He looked worried. I began to feel it myself. "I've started this point board, did you see it? We'll be taking bets on single games, point spreads, you name it!" He blinked with some excitement, clacking a pair of dice nervously in his puffy pink hand.

"How the hell do you cover that kind of action?" I wondered aloud. I'd never heard of its being done before and the task of setting odds and determining payoffs on such matters seemed near impossible.

"Sitizar is a numbers man, above all," Justine said to me, her first words, in fact, since I'd joined them.

I looked at Sitizar in an entirely different light. "That's right," he said. "I will set all odds on individual games. Post them on the board. Combos, if you have the fortitude, I would even bet dice rolls—but that would intrude too much on the game."

"But that means—" I began to realize.

"Exactly. Me—us—against the gallery." He laughed. Patrons turned to look briefly.

"But they could wipe you out. The whole casino. Everything," I said.

"Never." Justine smiled knowingly to me. I was impressed. What Sitizar was attempting was nothing more than miraculous. They'd keep him on his toes, if nothing else. I guessed he would set odds solely on inside information from Justine and other players and, more important, by the way the betting was running during each round. The feat was staggering and almost seemed to overshadow the paltry skill needed to win an individual game. It was almost as if Sitizar were playing off all of us *and* the gallery. I finished my drink.

"This backgammon, a heavy-shit proposition, heh?" Sitizar winked and excused himself as there was business to attend to—the judges were selecting match-ups in the arena based on random selection. Sitizar was to pull names from a hat, each contestant was then given a number and identified by that number until his ultimate end came.

"I never said he wasn't without his talents." Justine said, shrugging. "After all, his skill with numbers *and* judging gems would come in handy if you were to need such a person."

"Yeah, if you happened to want someone with such skills," I agreed.

"Did you know that he can guess the weight of a diamond within a quarter carat by bouncing it along his tongue?" she asked.

"You have to be kidding me," I said. It was a little far-fetched.

"You should see him; he puts the diamond—cut or uncut—into his mouth, rolls it around, across his teeth, takes it out, and gives it the once-over with those eyes of his." She laughed, I had to admit it sounded a bit bizzarre and could imagine those bug eyes of his rolling, the goiter shaking in earnest . . .

"But seriously, he's that good with gems. Any gem." She nodded in affection. She was dressed in a long black gown, the neckline conservatively above her considerable cleavage and marked with an ivory cameo.

"Where is your secret weapon?" I said, staring at the Victorian neckline.

"You should talk." She smiled once again, a near record number for her, I decided. "Frankenstein's monster."

"I need every angle I can get," I told her, and began to feel a bit inadequate; the very *smell* of the tournament was gritty. I was beginning to feel as if I were physically sinking, and I couldn't chalk all that up to my injuries either. Pressure: I'd forgotten what it was like in a major tournament. And Gregory's backgammon board. We were on his board. What *did* he have planned? I saw Dalva across the room, making for the gallery, leaving the bar. I didn't see Caroline.

"What's the matter?" she asked.

"Dalva. I don't see Caroline, though."

"I'm sure she's here. Saw the two of them together at the bar. Don't worry about them. We'll take care of that business after the tournament."

"Yeah, sure."

"About last night," she said, her tone serious, her gaze intently focused on a cherry stem she'd discarded into the ashtray from her drink. I'd been hoping she wouldn't bring up last night. I like to close things off neat and clean. Today was backgammon, nothing more to me.

"Yeah, well I got a little wet and lost a little sleep but feel, really, quite good today. I'm nervous about the tournament, of course. But last night . . ." I trailed off.

"It . . . was just an accident," she said tentatively. I knew she wanted me to correct her.

"Right, an accident," I agreed quickly. "Low-pressure system and all. Rain. Never rains in the Algarve, so you have to expect such things . . ." She stood, tossed another stem to the table and disappeared into the crowd. I hoped whatever they had planned wouldn't spoil *my* game. I wanted a good game. And I wanted her.

The numbers had been assigned, and the beginning of the first round was announced by one of the three refs. I took my assigned table and lined up opposite my opponent—a squat banker (as promised) from Brazil who tried to speak to me in Portuguese. I shook his wet hand and grinned as politely as my stitches would allow. He observed them with a wary glance and took his seat, bit at his lip, and rolled his die to determine the first play. I won and made a fast point on the sixth spot. He smiled, his teeth wide, white, and too friendly for the move I'd just made. The game continued along those lines: whenever I made a decisive move or the odds seemed to be going in my favor, my chubby, cherubic opponent would infuriate me with an ingratiating smile. I racked up a quick two points in the first game, and needed only thirteen more to win my round. In tournament play, each game is a point, and the doubling cube is used to advance any point value.

The next game was tighter, and therefore fewer of the Brazilian's teeth were glinting. I began to lose some of my concentration as the gallery buzzed and the painkillers numbed. My mind and eye wandered to Justine two tables over and marched up to Lord Alfred and then to Sitizar, who paced the sidelines, signaling numbers that his aides scribbled in crayon on the tote boards. I looked for my name—I was five to three to lose. The Brazilian caught my attention by rapping his knuckle on the table and pointing to the board with his sweaty hand. Right, play.

I lost that game even though I tried to double him out, knocking the point value of the game up to four. Four points to my two, nearly the odds that Sitizar had posted on me. He wouldn't get the satisfaction. I'd make damned sure he lost on me. I wasn't going to get careless that early, and hung back on the next two games, posting modest two- and one-point wins: four to my five. I smiled broadly, feeling my stitches pull at the crusty, healing skin at the corner of my mouth. My opponent's smile eased, fell flat; my stitches had begun to ooze, just a tad, just enough. I had a clear and open field to bear off, take my men off board during that game, and felt confident enough to double after he doubled me. I won, and the point total on that game was four—I was nine points to his four, and easily won the next two games at four points apiece. I stood too fast, very dizzy, shook his hand, swabbed my face with my handkerchief, and proceeded to trip over my chair and onto the carpet. The gallery murmured; a few people shrieked as they are wont to do in such situations; a group gathered around me, including my opponent, who felt obliged to turn me over like a sack of old potatoes and fan me with his score pad. From my position on the floor I could see the pantlegs of some pretty good tuxes and not much more; the crowd stirred with hushed conversation, whispers, and a few chuckles; the men crowded around me offered first-aid suggestions. My opponent touchingly knelt beside me, his smile gone but his face animated with commands and a long string of expletives. He continued to fan me with the score.

A glass of water appeared and then I heard an explosion that I felt more than heard. The impact was so great that my chest was forced inward and I lost breath. It seemed the entire ceiling had vaporized and the smoke and flames that followed the burst were rolling down to those hovering above me. My attendants crouched as the fireball billowed downward, yet several were caught in its outward, explosive fingers before it subsided, including my opponent. His shoulder was smoking and sparks showered down from his hair. The man standing next to him was ablaze, his back licked with flames as the rest of the crowd backed away from him in horror. The stench of burning plastic and metal was suffocating, and the air was fogged with the sting and singe of smoke, the chalky powder of pulverized plaster.

I groped to my feet helped by the back of a chair: from lying on the floor I was relatively unaffected by the smoke and fumes of the initial blast. The lights had gone out with the explosion, but the fire above lit the entire room eerily. I covered my face with the handkerchief I had clutched in my fist during my fall and ran toward the man who was aflame, throwing him to the carpet and smothering the flames with a linen tablecloth. The gallery pressed against the far wall; screams and groans rose in the tight room. People panicked in the back as they surged away from the explosion and toward the bar entrance, which was obscured by smoke and flame. The crowd nearest the ceiling explosion pushed toward the bar; the people nearest the fire in the bar entrance were trampled, thrown underfoot by the tide of people running through the flames for the exit. I grabbed a backgammon board and pushed through the front of the crowd indiscriminately beating back the people who looked the most terror-stricken. It's amazing how suddenly, in a crisis, someone will respond to a totally different stimulus; one guy was so frozen that when I struck him on the shoulder he recoiled from me as though I were another explosion. I beat my way to the teller cage as the flames over the bar entrance thickened to a wall. I climbed the grate of the cage, swung myself onto the top, and surveyed the crowd in the reddish fire glow. I did not see Justine or Sitizar. I swung behind the cage and into the hallway to Sitizar's office; Gregory was crouched behind Sitizar's desk, crying that someone had shot him. He was hysterical, wild-eyed with dope and fear. His arm bled heavily through the fingers that clutched at the wound.

He looked at me: would I leave him here to go up with the building? There was a lot of blood for just an arm wound. I moved toward him, smoke beginning to move down in a thick blanket from the ceiling.

"Let's get out of here. Can you move?" I said. Yeah, I'd thought about leaving him there in his own hell, but I only considered it for a moment. I crawled over to him. He was hurt badly, the bullet had traveled through the arm and made a damn righteous hole in his left rib cage. But he was clutching his arm. "The money, out there, get the money!" he managed when he found it in my eyes that I wasn't going to leave him there.

"Fuck the money! Crawl!" I tried to help him, supporting the arm with my own, crawling along with him. The smoke was too thick. We turned back, choking. I stood long enough to throw Sitizar's leather chair through the narrow slit window that ran along the one corner. We made it through the glass with the help of a fireman: they were there already. Gregory was rushed off in an ambulance. I went back in looking for Sitizar, Justine, everyone I hadn't seen outside. I crawled down the corridor from the office to the tellers' cages on hands and knees. The smoke was black; no doubt the fire was burning wiring, carpeting, and other plastics. I wound through the teller cage and into the casino, the walls fully ablaze. A gaping hole in the ceiling acted like a flue through which smoke poured. I found Sitizar just outside the cage, his eyes wide, jaw slack. I tugged him into the relative shelter of the tellers' cage by his lapels. I felt for a pulse, listened for a telltale breath or heartbeat. There was none. I searched his inner coat pockets and came up with a handful of blood. I ripped the coat open. He'd been shot, point-blank, no doubt during the stampede. I crawled out of the building, back through the office, leaving Sitizar to the flames. The police and a fire crew could do little more than watch the squat gray building burn down. Ambulances, private cars, trucks, and police jeeps carried the injured to Faro, fifteen minutes down the coast where there was an adequate hospital.

I made it back to the Massads', where I showered the grime off, but the smell of smoke clung to me no matter how much soap I used. I heard Desmiaou preparing dinner in the kitchen and someone humming in the dining room. It was Justine, her hair wet and darkly clinging to her scalp from her showering; she wore a plain white terry robe: I recognized it as Caroline's. She had the casino strongboxes laid out on the table, the contents in piles before her: francs, deutschemarks, dollars. I walked over, my hands in my robe pockets; she scarcely looked up from thumbing a stack of bills.

"I saved it, saved the money," she said.

"It would look that way." I found a velour sack and, unfastening the drawstring, poured a mound of uncut diamonds onto the table next to a stack of bills.

"And they didn't get the diamonds," she went on, still bent over the money, moving from pile to pile, counting, scribbling on a yellow paid of paper.

"They?"

"Caroline. That Angolan friend of hers, of course."

Here I was still reeling from the explosion, and she was already sure of who did what to whom. My guess would have been Gregory. This was the revenge he spoke of.

"Listen, lady, Sitizar died back there. And Gregory . . . hell, he might be dead by now too."

"It was an awful explosion," she said, not skipping a bill.

"Yeah, I guess you could say 'awful,' but the explosion isn't what killed anyone."

"No?" she stopped to tuck a stray strand of hair back behind her ear.

"No." How could she be doing this? How could she be stacking up the bills? Didn't she realize what had happened?

She looked up from the books, black pen in hand, tapped her tooth in contemplation, and shrugged. "He knew what the score was," she said flatly.

"Score." I nodded my head in disbelief.

"Yes, score. Like the games. Our side versus their side. Guess who won today? Lord Lingon? Brady Palts? No . . ." she fixed me with a steely and frightening look. "Us. Gregory. Me. You."

"For chrissakes!" I said, getting to my feet. "You don't care who the hell gets it as long as you can sit at the sidelines and count the chips."

She brushed aside a lock of her hair, took a sip from her teacup resting so benignly in its delicately patterned saucer.

"Was Caroline even there?" I asked, suddenly aware that I had seen only Dalva. If she had not been in the casino, then . . .

"What do you mean, was she there?" she asked.

"I mean, was she ever in the casino?"

"Of course. Who do you think set the explosives, shot Sitizar and Gregory? Tried to run off with all the money and diamonds?" she asked with a decisive arch to her eyebrows. "That explosion . . ."

"Must have knocked something loose," I said uneasily, pointing to my head and taking my seat. I watched her as she hummed and chirped happily over the ledgers and moment by moment, bill by bill, I became more uneasy. She paused from her counting, a blissful, almost sexual bloom across her cheeks as she surfaced from the money and the books.

"But I never saw Caroline. She wasn't there."

"Are you sure? In the confusion?"

And I recalled the blueprints once more and the configuration of tables as if they themselves were a backgammon board. The blast had come down just over us at the tables. Wasn't the explosion the *real* revenge that Gregory had in mind?

SEVENTEEN

I sat and had a drink or two with Desmiaou, neither of us saying a word, taking turns pouring until I had had enough: enough of the brandy, enough of the sounds of Justine counting the booty in the next room, enough of sitting and doing nothing about nothing.

So I got in my sweet rented Alfa Romeo and drove. Night air and clear thinking were what I needed at that point. I was feeling paranoid, useless, and totally wiped out. I realized how much I had hung on the tournament: and it was a washout . . . a setup. The wind whipped across my stitches as I drove toward the casino and marina.

Yeah, the tournament was my justification, I guess. I might have convinced myself at first that I was after Toby's murderer, but . . . I was running, really. The hardest to admit, I was no friend. I certainly was no friend to Toby; I was not one shake of the dice closer to solving his death than when I had stepped off the plane in Lisbon. And I had not put my mind to it, I mean a real hunkering down over the board to see where the blocks were and would be, who was shaking the high numbers, where the game was running . . .

And I was no friend to Caroline. Someone I'd known for so long—and all it took to turn me was a few porno snapshots taken back when we all were a little too young and a whole lot foolish. Snapshots and her associations. Dalva. It was a sure thing that Dalva was up to his neck in this.

You couldn't pick a better way to draw attention. I crawled to a halt near the ruins of the casino; thin plumes of smoke wandered up through the collapsed heap of the roof and walls. Militia with automatic rifles slung across their shoulders passed water bottles, casually guarding the charred building. No doubt they'd found Sitizar's body; authorities had blocked off the area for evidence and to prevent looting. I rounded the corner of the hotel, turned around behind the marina concourse, and went back and out the Apontarleve complex toward Albufeira along the coast highway. *Sitizar was dead and there was no better way to draw attention* . . . I found myself going over it in my mind as the car hugged the curves along the top of the bluffs, the ocean gleaming a grassy green below. *Attention* . . . Yeah, Caroline was in trouble all right. And not just as an accomplice or a poor, misled lover. It figured to me that she might have to stand for everything that had been happening: both murders, the theft. Christ, there was no telling.

An uncomfortable shiver ran through me. I recalled what Gregory had said to me on the golf course: *Save her, save her.* If everything was to pan out the way I thought just then, Caroline was being framed royally, with gold leaf and velvet matting. *Save her,* Gregory had said, and all this time I thought he meant from the affair she was having.

I wondered if Dalva had her shacked up at his place and took a spin by. The driveway was empty, and I prowled through broken pottery and those green-flowered vines from shuttered window to window, peering in through gaps in the broken slats and listening for any sign of life. Nothing. I decided that either Caroline was out on her own or Dalva had her stashed somewhere safe until he could put the fix on her and then turn her in. I cruised the streets of Albufeira and the outlying hills looking for her Porsche. I was about to run down to Quarteira, Faro, or back to the Apontarleve compound when I remembered the hotel Balaia-Penta, where we'd all had those stomach-wrenching whiskey-and-flat-Cokes. I pulled around the corner, up an alley, and parked the car where it wouldn't be noticed from the street. I hadn't been using it enough to be recognized by it, but I wasn't taking chances.

I asked a dark, pinch-faced clerk if he had a Caroline Massad as his guest, and he made like he couldn't understand English.

"This is all I've got—in money and in patience," I said,

emptying my pocket, prying one of his hands loose from the register and placing the loose bridge teeth and some stray escudos into his sweaty palm. He dropped them and jumped back in disgust. I searched out the last few days in the register as he inspected the teeth, scattered like stones, tinged pink from my blood. She was listed under Brodin, her maiden name. Room 519. I called up on the house phone and there was no answer. I went up and knocked on the door. No answer. I pounded on the door until the heel of my hand went red and numb. I leaned against it, pressed my cheek to it, and then I heard it: the distinctive plop of a plastic hotel glass hitting a bathroom floor. That cheap plastic plop. I kicked on the door, calling Caroline's name. She didn't answer. I tried to kick the door down, but my feet already ached, and this place had decided to buy good doors—the damned thing refused to be kicked in.

"Caroline," I said softly, breathing as if I'd swum across from Morocco. "Caroline," I said again, nearly as quiet as the plop of that hotel cup on the other side of the door. I heard her whimper. A faint, subtle squeak, muffled, I imagined, in the folds of a hotel towel.

"Caroline, let me in," I whispered. "Let me help. I'm sorry. I'm sorry I dumped on you like this, not believing in you."

"Fuck you," she complained in a sob-soaked voice, echoing in what had to be the bathroom.

"Damn it, Caroline." I kicked at the door in anger.

"I'm trying," she sobbed. I waited. After a time I heard the latch click and I opened up the door, right into Caroline who had collapsed in a heap. I pushed my way in, peeled her up off the floor, and dragged her into the bathroom.

The hotel cup was on the floor, spilled whiskey on the cold tiles. I propped her up against the bidet; her hair was going in every conceivable tangle and direction, her eyes bruised and swollen-looking, eyelids and hands quivering uncontrollably. Her eyes were wide open despite the fact that she could barely move or speak. There was more than whiskey in her. I took off her clothes and stood her in the shower, her skin bluish, dimpled, her eyes dilated despite the bright overhead lights in the john.

She was naked and shivering, going stiff. She slid down the tile wall into the tub. Her eyes rolled back into her head and huge goose pimples rose over her whole body; her skin toughened, I gripped her and shook her. She began to gasp heavily, quickly, as if she were having trouble breathing. She had begun to shiver—wave after wave of trembling rippled the taut muscles in her thighs, as if they had been touched with electric shock. Her arms clutched at her chest and she rolled over on her side in the tub, legs drawn up, her fingers digging into her heaving chest as if trying to press air into her lungs. I slapped her, then sat her up. I ran the hottest water I could on her, holding her head up out of the tub. I finally propped it up with the wastebasket, keeping her head out of the water, massaging her trembling limbs, her taut abdomen. Every muscle seemed tense with shock and cold and hard as rocks. Vapor rose from the water, and I pried her hands loose from her ribs, blood trickling down where her nails had broken the skin. She closed her eyes, moaned. Her breathing deepened, relaxed. I massaged her legs, their spasms subsiding, the skin grew pliable in my hands. I made her stand up when I felt she was able, stood her and made her grip the shower nozzle for support. I was soaking wet. I held her for a long, long time under that water. She was out. I kept her under the nozzle, turning her face to the jet, one arm around her waist, until I heard her sputter and finally say, "Shit, shit," in crisp, clear, Carolinelike tones. She pushed off from me and turned into a corner of the shower stall.

"Get out of the stall, you prick. What hit me?" she asked, hugging at her breasts.

I sent down for a bottle of brandy and bread and cheese then I poured the whiskey down the sink. American whiskey.

"Dalva gave—" she protested, toweling herself off as I got rid of it. I tossed her the dressing gown.

"If you want to know what hit you, it was the bottle," I told her. I wasn't about to sample it for myself.

"So I had a few and passed out," she said, shrugging into the nightgown.

"You feel like you just had a few too many?"

"No," she admitted, rubbing her eyes. "Christ, the fucking nightmares," she said.

"Nightmares, huh," I tossed the bottle into the basket under the sink. "Hallucinations, more likely."

We went into the next room, Caroline gripping the walls along the way. I found the vial, the same as those in Gregory's case, left on the rumpled bedspread. I sniffed it: the same acrid odor. Morphine and what else? Caroline watched me, weaving on unsteady legs.

"Dalva and me did some of that. Wild stuff. He's hit me up before," she went on, wriggling the toes on her right foot. She climbed onto the bed with a groan. I spread her toes apart: he sure had hit her up before. She giggled and withdrew her foot.

"So he hit you up and left?"

"Not exactly." She laughed huskily and then moaned, holding her temples.

I checked the end-table drawers, and what I found made me sit back down on the bed: a stack of crisp escudos and a small, tapered beige lump that could only be plastic explosive. I sniffed it.

"Let me smell," Caroline said.

"This is no joke, babe. Frame-up," I told her, holding the explosive out in my palm for her to smell. She wrinkled her nose.

"That lump of plastic?"

"Explosive. The casino was just blown, and I'll bet this was the brand that did it. And the notes," I said, fingering the stack of bills. "That Dalva is a real sweetheart." I called room service about that food. She needed something besides drugs in her system.

"Ohhh," she moaned again. "I haven't been out of this room since Sunday. Since just a few hours after I left you at the villa. Dalva and me had a few, messed around . . ." she trailed off. I took a long while to tell her about the explosion at the casino, but I didn't mention Gregory. The brandy, soda, and cheese and bread arrived. I handed her the food, tipped the delivery boy, and cracked the bottle for myself.

She sat up cross-legged on the bed, cramming bread into her mouth. I got her a glass of water; she held it out for a touch of brandy.

"Sorry, whatever your buddy spiked you with is still in your system," I warned her. A slice of sunset light cut across the bed lighting her face and her tinted blond hair with a rosy pink. She ate and drank without speaking or looking up at me. I sat at the foot of the bed.

"So you know what's up, don't you?" I asked. She didn't answer me. "He's going to frame your ass," I tried again.

"Frame me?" she asked, bread crumbs spraying from her lips across the brown coverlet. The red slice of light from the balcony flashed at her moist tongue as it licked at the water glass.

"For Sitizar's murder and possibly Toby's," I said.

"But who?" she asked.

"How about Dalva," I suggested.

She paused for a minute, brushing crumbs from her gown while she sized me up. "Listen, you're quite the shit lately," she finally said. "Why don't you just get it all out in the open."

"I only want to get your ass out of this mess. I want to apologize."

"Apologize?" She laughed, her voice still heavy with the drugs and whiskey. "You don't even know what kind of trouble I'm in," she finally said, shaking her head sadly, drawing her feet up under her. Her legs quivering as her gown parted a bit.

"It was Dalva's idea? To rip off Gregory?" I asked, taking a quick shot.

"Nope, mine. All mine. Do you know I can't buy a box of Kleenex without asking for his money. Everything is tied up in Gregory's failing businesses. The diamonds. At least Dalva and I weren't ripping off those Africans. Not like Gregory."

"Yeah, they're so defenseless," I murmured, thinking of Mobotiak and Josef. Thinking of Toby.

"I bet. It's mercenary as hell, and I don't feel one bit guilty about trying to rip the shipment off. It was *already* stolen. Consider it my divorce decree. Reverse dowry or some such shit. You're not a doctor, give me a drink," she said. I handed her the bottle and she got up unsteadily. I helped her outside to the balcony. "I ripped them off from the villa. He wanted me to take them to New York, sell them, keep the money. Make things right. But I couldn't, I couldn't take them ever. He said he'd take care of it." She paused, took a breath before shouting in disgust over the railing into the cove below. "Stuck in this *glorified* Miami Beach." Her gown blew in the breeze; the sunset fell brightly on the white of it. She squinted and stood at the railing, handing me the bottle. Her eyes were puffy, painful to look at, I couldn't imagine how painful to look out of. "Don't get me wrong, Vern. Dalva is really into that Angolan shit. The ideals. He's so serious."

"Don't count on it," I said. "He just almost killed you." She had no reaction to that, staring blankly out over the bright ocean. I leaned against the balustrade, swishing the brandy in its bottle. She settled back in the chair, looked up at me, her face tightening in the bright sun. God, she looked awful.

"Why didn't you tell me," I asked her. "Why the damned masquerade in the back of Dalva's restaurant? All the Marxist bullshit. Revolution and all that crap. And Toby, you could have told me you had asked Toby to run the diamonds for you." I might have been suspicious of her . . . I might have felt turned on and kicked in the balls with those long-ago snapshots, but why did she end up lying to me?

"Slow down." She grimaced, putting out a feeble hand. "I told you before. I did not know that Toby was here until I saw him, strictly by accident, at the casino. Wasn't even sure it was him. And as for the Marxist bullshit, the diamonds were already stolen, I guess; like I said, I wanted to believe it anyway. I don't know now, though, what with Dalva." Her voice trailed off. I took the seat across from her. The lace of her gown, the loose fold that closed it in front, fluttered in the sea breeze, along with strands of her dyed hair that escaped across her forehead and cheek.

"Yeah, what with Dalva. The bastard O.D.d you, for chrissakes! And it's a safe bet he killed Toby." I didn't mention the blueprints of the casino; I still wasn't sure of Gregory's connection, and I kept everything about his mutilation and being shot at the explosion to myself. I needed at least one hole card; I couldn't force myself to tell her all, not just yet. And there was still Toby. "Don't bullshit me, Caroline, do not bullshit me on this next one. There's too much on the line here . . . Did you ask Toby to run the diamonds?"

"No, I told you, no! I never asked Toby to run the diamonds!" She got up, angry. I forced her to look at me, holding her face in my hand.

"You didn't ask him? I swear, Caroline . . ."

"No, damn it, no!" She hit me. Square in the jaw, pulled back to hit me again but I grabbed her in a bear hug. She tried to squirm free, swearing, kicking. The tantrum didn't last long, the drugs wouldn't allow it. She was finally still in my arms.

"What with Dalva . . . Gregory . . . I need you—who else do I have left?"

"You got that part right. You need me." And what if she had ripped off Gregory, wouldn't I have thought about doing the same? He was crazy as an ant farm, no telling what he could do, might as well salvage what was lying around loose. Maybe he had been rough with her, he'd proven he wasn't a pussycat that night on the golf course. And Dalva? She just got mixed up with the wrong guy: she'd been doing that all her life. I knew I was making excuses for her, even as I held her in my arms, swaying gently with her in my arms. Naw, I was making excuses for both of us, but wouldn't realize it at the time. So we made love in the sun after all, there on the balcony, a cool, generous breeze off the ocean washing over our tired, frightened asses. There's only a few sweet diversions in this world that can convince me everything has a chance of turning out all right.

We held each other and sat quietly watching the ocean before I finished telling her all I knew: the explosion being set according to Gregory's marked blueprints, what Josef and Mobotiak had told me about Moreno and the diamonds, Gregory's self-mutilation. I stood uneasily, tucking in my shirt and fixing my belt. She'd admitted that Dalva had set the explosives. But the blueprints, by *Gregory's* blueprints?

"Damn—" She hissed in anger, her head weaving. "Ripping Gregory off is one thing. I mean he practically deserted me. We lived in the same house and all but not seeing him . . . wandering at night. I thought if I didn't get to the money someone would. But people getting killed. Gregory getting shot. Damn." Her eyes teared. She shook her head. Some time to be thinking like that, I thought, taking another drink, feeling slow and uneasy, my stomach on fire with little food and too much brandy and inhaled smoke. I could still smell soot, burnt plastic. "So it's Dalva. Framing me. Why?" she asked, hugging her knees, my shadow cast over her.

"Maybe not just Dalva." I thought of the Moreno disfigurement, Sitizar's seemingly pointless death, and the tournament going up in smoke. I stretched a few kinks out of my body. The waters of the tiny cove formed by the beach and hotel and cliff were in shade and seemed incredibly dark and deep, feathery waves barely pocking the surface. "Shit," I groaned. "The way things are shaping up, dear heart, we might find both of our asses up for murder. And the bombing."

"One thing, though," she said, smiling up at me as I towered over her, "why the hell did you ever mail those pictures of me, the nudie shots, to Gregory? Did you want me back?"

"Me?" I asked, flabbergasted, flushing, suddenly surprised and angry. "I never even knew you sat for them. Remember, we were playing a monogamous-lovers-living-in-sin at Northwestern." I trailed off, getting more and more pissed by the second just thinking of her posing like that for—who was that guy Sandra mentioned?

"I was pretty good-looking then, huh?" she kidded, opening her dress front, her breasts sudden, stark in the sharp light, her nipples a brownish red. "I'm still not too bad."

"No," I admitted.

"Then whoever sent them to Gregory was out to get me. Not to blackmail me, mind you," she went on, her voice changing from teasing seduction to anger, "get me. And it nearly worked. Do you know he nearly gave me the divorce after that?" She suddenly stood and pulled the gown around her. She wavered as she held her chair back, looking down into the cove.

"But I thought you wanted—" I began, incredulous that she would be upset that the pictures would get her a divorce.

"Hell no, the divorce would have been just fine. I thought you . . . but whoever sent them . . . they meant business."

"Who?" I said.

"Didn't work," she shook her head and staggered. "Didn't get me." We went inside, and I wrapped the portion of hot money and plastic explosive into a few sheets torn from a phone directory, and stuffed the bundle in a pillowcase which I flung off the balcony into the dark waters of the cove. It wasn't until near seven that night that I finally got her straightened out, dressed, and checked out. If she were going to be framed or set up, there was no sense waiting around in the hotel for the police to come looking. In fact, the absence of any cops on our heels all that time was beginning to puzzle me. It could only mean that the last pieces were not in place, that the final move that would sew up Caroline, Caroline and possibly me with her, had not yet been made. And Dalva figured her to be long dead; there was no hurry to have her body found; the morning maid could take care of that little detail for him.

"We could sneak back to the villa for my passport. Your money. Get the first flight out of Lisbon. If we drove all night, we could make it," she said, getting into my car.

"Stay calm," I told her, backing out of the alley and squeezing out onto the narrow cobblestone street.

"Then what? What the hell do we do, if I'm going to get framed?" she pouted. I made my way out of town.

"Exactly. You *can't* leave. You know how bad that'll look?" I glanced over at her. She bit nervously at her lip.

"Then I have to stop that bastard," she told me. "Get to the restaurant."

I pulled back onto the coast road and turned off toward the village and bullring. Caroline got steadily more agitated as we approached the restaurant, and I did my best to calm her.

"He could be very dangerous if we corner him. We have to be cool, so very cool about this," I warned her.

"Yeah, yeah, yeah," she said impatiently. "What do *you* have to lose?"

"I already lost a partner," I said, pulling up in front of the restaurant and the souvenir stand that perched at the curb. "And I don't need to lose another."

The restaurant itself was nearly deserted: two Portuguese at a back table wrestled with one of Dalva's pizzas. I reminded her to be cool, calm. She blew past the bird cage, heels clacking on the tile.

When I caught up, Caroline had a meat cleaver in her hand and Dalva was sitting bolt upright on a stool, pressed against the dough table; the cook cowered at the door of the oven.

"Caroline!" I shouted and held her hand up before it took a whack at Dalva. I spotted the gun on the table, a forty-five automatic, resting next to a green velveteen pouch and a lump of pizza dough. Caroline strained at my hand as Dalva reached for the gun. I let Caroline go and the cleaver came down hard on the board, narrowly missing Dalva's fingers. He drew back to the stool and then suddenly stood.

He had not been fast enough to get the gun, and he was slower still trying to make his getaway; Caroline had cornered him, pushed him up against the wall. His eyes bulged out as he watched her wielding the cleaver, her puffy eyes filled with tears, rage. The cook took that opportunity to make for the back door and out into the night. I inspected the gun gingerly, poking it about with my finger but being careful not to pick it up.

"You bastard," she breathed. "All that glorious talk about the revolution. The capitalists ripping off your people. Do you know I *believed* some of that bullshit myself?" She lowered the cleaver. "I believed in you. Maybe believed in you a whole lot."

"Caroline," he said sympathetically, holding out his arms, "what do you mean? I have the diamonds. They're over there on the table. I was just on my way to the hotel to get you. We could leave tonight, on our way to Luanda." The velveteen pouch was just like the one I'd seen earlier, in the strongbox at the villa. Had he already taken care of Justine? Here were the rest of the goddamned stones, right at my fingertips.

"But why did you try to kill me?" she asked. She was beginning to ask the wrong questions, questions that the slob would have answers to, and it was plain that she wanted to believe everything the creep was telling her. He looked over at me and then to the gun.

I decided to buck Caroline up a bit. "You mean you were going to leave this restaurant, just fly off to Luanda, to Angola, and the two of you would live happily ever after?" I asked resting my hand discreetly beside the pistol after pocketing the diamonds.

I wondered if I should let him make a break for it if Caroline let him pass. Did *he* think I would let him waltz out? I hadn't entirely made up my mind if I would reach for the gun if he made a break.

"Don't cut him, Caroline. Be careful. You'll need him in court. Your friend here was going to plant this gun." I paused. "Where were you going to plant it, Dalva? The villa?" I guessed that this was the gun that had killed Sitizar, perhaps Toby. And with the diamonds here, Justine. Another corpse to look forward to. Dalva was our man, but I had a feeling there was more to it, more to him.

Dalva went back to the wall. Caroline came right up on him, the cleaver again held high.

"Where?" she said coolly. Too coolly. Cool like the voice of a callous, calculating killer. I felt I couldn't let Dalva go, and yet I couldn't let Caroline really have at him. Hell, she just *might* kill him. And he had real answers. Best to leave him play out the board. I was in a precarious position, because by then I decided that I wouldn't use the gun. But Dalva decided everything on his own.

"Your car. I was going to leave it in your car."

I waited for the cleaver to come down with a *thwack* but it did not budge from its ominous position.

"Nice touch," I said. She struck at him and missed; the blade sliced into the Michelin calendar on the wall. Dalva ducked under her and looked at me and the gun once again. I lifted my hand from the table. I wasn't going to go for it, but I stood in front of the gun to let him know I wouldn't let him have it either. He ran toward the door leading into the restaurant, and Caroline followed. I called after her. He was best left on the loose, alive. For our sakes. The customers stood and stumbled out of their way. Caroline headed straight for Dalva and lunged at his legs. That launched both of them at the cockatoo cage. The bird screeched as it toppled, cage clanging. Dalva got to his feet and headed once again for the door, but Caroline was slow getting up. By the time I got to the street, Dalva had made it into the safety of his beat-up Mercedes, parked a storefront down from my car. Caroline beat at the window.

"You Judas sonofabitch!" she screamed at him, her voice echoing in the deserted street. She hacked at the glass with the cleaver; it lodged in the glass; Dalva cringed away from the window. The car finally coughed to a start. He put the car into gear. Caroline fell to the pavement. The car jerked forward, sputtered, then lurched forward again into the souvenir stall, the flimsy enclosure splintering apart as the car rammed through it. The weathered wood of the stall and red-sequined souvenir stuffed bulls spilled everywhere in the street. The car made off to the corner, squealed around the bend, and then clattered off into the street. Dalva was gone. Caroline stood at the curb, huffing.

"I told you to be cool," I said, coming up to her to make sure she was all right. "And look what you do." The customers had come out on the curb and they munched on their pizza, standing on the wood-littered sidewalk. They cheered Caroline as she passed them. We jumped in my car, and I handed the pouch of diamonds to her as I started the car. "If this is the other half of the diamonds, man!" I whistled. I brought my thought to an abrupt halt as I sat on something. Reaching around under me,

I pulled out a souvenir red bull. I tossed it toward the customers, still loitering on the sidewalk.

"What other half?"

"The other half of the diamonds Moreno had stolen. You only got half of them when you ripped off Gregory."

"How do you know?"

"I know, believe me, I know." She looked at me oddly. She was shocked, I guessed, that I wasn't telling her all I knew. To hell with it—she hadn't exactly been a straight arrow with me either. "We have the second half of the diamonds, but do we have the murder weapon?" I held the gun up.

"What do you mean?"

"Guns is guns . . . maybe the murder weapon is already planted in your car. We'd better check."

"Relax," she assured me. "My car is in back. Behind the restaurant."

I pulled around into the alley. Caroline's car was not there. The back door of the kitchen was still open from when the cook made his getaway. She got out of my car as if she didn't believe it, stood in the empty alley in the sharp glare of my headlights. There was no Porsche.

"What do I do now, Vernon?" Her voice trembled.

I stood in my seat, arms crossed over the windshield frame, the car idling. "My father had a favorite saying at times like this: 'Shit in one hand and wish in the other and see which one gets filled first.'"

"Cut the damned homilies," she said, still frightened, making her way toward the car. "What am I going to do?"

"Get in the car. We've got some hustling to do. And fast." I got back into my seat and threw her door open for her.

We made it back to the villa. As I expected, the cops were there: two militia jeeps and a police car were parked outside the gates. Caroline's Porsche glinted in the driveway. I stopped at the gate.

"Damn," she said, her voice quavering. She held onto the dash.

"Hey," I told her, grabbing her firmly by the other arm, "we both knew the cops would be here. Dalva practically guaranteed that. But think about it for a moment. The safest place in the world for you right now might be with the cops, while I try to straighten things out." I didn't mention that I thought the cops were probably finding Justine's body about this time. But it didn't look good for Caroline, and I could help both of us if I were on my own.

Two figures stepped out of the house onto the darkened driveway. Cops.

"You're nuts if you think I'm going to turn myself in," she whispered. I could hear voices as the cops made their way back to their cars. "Get the hell out of here before both of us are locked up," she said. I turned the car around and left, looking behind and holding my breath. They hadn't seen us, weren't following.

I went to look for Dalva, and the marina seemed the best bet. I parked behind the concourse and dragged Caroline behind me. If she didn't want the cozy comforts of a jail cell, than she'd have to play sidekick and dance through the same flak as me. The shops and cafés had all been closed for hours and the lamps on the piers and a pale moon were the only light. The water was still choppy from the storm the night before, and at the waterfront the wind was picking up, bobbing the sailboats, cabin cruisers, and yachts in an odd, jerky syncopation. Waves slapped up at the hulls and pilings. A few of the boats had their interior lights on; a radio was playing a few piers down, the weak music fighting through the gusts of wind.

"Where the hell we going?" Caroline whispered harshly, ripping her hand from mine.

"Your sweetheart's boat," I told her.

"I thought we agreed to let him go. You're the one that wouldn't help me kill the bastard back at his restaurant," she said.

"Kill him? No. But have him help us straighten up this whole mess? Maybe . . . If he's still here," I made my way down to the boat. The *Embora* was still docked and the cabin lights were on. I crept up to the boat and took the gun out of my coat.

Christ, it was heavy. I just stood there a minute, realizing it was the first time I'd ever really held a gun. Did I even look like I could use one? I boarded the ship, stepping over the railing in back; my shoe squeaked on the wet deck. I winced and motioned for Caroline to stay.

I nosed up to the cabin window and dropped my gun. Those cold, cold eyes of Justine's were sighting me down the barrel of her gun: right between the eyes if I wanted her to try a shot or two.

—— EIGHTEEN ——

I heard Dalva snicker behind me. He jumped from the wheelhouse above and picked up the gun.

"Nice," I heard Caroline moan.

"Come on in for a nightcap," Justine offered, sliding open the cabin door and waving us in with the gun barrel.

"Yes, have a drink with us," Dalva repeated. He slammed the door shut behind us and disappeared above the deck. The engines rumbled to a start. Caroline and I took seats opposite each other in the galley booth. There was a bottle of American whiskey and two clean glasses on the table.

"I know how you appreciate having drinks ready for you." Justine nodded to the bottle. Caroline did as she was told. I passed, twisting my empty glass around the tabletop. Justine pulled a stool up and took my glass and poured herself a drink. The gun casually yet thoughtfully rested in her lap, pointed in my direction. I knew I couldn't beat her to it.

"Surprise, surprise," Justine toasted me. Even there in the poor cabin light, knowing full well that it was she who was behind the killings, Christ yes, even then she was beautiful. Beauty and malevolence, her coldness. It was Justine behind

Dalva. I knew someone had called the moves for him. Justine. And I recalled how, back in the cozy, warm confines of Zorine's, I had felt that she was calling the moves in the backgammon game. Suggesting the moves. Hell yes, Justine all along. She drank slowly and got up, the navy jumpsuit she was wearing hugging her like rain-soaked clothes.

The boat was making its way out into the blackness of the ocean, the pier falling away behind us, the two spires of the hotel a mosaic of green-gold against the night sky. We skitted roughly over waves and the boat turned to move parallel to the shore. Caroline sighed and then shivered. I poured her another drink and she took it eagerly. She had a look in her eyes that scared the shit out of me: a little girl inside of her was looking up at me, a little girl frightened beyond crying, struck mute and cowering, waiting for the end.

"That's it," Justine urged Caroline to drink, her voice soft, agreeable.

"Where we going?" I asked, watching as she leaned against the galley stove, gun still pointed in our direction.

"I want to make sure you wash up fairly close to a good beach," she said in the same even tone she'd comforted Caroline with.

"A good beach?" What the hell did the quality of the beach have to do with it?—I knew we weren't out for a moonlit swim.

"I mean I don't want the police, the militia to have to look long or hard for either of you. Fishing for bodies is a tiresome job around those cliffs, and I want to make sure they don't lose patience and give up before they can recover you."

"And we've committed suicide, I suppose?" I prodded her, hoping I was wrong about what was coming, but knowing I wasn't.

"No, no. Not neat. Too many loose ends," she chuckled. "I mean, if I really want you to take a fall for all this, you and Mrs. Massad, why would you commit suicide after I make it look as if you two robbed the casino? Try again, Vernon. You can do better than that."

Caroline cleared her throat. Her eyes filled with tears, she pressed the top knuckles of her fist to her trembling mouth. The boat rocked over tough waves.

"You've planted the gun in the Porsche, the gun that killed Sitizar," I began to check off, actually indicating that pretty item on my finger. "Ah," I stumbled. "And that leaves *you* with the money from the casino, the real diamonds and . . ." I paused. She shook her head, the smile fading.

"That's part of it, Vernon. Yes, we'll have the casino money and the diamonds." She snapped her fingers and held her hand out. I surrendered the velour sack; she hefted it in her hand before tucking it into her jumpsuit pocket. "But there's a lot more to it than that. Believe me, if you only had an imagination as sharp as your backgammon."

The engine cut to a high throttle and I looked out the porthole: blackness over the ocean was all I could see.

"Suppose you tell me, last rites and all that. I'll pass up the cigarette and a blindfold just to find out why my buddy, Sitizar, and now me and Caroline are going to get our asses blown away." I wanted a drink. God, how I wanted one, but I knew I couldn't.

"You have no idea?" She seemed genuinely surprised. "You will be very important elements in what the police will determine was a terrorist smuggling operation run by not only our good friends the Angolan revolutionaires but three good little Americans from Chicago who, apparently, got in way over their heads and were, by all appearances, killed by their Angolan bedfellows. Let us say executed," she corrected, tapping the gun with the nail of her index finger. "Yes, executed."

"Like Toby," I said. Caroline took another drink, tears flowing freely down her cheeks. I took her hands in mine as they rested around her whiskey glass. I was scared too. And I knew it was starting to show. She pulled away from me, taking a drink. Dalva slid the door wide open, a burst of cold, blustery ocean air rifling through the cabin. He trailed a length of rope with him, coiling it, taking ominous care as to where he placed a few knots.

Caroline saw the rope and the cold, raw gleam in Dalva's eyes and began to cry openly.

"You weak bitch! No stomach for what you've caused?" Justine sneered down at Caroline, hate creasing, erupting over her, dissolving the cold calmness she'd maintained for so long. "You stole those diamonds from your husband, Mrs. Massad!" She lingered hatefully over the word "Mrs."

"It didn't take me long to convince her," Dalva chuckled.

"I'm sure it didn't. Too bad we couldn't get your lover Dalva here to convince you to carry the diamonds over, eh, Mrs. Massad? Things would have been neater. We could have killed you instead of that dupe of yours." "So we have half of Moreno's diamonds, just half." She hefted the stones in her hand; the gun still pointed to my head with the other. "But half is better than none. Half the diamonds and all of the company. And to be rid of you, dear Mrs. Massad. If you'd only gone in the first place . . ." She turned to me. "Tell us, Mr. Bradlusky. Tell us where Toby put the first shipment of diamonds."

I'd been brought up a nonpracticing Catholic and was not overly fond of the notion of confession, but I wished I'd had the whereabouts of those other fucking rocks to confess then and there. Not that Justine would let me go with a thank-you and a few Hail Marys, but even a minute or two of breathing and being would have been worth it. I knew I didn't have them, knew that Josef and Mobotiak didn't. Now it seemed that Justine and Dalva didn't have them either.

"I thought, no . . . I—I," I stammered.

"That seals it. Just as I have been telling you, Justine. The rebels that spoke with Mr. Kale. They have them." Dalva pleaded his case to her, seemed desperate to convince her.

"All right. I'm sure of it too, now. But you shouldn't have killed Mr. Kale until we knew. Until we were certain!" She'd turned her anger on him, and he looked down at the rope in his hands, setting one more knot. "No matter," Justine said, turning to us again. "Wouldn't it have been cleaner, easier if you had brought the diamonds over when Dalva asked you, Mrs.

Massad? We could have killed you, left *your* body and impli-
cated the rebels for your death? But you had to say no, had to get
another person involved." She had the gun pressed to Caroline's
forehead, tilting her head up with the gun barrel so that Caroline
was forced to look at her. "And such a stupid fool Mr. Kale was
for you, he couldn't follow plans either. Didn't you tell him to
get off the plane in New York, deliver the diamonds to us in
New York?"

"Yes, I told him, damn, I told him! I didn't know he was
going to take off to Chicago, please, I did what Dalva told me to,
Dalva told him!" She gulped out her words. Christ, Caroline. I
couldn't even go to my grave knowing she'd been straight with
me; she'd told me she never asked Toby to run the diamonds. I
guess all it took to get Caroline to work at an honest relationship was a loaded gun pressed to her face.

"She's been working with you all along?" I watched as Justine let Caroline's face down with the gun, let her collapse her
face into the comfort of her arms where she continued to cry.

"Sure. Although she never knew as much. She thought her
and her precious Dalva would get the diamonds and live happily
ever after. Mrs. Massad thinks she will always live happily ever
after, no matter who she steps on. But these diamonds, were
they worth all this, Mrs. Massad?" She held the diamond pouch
by the drawstring, running the bag through Caroline's hair as
she held her head down in the cover of her arms. "Would these
diamonds be worth it? Do you know how much Moreno was
worth to me? Do you know what he *meant* to me, Mrs. Massad?
My husband, Moreno Massad?"

Caroline jerked up suddenly, staring up in disbelief at Justine, tears streaming down her reddened face. Justine backed
away, gun leveled at Caroline. "You're not the only *Mrs.*
Massad. I loved Moreno, damn you! Why did you go with him?
Gregory never would have made that call, he never would have
turned in his own brother . . . but for you."

The filth was getting about knee deep. I glared at Caroline
and she turned her face from me. How touching, such a sudden
display of humility in the face of death. Goddamned Caroline.

"But Mr. Kale's death won't be in vain, Mr. Bradlusky. Nor yours. I'll get the revenge that Gregory hoped for. Yes, it was Gregory who turned his brother over to the rebels, but even he is at peace now. I can forgive him . . . his motives . . . almost forgive him. Now even you must be figured into the equation, Mr. Bradlusky. We have witnesses that will testify that Mr. Kale was in Lisbon and Chicago with the rebels. You and Mrs. Massad are ex-lovers, that is well known. Mr. Kale and you have been associates for years, and your activities have always been, even though not entirely illegal, very shady. Gambling and setting up patsies at backgammon. The casino bombing and theft will certainly be linked to the rebels and you two. Only a few stray diamonds in your pockets as you wash ashore. The diamonds and some of the casino cash, a sample plastic explosive in Mrs. Massad's car . . . they'll do a fine job of talking. That and your mutilated bodies, faces slashed to resemble what happened to Mr. Kale. The authorities know the rebels are here, but they have behaved themselves up to now, eh?" Justine and Dalva both laughed aloud.

"And with Sitizar out of the way you are the only heir left, don't you think that looks a little suspicious?" I managed; my voice was weaker, smaller than I'd ever heard it. I was blue with fright, cold head to toe, lucky, actually, that I could talk at all.

"You think I did all this for the business, the money, the diamonds? I get the sweetest, *real* revenge here, Mr. Bradlusky. Everyone responsible for my husband's death gets what they deserved for so long. The rebels, Gregory, that slut!" She pointed the gun at Caroline. "I get everyone and everything in one, swift, final move! You, of all people should appreciate that kind of economy!"

"Toby and I will really marvel at your deftness."

"You won't believe me, but I'm sorry you and Mr. Kale became involved in the first place. Things didn't have to come to this if Mrs. Massad had been more cooperative with Dalva here. You can thank your sweetheart there for you . . ." Her voice trailed off, her anger seemed to subside a bit. She bolstered it again by looking over at Caroline. "The intrigues . . . between you and your husband, I don't know who was the weaker. You thought this little diamond stealing would be a lark, a rich little lark. And he thought we needed the blueprints to set up the casino for cheating the bankers! Tame games to play when you've been responsible for someone's death, Mrs. Massad. Everything that could possibly appeal to the bored, decadent slobs," Justine said with clear contempt. "The damned silly games and intrigues. It was so easy. I imagine the police will have found some of the pictures of you, also, Mrs. Massad. You know the ones. Found them on the golf course, a stroke of luck. I'm sure they'll figure blackmail into the equation also. Perhaps the terrorists *blackmailed* Mrs. Massad into helping their cause. Do you think the police might suspect something along those lines?" Dalva produced the packet of Caroline's pictures: the sad, drunk face, the spread legs, the sixties bouffant. Caroline turned away. "And those pictures along with these," Justine went on, producing her own set of pictures, three in all, which she threw onto the stack: shots of Mobotiak and Josef and me under the café umbrella in the Lisbon café. They were obviously telephoto; the picture lacked the clarity of a closer shot, yet there was no mistaking Mobotiak's broad shoulders, the beak nose and yellow eyes of Josef, and me, me sitting there with a pasty, hangdog look, piles of escudos sitting up tall and pretty on the table. Three angles on all this, including a long shot to obviously identify, without a doubt, which street the picture was taken on. I let that last photo drop over the picture of Caroline, only her half-closed eyes, drunken smile peering from the stack of photos. "The authorities will be interested that the two Angolan gentlemen were in the country at all to begin with, let alone that you have been seen with them, don't you think?" Justine asked, raising my chin with a long-nailed finger so that I had to look her in those eyes. She blinked, she seemed to flash a sudden concern before turning quickly from me and nodding to Dalva, who sighed, as if tired, bored. But he took her cue.

Once he had us tied side to side and loosely at our feet, he managed to squeeze us onto the back deck, Justine following, gun pointed at my chest, her cold smile pointed a lot deeper.

The air on deck was thick, sending the oily spray of the Atlantic up on deck, dousing us all. The waves were high, the boat rocking.

"It's a bet you'll have to do all the dirty work again," I said to Dalva as Justine motioned for him to make us kneel down on deck. He looked at me long and hard, his eyes emotionless. Then I thought that it was only because he didn't want to, couldn't look Caroline in the eyes that he averted his. Sure, he'd been keeping her bed warm for his cut in the whole project, but I suspected he was more than a little skittish about slicing her up.

"Did Toby give you a hard time? Did he make a lot of noise when you did him in?" I asked, just as long as I had the sonofabitch's attention. My mind was on the way he'd be slicing the two of us. He pushed us down onto the deck without answering. Caroline began to cry loudly, almost a seizure of sobs that wracked against me.

"What makes you think I killed your friend? Gregory is crazy enough to have done it. Crazy from turning in his brother to the people he'd doubled," Dalva sneered at me then, before turning away. I saw Justine walk up.

"But he didn't, did he?" He didn't answer. She squatted in front of me, barrel of the gun pointed at my head.

"Why all the questions, Vernon?" she nearly purred. "You'll be dead in minutes."

"I want to go informed." I managed to smile into her gun and ice-smooth face. I was sick and felt a sourness rise in my throat. The boat lurched and Caroline and I were pitched forward. She landed face to deck, her hands trapped under her. I had managed to catch my fall with my tied hands acting like some stunted leg that grew from my chest. Caroline was pulling me down though. And her crying grew hoarse, animal-sounding, coming from some raw, buried part of her. I struggled to keep myself up on those tied hands, to look Justine in the eye. I wanted to look her right in the eye as she pulled the trigger. My clothes were soaking in the spray. I was shivering, had been shivering, for how long I had no idea.

"So Gregory might be dead too? You do neat work. You

could probably knock off half the Algarve if you put your mind to it." I managed to pull myself to my knees; Caroline wriggled up also. I felt Dalva behind us.

"The poor bastard," she continued her purr. "But he had turned in Moreno. And I vowed he'd pay. And oh how he paid. It wasn't hard getting him on the needles. So easy. And I'd remind him how he turned in his own brother to the people who killed him. How his wife was slutting around with some of the same people that had caused his brother's murder. Angolans. Source of a lot of trouble for him. I reminded him and reminded him. And I put another needle in his arm and cooed in his ear and he signed papers and went deeper and deeper and deeper." Her voice was dreamy, pleasant. It was as though she were recounting a languorous summer cruise she'd taken; the gun was loose and waggled in her slender hand. She was obviously proud of how she had controlled Caroline's husband. She was rubbing this into Caroline as deep as it would go before she finally killed her. There was a real pleasure in her story. "But no matter how much I persuaded, cajoled, took him to bed, he would not believe you were the one who stole the diamonds. It's amusing, the only thing he wouldn't believe was the truth. When Sitizar suggested the masquerade, I encouraged Gregory to do it for real. To mutilate himself. Bring his brother alive! To bring Moreno alive! Why would anyone set up his own brother to be killed? Do you know that, Mrs. Massad?"

Caroline whimpered.

"Have you seen the job we did on that face? The scars are impressive. It took days of work. Days of morphine. Months of healing. He seemed to get some perverse tranquillity. The fucking coward," she sneered. I felt that she was stalling, that she would turn us over to Dalva after she'd had her say and leave him to do the job. When was she going to give the gun to Dalva? The boat rocked again and I waited for the next wave. Justine pushed the hair up from her forehead and the boat rose up, and I lurched forward, just hoping to knock Justine down. I did better than I expected. I knocked the gun loose. She fell back on her ass with a look of true amazement on that cool-cool façade of hers.

Knocked cold on her ass. I looked over to see that Caroline had a grip on Justine's leg with her teeth: she was biting through Justine's pantleg and I fumbled for the gun, my wrists tied tight. I heard Justine scream and kick, and Dalva made his first mistake. He should have buried a knife in my back right then and gone on to do the same for Caroline. He should have buried that knife in up to the handle, but he turned me over instead, even as I gripped the handle of the gun. I fired right into his face.

I pulled the trigger of the automatic more than once but less than a hundred times is all I can say, because I don't remember how many bullets I pumped into him. I fired, and pieces of him flew. I fired and fired. He fell on top of us, and I felt his blood. Caroline held her grip on the hunk of Justine's leg. Justine howled and beat at Caroline's head with her fists, and Caroline made an odd, squeaking noise.

The boat had turned into the tide and was rolling on every wave. Finally Justine ripped free. She stumbled to her feet, grasping her upper thigh just above where Caroline had been biting. She stumbled backward and just kept going. Right over the rail.

I didn't see her go in, I couldn't lift my head high enough. But I heard her shriek taking a shrill upward sweep before ending completely. And I heard the roar of waves and Caroline gasping, blood on her chin and face, her eyes closed and nostrils flared, sea spray collecting on her as Dalva bled between us. I rested, and shouldn't have. The wet, bleeding weight should have moved me to action, but I sat there catching my breath. The bloody lump of Dalva's head had slid between Caroline's shoulder and mine. I squirmed against the ropes on my wrists, the gun still pressed in my fingers and into the blood-soaked cavity of Dalva's chest. My fingers were numb and then stung incredibly: I'd burned them, powder burns. An incredible rasp, like a saw buzzing through the deck, brought me around. A sharp jerk and the waves battered us up again. Another rasp. We were caught on the rocks. The boat listed, hung on a rock, and the aft swung and bounced into another rock. It was as if we'd been slammed into a brick wall from a speeding car. The waves rocked us back and then slammed us again. Caroline opened her eyes and looked at me dully, as if to say she'd done it all for nothing. She finally noticed Dalva, or what was left of him. The third slam sent us into action, squirming as best we could from under Dalva's corpse and straining at the ropes around our wrists, which had gradually loosened in our struggle. The rocking motion helped us from under Dalva's weight, until he finally lay splayed at our bound feet. I managed to worm the knife out of his pocket and cut Caroline's bonds. Then she cut mine. We were free. But free just as the boat listed farther to port and aft than it could without taking on water. We ran forward; water weighed her down. I gripped the board rails, pulling us toward the nose, but the water was too fast. The next wash and we were swept off and the *Embora* was engulfed. We were in the water and there was suddenly no boat deck left. I went from walking deck to treading water.

We ditched our clothes and swam toward land and the cliff face of the shore, the only direction the current would allow. We approached more rocks. A wave carried us up, I reached out to Caroline, my fingers numb with the cold and the burns. We rose, hands grabbing each other's wrists, and were smashed to the rock, yet not as hard as I had imagined; a cushion of water softened the blow. I reached for a handhold, but the surface I grasped at was smooth from erosion, my fingers slipping away as the wave carried us underwater and back out. I took in water, coughed, resurfaced. Caroline struggled in the water next to me, her arms flailing. The stitches in my mouth ached with the cold, stung from the salt. The waves lifted us again, and Caroline rose atop that one. I saw her hug at a slice of sandstone that protruded from the cliff face, but she fell from it as the water receded once again. The next wave was slow and not nearly as forceful, and it did not carry us up the cliff face; the current gathered its force and dragged us into the nearly submerged grotto that lay hidden under the waterline of high tide. What little light I'd grown accustomed to disappeared completely. I was pummeled into the cave, totally underwater until I burst to the surface gasping for air.

"Vern? Vern?" Caroline called, her voice echoing in what sounded to be a very large cavern.

The current didn't have nearly the undertow I'd experienced outside, yet it did drag me toward the opening and the sea. I held to the wall and found it easy to swim in the direction of Caroline's voice. I answered and felt my way along the sea-slickened rocks to the area where I finally found her clasping a rocky protuberance, her voice thin and tired. I grabbed her, moved in toward the relative warmth of her. I could scarcely feel my legs, the water was so bitterly cold. I knew that we'd both die of exposure if nothing else. I pushed off from her.

"Vernon!" Her scream echoed.

"I'm here, right here," I calmed her, feeling along the walls.

"Don't leave me!"

"Have to get out of the water. Out," I told her. I had nearly circled the entire grotto when I doubled back and found it: a deepening niche in the rock. I searched out a handhold, and after a few attempts pulled myself up, bracing my back to one wall of the niche and my feet to the other. My legs were heavy, clumsy weights to lift out and prop against the rock, but they held.

"Vern?"

"I'm all right." After a few minutes I managed to crawl farther up into the niche to where it provided a ledge of sorts: a three- or four-inch lip of stone and a few handholds. It wasn't much but it was better than the water. I went back for Caroline, leading her into the cleft in the rock, boosting her when I could, telling her where to feel for handholds and explaining where the narrow ledge of rock was. I climbed up after her, wedging myself between the crevice walls, my knees bent up, my back dug against the other wall. Caroline clung to her own perch next to me, water slithering up through the crevice and splashing up onto us from time to time, each wave sending a chill through us. We did not speak for a long time; all our energy was consumed with hanging on, with blocking the cold from our minds. The darkness was total and the waves roared outside our chamber, their thunder one long, low growl in the hollow of the cave. But waves began to subside, spewing less water up at us. My clothes dried gradually, the folds stiff with salt. Every ache and every bruise I had suffered the last week came back to me in renewed vigor; pain washed across me, into every joint. But as I began to dry, the cold became less severe.

From her perch, Caroline relaxed her head so that it rested against mine. I felt the warmth of her breath on my neck.

"How will we ever get out of here?" she asked. I was glad to hear such a question; I was lifted by hearing it: if she were too weak, had become resigned to dying there in that hollow of stone, she never would have asked how to get out. My resolve returned with hers.

"If the waters settle down, we may be able to swim out of the grotto and into the sea again," I told her. We could be miles from a safe landing or see one just around the corner.

"Which way?" Caroline said, her voice close and somehow hopeful. I could smell her hair and it was like a bouquet above the too familiar stench of seawater.

"The cliffs go on for miles. Caves and grottoes. Sudden beaches. There's no telling which way we should swim, what the currents will be like." I listed the dangers and the options laconically, in a weary singsong.

"We can wait for daylight."

"We can wait, huh?"

"I guess we have to."

It was a good long while before I saw the first deep green in the water. At first I thought it to be the false glow and light one usually sees in pitch dark, but the green deepened in color, wavered in the watery depths, and finally began to shine with the dawn: a radiant slice of sunlight diffused in water. Caroline, I don't know how, had managed to fall asleep. My back had gone from a dull ache, to a sharp pang, to paralysis.

"Caroline," I said in a harsh whisper.

She woke slowly, leaning against the rock wall and me, her feet splayed on the ledge, which was high above the waterline by then: the tide had begun to go out and our little dry nest was now five or so feet above the waterline. The waves that entered the cave were no more than frothy-white ruffles gently touring the circular walls of the grotto. The noise outside had subsided, replaced with a lulling, nearly silent rush of water. I could not let the serenity mislead us, though. Not only did we have to swim out of the cave but we had to swim along God knows how long a stretch of sea-smoothed and eroded rocks and cliffs until we could find an opening that would lead to shore, to safety; scaling the cliffs at this stretch of the shoreline was out of the question.

We lowered ourselves into the water, and this time the coldness seemed a relief. We swam out into the dawn, a white sun gleamed over the waters. I swam out from the cliffs, Caroline following, hoping to get a better perspective, hoping for an opening. Traces of the *Embora* were drifting in the water: a plastic glass, curtains from a window, a swarm of playing cards scattered on the surface. As I swam east, into the sunrise, the wreckage grew denser. Out nearly fifty yards from us around a bend, the *Embora* herself was lodged between two fingerlike protrusions of rock, split open and on her side. Little was left of her but the hull and a cross-section of the interior, a bunk and a bolted-down table exposed to the waves. A boat cushion floated nearby; I retrieved it and swam over to Caroline. We continued around the next bend, hopeful of a clearing in the solid rock wall, but found just more of the same reddish rock, rising over fifty feet above the sea, broken only by gaping entrances to grottoes like the one we'd just left.

I was ready to give up when, as we rounded the next cliff, suddenly a small boy on a red and yellow raft splashed over to us. Swimming, paddling furiously, laughing and squealing, he kicked up water, his eyes bright, his cheeks red with sunburn. He passed us without a word. He was a visitation! A dove with an olive branch. I yelped to him, excited, screaming, taking a mouthful of water. He paddled more quickly away, giving us a wary look. We paddled around the cliff and found ourselves swimming toward a narrow, nearly deserted beach, sheltered on each side by the cliffs. The back of the cove was a gently sloping mound of small boulders, sand, and gravel furrowed with the switchbacks of flagstone steps that led up to the crest from the beach. A pudgy, incredibly pale woman in a blue floppy hat and remarkably immodest bikini which, on her doughy body, looked like the minimal strap of a sumo wrestler, was cooing in a shrill voice after the sunburned boy Caroline and I had just passed.

"Ya-hooo! Brandon!" she called in a thick English accent, barely giving us a glance as we sputtered onto the beach nude. Caroline and I collapsed near the woman, in shock that we'd made it to safety. Finally the woman looked down at us, a set of gray eyes blinking over her biscuitlike cheeks.

"You didn't happen to pass my Brandon out on the water, did you?" she asked. I waved a hand in the direction that I'd seen the boy disappear around the rocks. I stood, grinning moronically at her. "He is giving me these fits all the time," she went on. "I say, do you need a hand with anything?"

I hugged her. "God bless that little Brandon, lady!" And I planted a kiss on her, smiling. She pulled away, shocked. "God bless Brandon, God bless!" I sang, waltzing the woman around the sand; Caroline laughed as she lay exhausted on the sand. "God bless the little Brandon!"

I grabbed a handful of flesh on each side of the woman and jiggled her until she, too, was laughing hysterically. Caroline grabbed me by the arm and we ran up to the hotel. She kissed me on the neck, giggling, as we entered; guests pretended not to be shocked, tried not to stare. We skipped up to the front desk and a clerk came around hurriedly with towels, bellboys gaped; the two of us were laughing, stark naked and laughing. They found us some swimwear and I got a cab out front, still high with relief. It didn't take much for reality to set in. We crawled into the cab, breathless. After a moment Caroline said, "About Toby, I didn't ask him."

I turned to her. "Shut up. I don't want to hear it."

"I didn't. And you've got to leave me out. Once he was here, though, I—"

"Shut the fuck up, Caroline." One moment we were the only two people alive in the world and the next I wished she'd gone down with the *Embora*. I found a perverse peace of mind in that wish. I was still catching my breath, staring blankly at her.

"We have two things going for us now. We're both alive and your husband *might* be. That's all we have, Caroline. All." My voice couldn't have sounded more wooden, dead, in the tight hollowness of the cab.

———— NINETEEN ————

I ran my hands over my salt-stiffened face. We still had a lot of ground to cover. The only people who knew Caroline was not responsible for the theft at the casino, the bombing, and now Dalva's death, were both floating in the Atlantic. We had to play as if the situation were at its worst: we had to prove that Caroline was not involved in the casino bombing and Sitizar's death, even if explosives had been planted in her car. Better yet, if we could prove she had nothing to do with Toby's death or his visit to the Algarve, perhaps then someone would listen. But as it stood then, Caroline and I were, as Justine had planned, prime suspects. Justine might have died, but her game plan was still playing itself out. It looked as if we were in on the smuggling and the murders. We looked to be up to our sweet little American asses in international terrorism too.

"So what next?" Caroline asked sadly, her eyes closed.

"We need to have a long talk with your husband. If he's alive, he can save us. If we can get him coherent." I paused. "Tell the driver to go to Faro. The police are sure to be at the villa."

Caroline stopped in town for cash, and we bought some clothes. The hospital was dark and cool. High, vaulted ceilings were hung with simple dim light fixtures, and the marble floors were spotless and buffed to a shine. A nurse at the front desk directed us to the second floor.

I was not entirely surprised to find a policeman stationed outside Gregory's door. No doubt the authorities were not pleased with Sitizar's smoldering corpse and the missing receipts, and Justine had seen to it that Gregory had little in the way of an alibi.

"What do we do now, smartass?" Caroline whispered.

We did something smart for a change: I had Caroline tell the cop who we were, and he told us to wait for his superior who was in the room with Gregory. We took a bench in the hallway. It was quiet and pleasantly dim in the corridor. Nurses glided by occasionally with a smile; a janitor mopped the far end. The captain came out of Gregory's room, breaking the calm with his gestures and a few commands to the two men who entered the hall with him. The cop stationed at the door nodded toward us. He told his superior, in a hushed voice, who we were.

The captain came over to introduce himself to me—it seems he and Caroline had met at any number of Algarve society occasions. Captain Hondre watched both of us carefully. "It is a shame about Mr. Massad," he said. "He is in very bad shape. His strength is not so good." And he stopped to look us both square in the eye, flashing a half smile of horselike teeth. "You will want to see him, Mrs. Massad? I am sure? But he is very weak. Take just a moment." He gestured toward the door.

I nearly had to force her through the doorway; she was stiff, nervously shaking under my arm as I pushed her by the shoulders and walked her through.

"And Mrs. Massad, Mr. Bradloozekey? I will want to talk with you, yes?" I closed the door after us. I had done nothing to prepare Caroline for what she was about to see: it was plain that she had never known of Gregory's self-mutilation; there was no telling how she would react.

The room was cold, and darker than the corridor. The walls, the floor were tiled and bare of pictures, fixtures. His bed sat facing us and we approached the side, her eyes wide and glistening with fear.

"Oh God," she said, and held the metal railing, putting a hand to her mouth. Gregory was propped up and breathing with difficulty, tubes running down both nostrils. An IV hung at the bedside. His eyes were only half opened and the lids seemed blued, almost as if done in eyeshadow, yet this was deeper, *of* the skin, not on it. The pits, the self-inflicted scars along the one cheek and jaw, looked to go through to the very jawbone. The light was casting a shadow over each crater that had been burned and gouged into his face. It reminded me of the way I had seen him that first time, in the back gallery of Zorine's . . . but he looked nothing like Moreno without the thick glasses, the mustache, and that confident stare. Here in the bed he looked like an old, tired, and frightened man, a fear trying to surface through the pain and fight that were scarcely left in him. I couldn't forgive him that night on the golf course, but I couldn't wish him dead either, not after looking on him in that shape.

Then Caroline did a peculiar thing: she let go the railing that was giving her so much support and went to his side and ran her fingers over the pits, the scars. "Oh God, why?" she said, and started crying.

Gregory looked up into her eyes and smiled. I swear he smiled, or what he could manage of a smile as she continued to lightly play her hand over the marks, the scars: you'd think she was trying to erase them.

"The company. My conscience," he began with a labored gust of speech, raspy and nearly unintelligible.

"Me," she sobbed. "And me." She straightened as Gregory turned his face from hers, out into the darkest corner of the room. A nurse came in, checked his IV, and left.

He motioned to me with his hand, swirling it lazily in the air in my direction. I drew closer, went to the other side of the bed. He struggled to gulp in enough air at nearly every word. "Did . . . catch Justine . . . double-cross?"

"I don't know. The last we saw her was in the ocean. Might be alive. We made it. But Hondre, the police . . . I don't know." He continued to look up at me, searching the scars on my own face, and I know I read an apology in that. I turned away and found myself looking across at Caroline on the other side of the bed. "Explosion. Wasn't my idea. Wanted only some restitution. No one killed. In fire. Shot me. She shot. Me." He began to gag. Each wrack pulled him up from the bed, and he worked harder and harder for breath. Caroline cried in a tight, wrenching squeal. The cop threw open the door, a doctor came rushing in; I helped Caroline to the corridor and back to the bench where I rocked her in my arms and let her cry it all out.

I talked to the doctor: it seemed whatever was mixed in with the morphine in Gregory was giving him problems; the lab was working on it. But the wound was deep and had done damage to the heart and liver. I asked if Gregory would make it, and he gave me a careful shake of the head that Caroline could not see. No.

We waited, the police keeping a respectful distance down the corridor. It took nearly six hours for him to die, the sound of his last coughs flicking brittlely into the hushed, tiled corridor. Head buried in my chest, Caroline held her breath, listening, hearing nothing from his room. "Oh God," she let out in a rush and tremble. I found myself patting her on the back.

Hondre talked to the doctor and then he very softly said, leaning over both of us, "I am sorry but I must be taking both of you in to go over Mr. Massad's statement. There are still questions."

"I'm not surprised."

"If Mrs. Massad would prefer to wait—"

"No. She's going."

TWENTY

Gregory was buried in the family plot: a hillside cemetery outside of the town of Loule. From the hill you could see all the way down to the ocean. Everything down there looked clean. We ate at a small restaurant and returned to the villa. I tried to go out to the balcony to write, but couldn't.

I spent the days in my room or in the marina bar or walking the grotto-etched beach. Caroline sat in the backyard and we did not speak much; breakfasts, lunches, and dinners that we ate together would pass with few words. I felt awkward and uneasy but unable to go back to Chicago just then. I knew where the uneasiness lay, and I needed to get it out of my system.

We had found ourselves on the back patio, another starful night arching above. We drank. And then she said:

"What am I going to do?"

"You could go back. Go back on the plane with me," I said, and wished I could retrieve my words. I didn't want her in the States with me; I realized I didn't want her with me ever again.

"No. I'll stay here; don't worry about me." And she went off on another crying jag.

"Quit bawling," I found myself saying, anger rising in me, the sound of her crying an insult.

"What? What am I going to do?" she moaned.

"Who the hell cares, Caroline? Who would want to care? Haven't you gotten every goddamned thing you deserve?"

"What, what do I deserve?"

"Of all the people who've died—" and I stopped myself. I hadn't meant that. But her whimpering, her self-pity infuriated me after all the misery she was a part of causing.

"So you think I should be dead, too? Say it! Go ahead and say it!"

"I just think you've got a hell of a nerve."

"Maybe I am a slob, maybe I did deserve to die with some of the others. But I didn't, and I don't know what to do with myself. With anything." She regained her composure, and took a drink, the house lights reflecting warmly in her brandy glass.

"In the hospital you said he mutilated himself because of you," I said, thinking about some things Justine had said as she was needling Caroline aboard the *Embora*: the night Moreno was killed, why Gregory had called the rebels, the pure hate she had for Caroline. "And those pictures," I said.

"Those pictures are from a long time ago. A photographer Sandy and I dated."

"Yeah, yeah," I said, those pictures still stirred something dark and ugly in me, just as they had in Gregory. "But disfiguring himself just for diamonds," I went on. "Or even for turning his brother in. And why would he turn his own brother over to Josef?"

She was silent, unmoving. I listened as I could hear her breathing: the night was that quiet.

"So is it true?" I finally asked, a half-assed question, but that was the only way I was going to back into the rest of the conversation with her.

"What? Is what true?" It took her too long to ask.

"That you were having an affair with Moreno. That you were in the hotel with him when Josef killed him."

"Why, you jealous?"

Maybe I was, but I doubted it then. "You were with Moreno, and Gregory found out, got pissed, and called Josef in on his own brother, right?" She squirmed, squared her shoulders and looked up into the sky and then slowly closed her eyes.

"Yeah, yeah. But I don't think Gregory knew Moreno would get killed by—what's his name?"

"Josef."

"Friend of yours?"

"So far."

"Nice friend . . . well, I don't think Gregory realized how rough Moreno had been playing in Africa. None of us did, really. So when Gregory turned over Moreno, he figured he'd just get roughed up a bit. Ho!" She opened her eyes, looked away, but not before I glimpsed the tears making their way down her cheeks. She was quiet.

"And you were there, in the room when—"

"Yeah. Was I ever there."

"Pretty bad?"

"I've been through worse. The last few days, for instance." She turned toward me, and I found myself holding her again. "Christ, I didn't realize Gregory was so much in love with me. I thought he was—"

"Like you?"

"Fuck you, Vernon. You make it sound like I don't even have a heart."

"You do, babe, you do. It's just buried a few feet deeper."

"So it's all my fault. Everything. It's like I killed . . ."

"You didn't kill anyone." I found myself stroking that damned bleached hair.

"But if I weren't so—so fucking stupid!"

"Yeah, if you call cheating on Gregory with his brother, stealing stolen diamonds, and then falling patsy to Dalva for Justine as stupidity. A little bit of an understatement if you ask me. You should have been straight with me, told me everything. Right from the start, as soon as I got down here." I peeled her away from me, held her out so we could look eye to eye.

"I did. I told you everything I knew, everything Dalva wanted me to believe. How was I supposed to know they were setting me up? Setting Gregory and Sitizar up?"

"And Toby? Toby was a reckless, greedy bastard, I know that. I'm not blaming you for him, but it wasn't until Justine had that forty-five shoved down your throat that you got religion and admitted in front of me that you had gotten him involved."

"No. I told you I never asked him over here. But once he *was* here, Dalva and I told him what to do."

"You were supposed to carry the diamonds over, and after they were delivered you would be—"

"Right, they were going to kill me. I didn't know that, I was just scared shitless to carry those diamonds over."

"And then you got Toby."

"Wrong, damn it!"

"Right." I pushed her away, and laughed just once, an angry laugh. "Wish I had a forty-five automatic on me. Make things between you and me a lot easier in the future."

"Think, damn you! If I didn't tell Toby to come over, who could have?" She grabbed me by the arm.

Sandra. She was trying to pin this one on Sandra. "Your sister? Come off it, dear heart." How the hell was I supposed to believe that? I was beginning to, though. I was beginning to. "Sandra?" I asked, really searching through those big blue-gray eyes of hers, though most times this was a pointless tactic.

"You didn't hear it from me."

"Sandra is mixed up in this?"

"Don't ask me again."

"Shit," I said under my breath, it was all I had in me to say. Even Sandra, the whole tangled mess winding back up in Chicago. Caroline walked away from me into the darkness of the yard, beyond the lights of the villa.

"I'm going to bed. I've got to leave in the morning. Christ, I might even leave tonight." She stopped suddenly and stood motionless. "I said I'm leaving. Probably in the morning."

"I heard you."

"You can come with me."

"No," she said without turning, walking farther out into the yard.

I packed in a hurry, throwing everything in and forcing the lid shut on the suitcase. I wanted to leave that night. If I didn't leave then, if I stayed one more night, I might find myself staying for a few more weeks. Months. Shit, forever. One sun-drugged day melting into another, one eucalyptus-scented night after night. There was already so little to go back to, and that frightened me. I went to the window and saw Caroline winding slowly through the yard, dreamily running one hand across the bushes as she strolled. But staying here, staying with Caroline would be a suntanned coma; I had little to go back to in Chicago, but it was better than the alternative. Once I realized that, staying was impossible, and leaving that night didn't seem as urgent. I could get out in the morning.

I loaded up the Alfa early and had a shave and a shower after daybreak. Caroline came out into the driveway, her kaftan clinging wonderfully, her face, her eyes alert: she'd been awake for at least a few hours.

"So you're leaving?" she said in a clear, clean voice.

"Yeah, I told you last night. You should come with me." I stuffed my suitcase in for a tight fit behind the driver's seat, gave the villa a once-over: it was small, actually. And too cute.

"No. I'd better stay. I've got things to take care of. The business—or what's left of it, for one. You could stay here. You could."

"I suppose." I jiggled the keys in my pocket.

"But you won't." She answered for me. "Visit sometime. Maybe in a few months."

"Yeah, I should do that," I lied.

She tiptoed gingerly over to me across the gravel in her bare feet. "This came for you. Before you got up." She handed me a telegram, already opened. It was from Sid. I was fired, or my columns were, actually. No more backgammon syndication. I balled up the cheap paper and tossed it to the gravel. That telegram didn't hurt as much as I had thought it would. Caroline gave me a peck on the cheek, I gave her an honest, loving hug and got my ass out of there as quickly as I could.

—— TWENTY-ONE ——

I made Lisbon in good time, checked into the Sheraton and went immediately to the rooftop bar to see Joao.

"We've got things to do," I told him.

"Do?" he asked, putting on his "civilian" jacket as he finished his shift at the lounge.

"We must pick up Camille, the girl my friend was with." He shrugged. "A night on the town. I pay."

He agreed.

We set off for bars and clubs that smoked with dancers, good food, and way too much wine and brandy. Camille became a permanent fixture on my lap, Joao my faithful guide and interpreter, as escudo after escudo tumbled from my palm, seeding all of Lisbon. When I was good and drunk, so drunk that even our cab driver suggested that he take us back to the hotel, I told Joao what I had planned to do.

"Bury him?" he said, his eyes widening despite the powerful gravity of his drunkenness.

"His coat. Like it was him. I missed the fuckin' funeral."
Camille was light on my lap, quietly brushing at my hair.

"The jacket? You want to bury the jacket?" He stared at the
blue-red plaid, rubbing the lapel of it between thumb and forefinger as though an appraisal of the quality of the material
would tell him where to bury it.

"What's a top-notch graveyard? We need to put Toby away
in a good place." I insisted.

Joao carefully considered the question, Camille stayed
quiet. "Off the bridge," he finally said. "We bury him in the
Tagus River. Off the big bridge into the river. That would be the
most glorious of places in the city." Camille agreed. Even the
cab driver agreed, and took us out to the toll bridge. Halfway
across he pulled to the side, glancing repeatedly in the rearview
mirror. We all stumbled out onto the asphalt, the wind whip-
ping in from the Atlantic and across the wide expanse of bridge
that breached the river's mouth. It was difficult to even talk.
Toby's coat flopped in the wind, blowing back toward the cab.

"Ballast!" I screamed. "We need ballast or it'll come back at
us!"

Joao lunged into the cab and produced one empty and one
full bottle of wine. He jammed both in the sleeves of the coat
and tied the ends. He handed me one arm of the coat as he
gripped the other, his hair splayed and covering his eyes, his
shirt collar flapping.

"A prayer?" he asked.

"Camille?" I asked. She gazed out past the double railings
and wire suspension cables into the black water below.

She closed her eyes and said something in Portuguese.
When she stopped and opened her eyes Joao and I swung the
coat twice and released it.

"He's all gone now," Camille said to me.

"I know," I told her, and got back into the cab.

The next morning I soaked my head in the bathtub and had
brandy, soft-boiled eggs, and a hot towel sent to my room. But
that was comparable to fighting malaria with a Japanese fan. I

packed and grabbed a cab for the airport, my eyes closed behind
my dark glasses. In the plane, I pulled the shade on my window
and prayed for more sleep.

"Excuse me," a voice said next to me. I opened one eye,
rolled it in her direction. My seatmate was a modestly pretty
woman in her late twenties, good smile, clear blue eyes, perkish
and sprightly-looking. I must have had a terrible hangover to
miss her as I sat down.

"Mmmm?" I offered, and opened the other eye.

"I, I couldn't help but notice, I mean the way you were
slumped over, and the recent wounds on your face and all. If I
can get anything for you, if you need any help with anything, let
me know."

"Nurse?" I mumbled, and self-conciously drew a hand over
the scar on my mouth.

"Dental hygienist," she said with pride.

"Dental hygienist." I nodded gravely, tonguing the wide,
slick, blank expanse of gum where my bridge had been.

"But I'm studying to become a technician," she continued,
offering that tidbit with another nod to her head, her smile un-
flinching, permanently affixed.

"Technician." I raised an impressed eyebrow.

"They take X rays, develop them, make teeth," she went
on. "Like the ones you don't have."

"Like these?" I pointed two fingers at the sunken section of
my face.

"Yep. They were destroyed in the accident?" she asked, saying "destroyed" as if we were speaking of gassing puppies at an
animal shelter.

"No. I had a bridge, but it was knocked loose and bent up
and, well . . ." I reached into my pocket and retrieved them in
my handkerchief. She took them out of the handkerchief and
pushed them around the palm of her hand.

"Mmmm," she finally said, picking one up and eyeing it as
one would a gem. Her appraisal seemed very critical, very de-
manding.

"Well, what do you think? Friend of mine had a cousin do the job for me. By mail no less. Took the impression."

"It must have been a horrible impression. No definition. And look at this seam," she said. I nodded. "These plastics are hard to work with, though. They set fast, so you *must* work fast," she instructed me, handing me back my loose teeth.

"Work fast," I repeated graciously, tucking the teeth away.

Work fast. Plastic teeth. Plastic! That was it! I had no recourse but to calm myself with a drink and wait to get home.

———— TWENTY-TWO ————

I phoned Toby's cousin as soon as I hit Kennedy for my connection to Chicago, but the operator informed me the number was still disconnected. No office number, no home number. I was first on the plane for Chicago and first to ask for a drink. In Chicago, I claimed my luggage and fumed as we had to buck weekend traffic and heavy rain back into the city. I dashed into the building in the downpour and waded through the debris of my torn-up apartment to the dining room, where the copy of my old column, the one Toby had sent in the P.O. box with the old backgammon board, was atop the junk where I'd left it.

White had three men blocked off the board. Knocked off by black and waiting to come back on board, I reasoned as I sat at a table, article in hand. I set the column aside and gathered the pieces of the set together, the leather strips, the frame and men that I had dismantled. White has three men off the board. But which three? I looked over the white pieces again.

Plastic! In the pieces! I don't know why I didn't realize all that before. I sat out on the back stoop, in the rain, with a hammer. Some smashed up easily, others were stubborn. I was scared to death that they would splatter and I'd lose a diamond.

But I sat out there on the alley stoop, hammer in hand, and after every white man had been smashed, I went on to the black. No diamonds. I was beginning to suspect that I was wrong, my hunch was all wrong: that Dalva, when he had searched the apartment or when he killed Toby, had found the diamonds. But Dalva had said that he didn't get them from Toby that night, in fact, he thought Toby had passed them to Josef and Mobotiak. And Josef had thought that Dalva had taken them from Toby before killing him. They had to be here, had to have something to do with the column. They *had* to be in the plastic pieces. Why tear up my apartment unless the first batch of diamonds had *not* been located? I went back into the house.

As I reread the column it became clear: the three white men were knocked off the board and sent to the *Bar*. Black has the clear advantage.

He should use the doubling cube.

I ripped out the plastic spines that were the bar of the board and took them and the doubling cube back out into the rain. Neither would yield to the hammer. This was the dental plastic—enamel-hard and nearly unbreakable. I went through my tools and tried a hacksaw but early on realized that it would be impossible to saw the whole bar and relatively tiny cube. I put both under the broiler in the stove and made some progress, but not enough. Heat it had to be. I dumped charcoal briquettes into the kitchen sink, soaked them a long time in fluid, and, opening the transom over the kitchen door, lit the coals. The initial flames left the ceiling black; but soon the smoke subsided. As the plastic melted, it actually peeled away from the diamonds— I had expected the melted plastic to stick to the rocks, but it didn't.

I burned the doubling cube; one huge diamond. I burned the midbar. The plastic peeled away in thick, charred petals to reveal the biggest of the diamonds and dozens of smaller ones nestled in the midst of the plastic like some blue bird's eggs. I chipped them loose and had a good long drink, carefully lining all of the gems up on the end of the dining room table. Other parts of the frame yielded more. I put the largest of them—

nearly the size of my thumb—in the middle, flanked by the others. I drank and watched them and drank and watched them and counted them: thirty-eight. Some of the biggest had to be worth—Christ, I couldn't even guess and got a knot in my stomach just imagining the prices. I satisfied myself with examining them, rattling them in my hands, and then putting them back in line. I watched how the dim light overhead caught the dull, uncut surfaces. They were really just stones. But those stones seemed, at that point, to be the pieces they had been hidden in—game pieces, markers. A system to determine who won and lost, who was likely to win again, who bet the highest. Toby had picked a better place to hide them than he could have ever imagined. I was real drunk when the phone rang. It was my father.

"I read in the papers, you jackass," he started off, without even his customery curt hello.

"What did you read?" I slurred.

"Your column canceled. You're drunk?" he asked, his voice a little softer.

"Yeah. Real drunk, Dad."

"You should be. What you gonna do now, the column gone and all?"

I fingered one of the creamy blue diamonds on the table. "The reason I got fired. Well, listen, Dad, it's a long, long, tiring story. But I got fired because—"

"Because you got mixed up with that chippie in Portugal. I told you didn't I?"

"But the whole thing left me with some diamonds."

"Yeah," he said matter-of-factly, and I was sure he hadn't heard what I said.

"That is, these diamonds don't belong to me. But I might be the only person alive that knows or cares they exist. I mean things have been pretty confusing and I might be able to get away with hanging on to them. I have a whole slew of these here diamonds that I can fence. Hot diamonds." There was a long, parental silence which he finally broke in a patient and soothing voice.

"I want you to think carefully about your life, how you have led your life up to this point."

"I can't think past my nose at this point," I told him.

"I want you to think about how you have handled things in the past, and answer me honestly. If you hang on to these diamonds don't you really think you'll just fuck things up royally for yourself?"

"I guess you're right," I found myself agreeing. "I'd probably fuck things up."

"Good. Return the diamonds, Vern. And now that you're so broke you can't afford a soup bone, why don't you come out to Phoenix here. We could use you. I'm getting too old to handle all these dogs by myself. And Doris isn't getting younger."

"Greyhounds? Racing dogs? What do I know about racing dogs," I protested. "I thought Doris was the expert."

"We could use a hand."

I was looking out past the dining room into the piled debris in the hallway. The rain outside was slowing. I took the last of my drink. What the hell, what did I have to keep me?

"I could use the work," I told him.

TWENTY-THREE

I was growing tired of my own company and had a few loose ends to tidy up besides. I pocketed the diamonds and walked through a light drizzle to Murphy's. The night air was, unfortunately, sobering.

The bar was cozy that night—the beer signs a pleasant glow, people talking in small groups, faces flushed from the cold rain. Even the visage of Hizzoner smiling down from the clock seemed in a sleepy, benevolent mood. I drank myself enough courage to go upstairs and tell Sandra all that had happened. How Justine got Dalva to honey up Caroline, get her to lift the diamonds from her husband, but, she had refused to bring the diamonds over to be fenced, and saved herself from being murdered. Justine had to find another way to get Caroline. Toby and I had worked neatly into her plans: place all the blame on the dead and the revolutionaries. And then she told me how the nude photos had gone to the Algarve via her. She'd mailed them: that photography boyfriend had taken them. It was all in the name of revenge.

And Toby, who had set him up? Sure it was all in Justine's game plan, but who got him to play?

"I got Toby to go over," she admitted plainly, curled up on her bed in her terry-cloth robe.

"Why?" I asked.

"You're standing over it," she shrugged.

"The bar?"

"Doing pretty bad . . . and suddenly Caroline tells me we could both get rich, forever. Find someone to bring these diamonds to New York for her and that new boyfriend of hers. Shit. Who did I know?"

"Toby."

"Yeah, Toby. And when he gets here he says he's double-crossed some foreigners, put diamonds where no one could find them. Said we might as well cross Caroline, too. Keep them for ourselves. Stupid, fat . . ." Her voice trailed off; she drew in her robe. "What did Caroline need with the money? Toby said so many people were after the diamonds to begin with, so many people screwing each other for them, what was one more? Caroline had it coming, if you ask me."

Caroline and Sandra didn't look a bit alike, I thought, looking at Sandra hunched there on the bed, her red hair tousled, unwashed, her skin that gorgeous, freckled pale; but they had the same blood, the same thin blood.

"And Toby, he had it coming too?"

She stared at me. "We all did, Vern. None of us are sweethearts, you know. Not even you. But look who comes out on top, Caroline! Again, damn her! If anyone deserved . . ." She stopped herself short, more for my sake than hers, I'm sure: she had to know how ugly petty jealousy looked on her.

"Coming out ahead of Caroline means that much to you?"

"She took what she wanted, always did. Even you, right?" The sarcasm in her voice turned something over in me, and I lost what little cool I'd tucked away in reserve. I began to pluck the diamonds, one by one, from my pocket, tossing them lightly at her. The first one bounced into her lap, and she flinched before picking it up. The next bounced off her head onto the bedspread. "These things are worth a lot of money, but all anyone wants to do is keep score with 'em. So there you go, another one, another one, one more," I said, flipping them faster and faster at her until she ducked her head when I took the last small handful out of my pocket and lined them at her. She kept down. I sulked out of the room.

"Vern!" she screamed. I could hear her rustling through the covers, scrambling on the bed for the diamonds. "Hold it, stop!" And she came running down the hall, the stones cupped in both hands. "Take the damned things, you righteous bastard, take them, get rid of them!" She'd caught up to me in the doorway, stuffing the gems back into my coat pocket. She took my arm and brushed a hand over the scar on my forehead as if she were brushing back a stray lock of hair. "Get rid of the damned things, throw them in the lake for all I care, but come on back, come back."

I had one foot on the landing; my shoulder was holding the door open. She snuggled up to me and waited for an answer, eyes wide as a pure, clean emerald. Someone in the bar downstairs laughed himself into a coughing jag. I shook my head. I was always coming back to one bad bet or another.

"Why don't you come with me. To Arizona."

She laughed lightly, patted the pocketful of diamonds. "What would I do with a broke, beat-up backgammon player in Arizona?"

I shrugged and started down the stairs, feeling about as good as her description of me.

TWENTY-FOUR

I had a long, cold, and slow Bass ale at the bar. What Sandra had said about us upstairs was oddly comforting: none of us were sweethearts. She had that part right.

"Mr. Bradlusky." I felt a hand on my shoulder. I turned and saw Josef, wide-eyed, smiling, and genuinely glad to see me.

"You're back! My work is healing nicely!" he said, pointing to my face, shifting from foot to foot. Mobotiak sniffled, his quivering face wet from the damp. Both were decked out in jeans and button-down white shirts. They looked uncomfortable.

"You must know what I want," Josef said.

"Outside?" I pointed past the screen door at the sidewalk outside. Josef nodded with a broad smile, and we stepped out on the sidewalk and to the corner, out of the light.

"You have been through a great deal, I know. I feel terrible about you—" Josef stammered, embarrassed.

"Injuries," Mobotiak said, nodding to my scars, "deep injuries."

"Yes. Injuries. Did you have any luck finding any of our belongings?" Josef asked, his eyes eager and worried. He bounced lightly in anticipation.

Here were the only people I felt had any right to the diamonds. Someone—Gregory, Moreno, or the man on the moon for that matter—had told them they'd get a fair price for their diamonds, and they were cheated. Simple as that. I had been their only way into the Algarve, into the lives of the people who ripped them off.

"You didn't find our property, did you?" Josef said sadly, interpreting my silence for failure.

"No. I have some of the diamonds," I said casually, and began taking them from my pocket. I carefully plunked each one into his palms. I explained how the rest had gone down on the *Embora* with Justine. He said something in Angolan or Portuguese to Mobotiak, who then produced a fat roll of American money.

"Is forty thousand an insult?" he asked. Mobotiak held out a wad of hundreds, five hundreds. It didn't look real. I laughed and they both looked up at me, hurt in their eyes.

"More?" he asked.

"None," I said, looking at both of them. "None, and please put it away before I change my goddamned mind." I looked at Mobotiak, shoving the money and his outstretched hand back toward him.

"You must know that you have helped a righteous cause," Josef began.

"I don't want to hear about the cause," I answered, trying my friendliest tone. I turned to leave. They just stood there on the sidewalk, the blue and red beer signs reflecting off their shirts.

"But, hey," I said, walking back, "my bridgework. Maybe five thousand for some decent teeth and an airplane ticket out of here," I said, and put my hand out.

"Certainly!" Josef beamed, and took the appropriate bills from the wad in Mobotiak's hand. "Certainly for your new teeth," laying each bill proudly in my palm.

They thanked me three or four dozen times before taking off. I found myself wandering back toward the bar, standing in a slice of light from the front window and gazing through the gilded U of MURPHY'S, past the few drunks marooned on their barstools, to the back curtain. I half hoped Sandra would come bursting through at any second, tossing the keys to the joint on her way out the front door. When I realized that might actually happen, I turned and cut down Devon to the nearest side street, clutching the crisp bills in my pocket. Yeah, beaten up, not exactly broke. But alone, for a change. That last condition, that final, low roll was going to be the easiest one to play.